Brewing & Betrayal

A Sarah's Secrets Mystery

by

Sarah Macey

Published by Brew & Clue Publishing Ltd in 2025

Copyright © Brew & Clue Publishing Ltd
All rights reserved.

This book is a work of fiction. Names, characters, businesses, organisations, places, and events are either the product of the author's imagination or are used fictitiously. Any resemblance to actual persons, living or dead, events or locales is entirely coincidental.

No part of this publication may be reproduced, stored in a retrieval system, or transmitted in any form or by any means electronic, mechanical, or photocopying, recording or otherwise, without the prior permission of the publisher and author.

For Kim

If you hadn't been so kind about that first, scrappy attempt at a novel, handwritten between college classes, I'm not sure I'd have tried again. Thank you for being the first person to believe in my writing, even when it was just for fun.

Contents

Chapter 1 3

Chapter 2 16

Chapter 3 32

Chapter 4 41

Chapter 5 59

Chapter 6 77

Chapter 7 94

Chapter 8 105

Chapter 9 118

Chapter 10 131

Chapter 11 143

Chapter 12 156

Chapter 13 165

Chapter 14 178

Chapter 15 200

Chapter 16 214

Chapter 17 231

Chapter 18 247

Chapter 19 263

Chapter 20 274

Chapter 21 285
Chapter 22 299
Chapter 23 307
Chapter 24 319

Chapter 1

Sarah Meadows stood on the pavement of Castle Road, her gaze fixed on the front of the small coffee shop. She watched on with a mix of excitement and nervousness as the beautiful driftwood sign for '*Sarah's Secrets*' was hoisted up into place above the shop window. This was it, the beginning of a new chapter in her life.

"Sorry, erm," Sarah called out to the workmen as they manoeuvred the sign into position. "Could you tilt it slightly to the right? I think it'll look better that way."

The two workmen currently at each end of the big sign, exchanged a glance, their brows furrowing slightly as they adjusted the angle of the sign once more. Sarah's suggestion seemed simple enough but having spent the last half an hour balancing the sign between them, finding the perfect spot was proving to be more challenging than anticipated.

"Maybe a tad to the left?" suggested the heavier of the two, his voice tinged with a hint of frustration. He wiped the sweat from his brow with the back of his hand, leaving a streak of dirt on his forehead.

His companion, balancing precariously on the ladder opposite him like a mirrored reflection, let out a sigh. "Or maybe a touch higher?" he countered, adjusting his grip on the sign with a slight shake of his head. Their exchanges grew shorter, their movements more deliberate, as the sun beat down on them, intensifying their frustration with each passing moment.

"I'm sorry," Sarah said, apologising for what felt like the twentieth time this afternoon. "I promise that we're nearly there. And then I'll get us a drink to cool down."

A look passed between the two men, standing like two bookends, their patience wearing thin as they waited to see if they could finally come down from their respective ladders. With each minor adjustment, the sign seemed to mock their efforts, refusing to cooperate and settle into its designated spot.

Sarah stepped back and squinted, examining the sign from different angles. "Yes, that's perfect," she replied with a smile. "Thank you."

Just as she was about to turn back to the sign, a voice behind her made her jump. "Mum!"

Startled, Sarah spun around to see her son Charlie standing behind her, grinning mischievously.

"Charlie! You scared me," Sarah exclaimed, her heart racing from the surprise. "What are you doing here? I wasn't expecting to see you until tomorrow."

"I wanted to see the sign go up," Charlie replied, gesturing towards the coffee shop. "It looks great, Mum."

"Thanks, Charlie," she said, reaching up to ruffle his hair affectionately. "I mean, I still think it has a slight hint of a lingerie shop or something like that", he laughed, "But it's nice to see that it's finally happening."

Sarah laughed, the sound light and melodic. "Oh, Charlie, you always know how to tease me. You and your wild imagination."

Charlie grinned. "Mum, remind me again why it's called *'Sarah's Secrets'*? I mean, what's the big secret?"

She laughed even harder, shaking her head. "Well, that's kind of the point about secrets, isn't it.... I can't tell you, otherwise I'd have to kill you!"

Charlie groaned theatrically. "Come on, seriously. What's the story behind it?"

Sarah's eyes twinkled with mischief. "Well, I hope that eventually this shop will be a cosy little hideaway, people's secret place to come and escape from their lives."

Charlie looked at her thoughtfully, recognising the deeper meaning behind her words. "You know, Mum, that's pretty much what you're doing, isn't it? Setting up this shop to escape from your past life."

Sarah's smile softened, and she nodded. "Well, that makes me sound like I'm running away from something criminal, or scary.... but yes, I guess you're right. After all those years sitting behind a desk, it was time for a change. You know that I've wanted something different, something that felt more like... me. And if I can create a space where others can find a bit of peace and joy, then I will be happy, and it will all be worth it."

Charlie slipped his arm around Sarah's shoulders, giving her a supportive squeeze. "Well, I think that you're doing an amazing job. And hey, even if it does sound like a lingerie shop, it's still going to be the best shop in town."

Sarah chuckled, leaning into her son's embrace, the warmth of his support fortifying her against her own nerves. "Thanks, Charlie. That means a lot," she murmured, her voice filled with affection.

Charlie was Sarah's middle son, the one who always seemed to get the family's sense of humour and share her passion for new ideas. They were close—almost too close at times, bound together by a shared love of coffee, music, and their constant quest to find the best new places to eat and hang out in Southsea. Over the years, he'd become her sounding board, someone she could turn to for both advice and comfort.

Sarah, though proud of her son's growth, couldn't help but feel a flutter of nerves as she thought about their new working dynamic. She knew that being partners in a coffee shop would be a whole new experience. It would be exciting, but also challenging. She'd need to strike a balance between being the business partner and not slipping into "mum mode", and she reminded herself that she'd need to make sure her advice and guidance came across in the way it was intended. It would take work, but Sarah was confident that they could make it happen.

She took a deep breath, letting the anticipation of the future wash over her as she gazed at Charlie, who was already looking around, surveying their work with a hint of pride in his eyes.

"Charlie," she said, her eyes sparkling with a mix of excitement and a trace of nervousness, "we're going to be an awesome team, aren't we?"

Charlie smiled back, his confidence unshaken. "Absolutely, Mum. We've got this," he reassured her, giving her a quick, encouraging wink. "No matter what happens, we'll have fun and show them what *Sarah's Secrets* is all about."

Sarah couldn't help but smile at his optimism. With Charlie by her side, she knew they could handle whatever came their way. As she watched him chatting to the sign makers, she felt his infectious enthusiasm and realized that this was only the beginning of an exciting new chapter—one that was going to bring them both closer than ever.

She felt a surge of happiness wash over her. Here she was, standing in the very coffee shop she had dreamed of opening with her son by her side. She glanced around at the chaos of a shop mid-construction, the piles of boxes, the half-finished counters, and the still-unhung artwork. It wasn't just any coffee shop, it was their coffee shop.

As Sarah stood on the cobbled pedestrian area of Castle Road, she was reminded of everything that made her love her home in Southsea. She was transported back to fond memories of walking hand in hand to the school just round the corner and summer afternoons spent eating fish and chips on the beach. With its gentle rhythm of life by the sea, Southsea was the perfect setting for her dream to take root and flourish.

Tucked away in a side road off Southsea Common, Castle Road was an eclectic mix of shops, each one's individual personality adding to the vibrant community spirit that made Southsea unique. There was a little wine bar on the corner, its warm lights spilling onto the pavement, inviting and cosy. Next door, a ceramic painting shop, run by her friend Amy, and always filled with laughter and creativity. Further down, to the right side of road was a hairdresser with its sleek, modern interior contrasting the historic charm of the street. And right across from her, a tiny boutique art gallery displayed a rotation of local artists' works.

When the opportunity to buy the shop had come up, Sarah had jumped at the chance. For years, she'd been envisioning this moment—dreaming of the day when she could finally step away from the demands of her office job and dive into the world of coffee and community. She had always known that she wanted a shop close to the sea, somewhere that embodied the laid-back charm of Southsea. The idea of being able to walk to the seafront in just five minutes, breathing in the salty air and watching the waves crash against the shore, was a dream that felt almost too perfect to be true.

But it wasn't just the location that had drawn her in—it was the shop's potential. Tucked away in a tiny, quirky corner of Southsea, it was a place with character, hidden from the usual hustle and bustle but still part of the vibrant local community. It was the kind of place that felt personal, where every shop had its own story, and Sarah had imagined herself becoming a part of that narrative.

Charlie and Sarah had spent countless weekends together, trudging through empty shops in their search for the right one. There had been a few that had potential, but the majority were either too run-down and expensive to fix— or unsavoury—places that lacked any charm or character. They'd walked into these spaces with resigned sighs, knowing deep down that they weren't what they were looking for. It wasn't until they stepped into this shop that everything clicked.

The moment Sarah crossed the threshold, she knew. The space had a kind of magic to it. It was small, just the right size for them to manage on their own as they got the business off the ground, but it was big enough to give them room to grow. The layout was perfect for the coffee counter she had in mind, and the high ceilings and large windows bathed the shop in natural light, giving it an airy, welcoming feel. There were little touches that Sarah could already envision—the chalkboard menus on the walls, a cozy reading nook, and shelves lined with quirky coffee-related knick-knacks.

Charlie, standing beside her, had looked at her with that familiar grin, his eyes sparkling with the same excitement that bubbled in her chest. They didn't need to speak, they both knew instantly that this was the place. It was perfect for them.

This wasn't just a shop—it was a fresh start, a new adventure, and a place where Sarah and Charlie could finally put down roots, side by side, in the heart of the community they loved. And as Sarah stood there now, gazing around at the progress they'd already made, she couldn't help but smile, knowing that this tiny shop was about to become the foundation for everything they'd dreamed of—and so much more.

Sarah took a deep breath, letting the familiar scents and sounds wash over her. Southsea had a way of wrapping around her like a comforting blanket, offering a sense of belonging she had never found anywhere else. Here, she had built a life, rooted in the stability and community she had always longed for. It wasn't where she was born, but it was unequivocally home.

She couldn't help but compare it to the countless years spent feeling trapped in the confines of her corporate job. When every day felt like a case of the Sunday 'scaries' and the sense of disillusionment grew with each passing year. It wasn't that she'd hated her job, in fact there were many years where she'd loved being involved in everything that made manufacturing happen. She'd been driven and committed to it, but with the knowledge that retirement was still a couple of decades away, she had begun to wonder if there wasn't something more fulfilling that she could be doing with those years. The decision to leave it all behind and pursue her dream of opening a coffee shop had been a leap of faith, a bold step into the unknown.

But as she stood there on the cobbled street, doubts crept in, whispering tiny little thoughts of failure and regret. Was she making the right decision? Would she be able to succeed in her new venture, or was she simply trading one stress for another?

She knew that if she let them, the weight of her doubts would threaten to crush her spirit, but Sarah refused to let her fear of the unknown dictate her future. With a determined resolve, she pushed aside the lingering shadows of uncertainty and focused on the promise of a brighter tomorrow.

Sarah reminded herself why she had embarked on this journey in the first place. It wasn't just about escaping the confines of her old life, it was about embracing the freedom to pursue her passions and carve out a new path for herself.

Giving herself a little mental shake, she cast aside her doubts and prepared to embrace the unknown with open arms. The road ahead might be filled with challenges and obstacles, but she was ready to face them head-on. For the first time in a long while, Sarah allowed herself to believe that she could achieve her dreams, no matter how daunting they may seem.

Opening a coffee shop in Southsea was no small feat. The town was filled with quaint cafes and bustling eateries, each vying for the attention of locals and tourists alike. The fierce competition and the uncertainty of success weighed heavily on Sarah's mind. But as she looked at the street, with its colourful shop fronts and narrow winding pavements, Sarah couldn't help but feel a sense of hope.

She came from a military family, a childhood defined by constant relocation. From the bustling cities to the quiet bases nestled in the countryside, she had seen more places by the age of ten than most people did in a lifetime. Yet, none of those places had ever felt permanent. They were just temporary stops in a life of change, homes that never quite fit, no matter how many boxes they unpacked.

Southsea was different. It was the place where she had finally settled down, where she had raised her family. The street before her was more than just a picturesque scene, it was a tapestry woven with memories. She smiled as she passed the fish and chip shop, a quaint little place that hadn't changed much over the years. She remembered going there with her dad and sister, the two of them eagerly peering over the counter while their dad ordered. The smell of fresh, golden fish and crispy chips filled the air as they carried their treat home to share with her mum.

In her mind's eye, Sarah could already see her little coffee shop bustling with activity. It would be more than just a place to grab a cup of coffee, it would be a sanctuary where people could come together to share stories, laughter, and the simple joys of life. She envisioned cosy corners filled with comfortable chairs, and the aroma of freshly brewed coffee drifting through the air.

With a determined glint in her eye, she made a silent vow to herself. She would make *Sarah's Secrets* a success, no matter the challenges that lay ahead. Deciding that she'd spent enough time loitering in the street, Sarah reached down to affectionately ruffle the floppy ears of her ever-so-loyal chocolate labrador, Missy, who sat beside her, watching attentively. "Come on, it's not time for our walk yet... we've got work to do," Sarah said softly. With Missy padding along at heels, she pushed open the door to the shop.

༺━━༻

As Sarah opened the door Missy followed in after her, her tail wagging gently as she explored the space, sniffing at the boxes stacked in the corner. The sunlight streaming through the large windows illuminated the dust particles floating in the air, giving the shop an almost ethereal glow.

Sarah was about to set down her bag and get to work when she heard the distinct creak of the front door opening again. She turned around, half expecting Charlie to have followed her inside, but instead, she found herself face to face with a figure she hadn't seen in years but recognised instantly, Mr. Edward Barnes, the owner of *Barnes Curiosities*, the antiques shop that took centre stage in the fork of Castle Road.

Edward Barnes was a man who looked like he carried the strain of every one of his seventy plus years etched in the deep lines of his face. His weathered features and stern expression gave him an air of authority, like a statue that had stood guard over the street for decades. His clothes, a mix of old-world tweed and a well-worn waistcoat, spoke of another era, as did the cane he held in his right hand, though Sarah suspected he didn't truly need it.

"Mr. Barnes," Sarah greeted him with a warm, if slightly nervous, smile. "It's good to see you. I wasn't expecting any visitors just yet."

The old man stepped into the shop, his keen eyes scanning the space as if he were appraising an antique. "So, it's true, then," he said, his voice gravelly with age and a hint of disapproval. "You're opening a coffee shop here, of all places."

Sarah nodded, trying to keep her tone upbeat. "Yes, I am. I've always loved this street, and when the opportunity came up, I couldn't resist."

Mr. Barnes' gaze shifted to the sign outside the window, now hanging proudly above the door. He grunted, a sound that was neither approving nor disapproving, but something in between. "*Sarah's Secrets*, is it? Interesting name," he remarked, his tone suggesting he found it anything but.

Sarah bit back a nervous laugh. "It's meant to be a bit of a mystery. I want it to be a place where people can come and relax, maybe even find a bit of themselves they didn't know was lost."

Mr. Barnes didn't respond immediately. Instead, he took a few slow steps around the shop, his cane tapping lightly against the wooden floorboards. "You know," he began, "I've seen many businesses come and go on this street. People arrive with grand ideas and bright dreams, thinking they'll change the world, or at least this little corner of it. Most don't last."

Sarah's heart sank slightly at his words, but she refused to let it show. "I'm aware of the challenges," she said, her voice steady. "But I believe in this place. I believe it can be something really special."

Edward stopped his inspection and turned to face her, his expression unreadable. "Belief is a fine thing, Mrs Meadows, but it takes more than belief to keep a shop like this going." His gaze softened just a fraction, and for the briefest moment, Sarah thought she saw a glimmer of something almost like respect in his eyes. "Still, if you're serious about this, you'd better be prepared to work harder than you ever have. This street doesn't take kindly to half-hearted efforts."

Sarah met his gaze, a small smile playing on her lips. "I wouldn't have it any other way, Mr. Barnes."

He grunted again, then turned to leave. As he reached the door, he paused and looked back at her. "If you need anything—advice, or perhaps a bit of history about this place—you know where to find me."

With that, Edward Barnes stepped out of the shop, the bell above the door jingling in his wake. Sarah watched him go, her heart both heavy and light at the same time. It wasn't exactly a warm welcome, but she hadn't expected one.

Sarah turned back to her shop, her resolve stronger than ever. She had taken the first step, and now, there was no turning back.

Chapter 2

Inside the shop was a hive of activity. Mike, Sarah's husband, was hard at work, the radio blaring out as he drilled holes for shelves into the freshly painted walls. The sound of his tools echoed through the room as he focused intently on his task, muttering to himself as he worked. Despite the mess and chaos, there was something endearing about watching him. He was always so steady, so determined when it came to making things work.

"Hey, Mikey," Sarah called out, stepping further into the shop, her voice breaking through the clatter. "How's it going?"

Mike looked up from his work, a bead of sweat glistening on his brow. "Hey, baby," he replied, flashing her a tired but encouraging smile. "Making progress, slowly but surely."

Sarah nodded, her gaze sweeping across the room. The walls had been painted a rich, deep blue, which, far from feeling dark or oppressive, enveloped the space in a sense of intimacy and warmth. The colour was bold but inviting, creating a cocoon-like atmosphere that made the small shop feel like a hidden gem—somewhere people could retreat from the outside world and enjoy a moment of peace. Above them, the ceiling had been adorned with scattered stars and celestial patterns, carefully hand-painted to add a touch of whimsy and character, giving the whole room an almost dreamy feel. Sarah hoped that the combination of the deep blue walls and starry sky above lent the shop a sense of quiet magic, like stepping into a little corner of the universe.

At the back of the room, a walnut counter had been freshly installed, its rich, warm tones balancing the cool blue of the walls perfectly. The wood gleamed softly in the light, adding an earthy, natural touch to the space that felt both sophisticated and cozy. It was the heart of the coffee shop, with the shiny new coffee machine and till perched on top, ready for *Sarah's Secrets*' first customers. The counter was sturdy yet inviting, the perfect place for people to gather around, sip their coffee, and feel at home.

To the side of the room, a stack of wooden tables and chairs, all still in their protective wrapping, were pushed out of the way to make room for Mike's construction efforts. They would soon be arranged to create the ideal seating plan—small, intimate tables for two in the front, along with a larger communal table in the back of the shop. Sarah could already picture it, customers laughing over coffee, sharing stories, and becoming regulars in the close-knit community she had longed to create.

Despite the progress they had made, Sarah couldn't shake the feeling of overwhelming chaos. There was still so much to be done. Shelves to be hung, final touches to add, and the whole space still needed the personal touch that would turn it from a construction site into a welcoming haven. Time seemed to be slipping away faster than she could keep up with. Yet, as she stood in the middle of the room, looking at the beginnings of the space she had dreamed about for so long, a quiet sense of accomplishment crept in. She knew they were getting closer.

"Hey, are you ok?" Mike asked, noticing the furrow of concern on Sarah's brow as she surveyed the room.

Sarah sighed, her shoulders slumping slightly. "I don't know," she admitted, her voice tinged with uncertainty. "I just... I don't know if we're going to be ready in time."

Mike set down his tools and crossed the room to wrap Sarah in a comforting hug. As she leaned into him, seeking comfort and support, she couldn't help but laugh to herself at the height difference between them. Mike, with his tall, broad-shouldered frame, towered over her, while she had always been short, her head resting just under his chin. She craned her neck up to look at his face, and a familiar warmth spread through her as she met his reassuring smile.

Their first meeting hadn't been a conventional one. One night a friend had convinced her to go to a salsa class. "It'll be fun!" she had insisted, practically dragging Sarah out the door.

Enter Mike. He hadn't wanted to be there either, dragged along by his best friend who'd promised him a free drink if he came to the class. Mike had no rhythm and less enthusiasm. But as the class progressed, he ended up being paired with Sarah for one of the dances. Neither of them knew what they were doing, but they were both trying, laughing awkwardly at their own missteps.

"Just follow my lead," Sarah had said, a grin spreading across her face as they tried to figure out the steps. And Mike couldn't help but laugh along with her.

Somehow, despite the disaster of their first dance, there was an undeniable spark between them. Sarah's easy-going attitude and Mike's dry sense of humour seemed to balance each other out perfectly.

Fast forward a few months, and Mike was getting used to dancing—well, at least to being dragged to salsa classes with Sarah. But let's face it, once he'd bagged a wife out of it, Mike hadn't been back on a dance floor since. "I'll leave the dancing to you, babe," he'd said, and Sarah had agreed, content with the fact that their connection was built on far more than dance steps.

Now, as they stood together in their very own coffee shop, Sarah couldn't help but reflect on how grateful she was for the serendipity of that first meeting. As Mike hugged her tighter, a chuckle from Sarah rumbled against his chest. "What's so funny?" he asked, looking down at her with amusement.

Sarah shook her head, still smiling. "Oh, just thinking about how I used to wear heels all the time to try and keep up with you. Now, the lack of inches in my height is even more apparent."

Mike laughed softly, tightening his arms around her. "I never minded the height difference. Besides, you always looked adorable trying to balance on those heels."

Sarah snorted in mock indignation. "Adorable? I was aiming for sophisticated."

"You were always both," he said, planting a gentle kiss on the top of her head.

Sarah sighed contentedly, feeling the tension of the day melt away. "It's nice not to worry about that anymore. My feet certainly appreciate it."

"Your feet and I both," Mike teased, giving her a playful squeeze.

Sarah laughed, the sound light and genuine. "Well, now I can focus on what really matters. But what if we need more time?" Sarah pressed, her voice barely above a whisper. "I don't want to rush things, especially if it means cutting corners."

Mike pulled back slightly, meeting Sarah's gaze with a determined expression. "Listen to me, Sarah," he said firmly. "I believe in you. We can do this, together. And if we need more time, then we'll take it. But I know you, and I know you'll make this place something truly special."

Sarah's heart swelled with gratitude as she looked into Mike's eyes. She knew she was lucky to have him by her side, supporting her every step of the way.

"Thank you, baby," she whispered, her voice thick with emotion. "I don't know what I'd do without you."

Mike smiled, pressing a gentle kiss to Sarah's forehead. "You'll never have to find out," he replied. "I'll always be here for you, no matter what."

They stood there for a moment, simply enjoying the closeness. Sarah felt a sense of peace she hadn't felt in a long time. Despite all the challenges they had faced, and the ones still to come, she knew she could handle anything with Mike by her side.

"You know," Mike began, his tone gentle yet firm, "you need to relax a little. Enjoy the process of doing something new. It's all going to come together beautifully, I promise."

Sarah nodded, a small smile tugging at the corners of her lips. "You're right," she conceded. "I just need to take a deep breath and trust that everything will work out in the end."

Mike's smile widened, pleased to see Sarah's spirits lifting. "Exactly," he replied. "And hey, speaking of relaxation, I think you deserve a little treat before the big opening day."

Sarah raised an eyebrow, curious. "Oh? What did you have in mind?"

"I was thinking," Mike began, "maybe you should book yourself into the local health spa for a bit of a pick-me-up. You know, pamper yourself a bit before the craziness begins."

Sarah's eyes lit up at the suggestion. "That sounds amazing," she exclaimed. "I could definitely use a spa day to recharge my batteries."

"Great," Mike agreed, nodding in approval. "And why not make a day of it? Take Robyn with you. She could use a break too, and it'll be good for you two to spend some quality time together before all the mayhem starts."

Sarah's smile widened at the thought of spending the day with her niece. "You know what? That's a fantastic idea," she declared. "Robyn's going to be my right-hand woman", she laughed and corrected herself, "I should make that left-hand woman at the coffee shop, so it'll be good for us to have a bonding session before the big opening."

Excited at the prospect of a bit of pampering, Sarah reached for her phone to text Robyn. As she typed out the message, another thought occurred to her.

"Actually," she said, glancing up at Mike, "maybe I should ask Charlie to come along too. After all, he's the coffee brains behind this adventure and he's the one that's going to be baking all the lovely cakes we'll be selling in the coffee shop."

As if summoned by the mention of his name, Charlie walked into the room, a box of mugs, cups, and saucers in hands.

"Hey, Mum," he greeted, wiping a bead of sweat from his brow. "Got the rest of the supplies from the car."

Sarah smiled warmly at her son, grateful for his hard work. "Thanks, Charlie," she said. "Listen, I was just thinking... Would you like to come with us to the spa? It could be a nice way to relax before the big day."

Charlie hesitated for a moment, considering the offer. "Thanks, Mum, but not this time," he replied, shaking his head. "I've still got a lot to do, and I want to make sure everything's perfect for the opening."

Sarah nodded understandingly, though a hint of disappointment flickered in her eyes. "Of course, sweetheart," she said. "Just let me know if you change your mind."

Charlie flashed her a grateful smile before disappearing into the back room to continue his work. Sarah sighed softly, feeling a pang of guilt for dragging him into the whirlwind of preparations. But she knew Charlie was just as committed to making *Sarah's Secrets* a success as she was, and that thought filled her with pride.

As Sarah watched Charlie disappear into the back room, a wave of conflicting emotions washed over her. On one hand, she felt an overwhelming sense of gratitude for the unwavering support of her son and niece. The fact that they were willing to give up their own jobs to join her on this venture filled her with love and appreciation. But on the other hand, she couldn't shake the nagging feeling of doubt and responsibility that gnawed at her from within.

She knew that Charlie and Robyn were taking a risk by investing their time and energy into *Sarah's Secrets*. They were both talented individuals with promising futures ahead of them, and Sarah couldn't help but worry that her dream might end up being a burden rather than a blessing for them.

As Sarah glanced around the shop, taking in the sight of the half-finished shelves and the stack of boxes waiting to be unpacked, a wave of frustration washed over her. It wasn't just the chaos that unsettled her—it was the growing sense of brain fog that had begun to cloud her thoughts over the past few days. She'd noticed it more and more lately, moments when her mind just stopped, like a computer freezing, unable to process what was in front of her. She couldn't tell if it was the weight of everything on her plate—the coffee shop, the upcoming opening, the responsibility she had to her family— or if it was just her age catching up with her. Maybe both. She wasn't sure. What she did know was that it was happening more often, and it was starting to worry her.

She sighed and ran a hand through her hair, hoping the motion would clear the cobwebs in her mind. It didn't. The lists were piling up—literally and figuratively—tasks that seemed simple enough but that, when she stared at them, only blurred into a haze. Opening day was getting closer, and every time she thought about what needed to be done, she froze. The mounting pressure made it hard to think straight.

A sense of panic began to creep back in, a sinking feeling in her stomach as she glanced at the calendar on the wall. Ten days until opening. Ten days. The panic bubbled up, and for a moment, she felt completely paralyzed. She was caught between the urge to do everything and the overwhelming realization that there was just too much to manage. Her brain felt like it had shut down completely, unable to prioritize or make decisions. How could she be so stuck, so unable to move forward?

Sarah clenched her fists at her sides, trying to fight off the growing tide of anxiety. *This isn't like you*, she thought. *You've handled bigger challenges before. You just need to get a grip.* Her old work persona—the one that had survived endless deadlines and corporate pressure—started to surface. She could feel that familiar sense of clarity begin to break through the fog.

She took a deep breath and forced herself to step back. She couldn't fix everything in one go. She needed to break things down into smaller pieces, just like she used to do with projects in her previous job. Step by step. She couldn't do it all herself, and trying to do so was only making her freeze up. It was time to prioritize, delegate, and focus.

She made her way to the counter, where she had a notebook ready and began to write, listing the most pressing tasks for the day. As she wrote, Sarah's mind cleared. The panic had receded, replaced by the methodical thinking she knew she needed to succeed. She glanced at the list and felt a surge of resolve. It wasn't going to be easy, and it certainly wasn't going to be perfect, but she could make it work. One task at a time.

With a mental kick up the backside, Sarah stood up straighter. This wasn't her first challenge, and it wouldn't be her last. The opening was days away, but she had the skills, the team, and the determination to make it happen. No more freezing. No more letting the chaos overwhelm her. She was in control. Drawing strength from her newfound resolve, Sarah turned back to Mike, her eyes shining with determination. "You know, you're right, Mike," she said, her voice steady. "I need to focus on making this work, not just for myself, but for Charlie and Robyn too. They've put so much on the line to help me, and I can't let them down."

Mike smiled, his eyes softening with affection. "You won't, Sarah," he said reassuringly. "You've got what it takes to make this place a success. And besides, you've got a whole team behind you, supporting you every step of the way."

The morning light filtered through the windows of *Sarah's Secrets*, casting a warm glow over the soon to be opened coffee shop. The aroma of coffee beans filled the air, mingling with the faint scent of paint. Sarah and Robyn stood by the counter, their eyes fixed on Charlie who was meticulously setting up the coffee grinder.

"All right," Charlie said with a serious expression, "today we're going to learn the fine art of coffee grinding and brewing. It's not just about pushing buttons, it's about crafting the perfect cup."

Sarah and Robyn exchanged amused glances, stifling giggles. Charlie's dedication was both endearing and impressive, and they couldn't help but appreciate how invested he was in ensuring the best quality for their customers, but he did tend to go into teacher mode when asked to explain everything.

"First, the grinder," Charlie began, demonstrating how to adjust the settings for different types of beans. "You want to get the grind size just right. Too fine, and it'll be over-extracted and bitter. Too coarse, and it'll be weak and watery."

Robyn nodded earnestly, trying to absorb all the information. Sarah, meanwhile, playfully mimicked taking notes in an invisible notebook, earning a light nudge from Robyn.

"Now, onto the machine," Charlie continued, moving to the espresso machine. "It's all about timing and pressure. Watch the gauge, make sure the water temperature is consistent, and always, always tamp the grounds evenly."

As Charlie demonstrated, Sarah and Robyn couldn't help but giggle at his intensity. "Charlie, you're like a coffee sensei," Sarah teased, her eyes twinkling with amusement.

Charlie grinned, a hint of blush creeping up his cheeks. "Hey, I take my coffee seriously. And you should too. Our customers deserve the best."

Sarah and Robyn exchanged another look, their giggles subsiding as they realized the truth in Charlie's words. The laughter that had bubbled up between them began to fade, replaced by a more reflective quiet. They both knew that, as much as they wanted to make light of the situation, this wasn't a joke.

Robyn, still smiling but with a hint of newfound determination, nodded first. "You're right, Charlie. We want to be the best." Her voice had shifted, no longer light-hearted, but earnest.

Charlie's face lit up with approval. "Good. Now, let's make some espresso."

As they worked together, Charlie guiding them through each step, the atmosphere in the coffee shop was filled with a sense of camaraderie and shared purpose. Sarah couldn't help but feel a swell of pride and excitement. They were building something special here, and she was grateful to have such dedicated family by her side.

After a successful round of espresso making, Charlie leaned against the counter, a satisfied smile on his face. "You two did great. If we keep this up we're going to make this place the go to spot for coffee in Southsea."

Sarah smiled, loving Charlie's sense of optimism. "Thanks, Charlie. And speaking of making this place great, I know you've mentioned wanting to roast your own coffee."

Charlie's eyes lit up with enthusiasm. "Yes! A roaster would allow us to control the entire process, from bean to cup. We could create our own unique blends."

Sarah held up a hand, a playful smile on her lips. "I think it's a fantastic idea, Charlie. But let's make a go of the basics first. If we can build a solid customer base and prove we're serious about quality, then we can think about investing in a roaster."

Charlie nodded, his excitement undiminished. "Deal. We'll focus on making the best coffee we can for now. But I'm going to hold you to that, Mum."

Sarah laughed. "I wouldn't expect anything less."

With their spirits high and their teamwork stronger than ever, the trio continued their practice, each step bringing them closer to their dream of making *Sarah's Secrets* a beloved fixture in Southsea.

Just then, the kitchen door swung open, and Mike emerged, wiping his hands on a rag. He had been servicing the gas oven, ensuring everything was in top working condition for the coffee shop's opening day. He paused, taking in the sight of Sarah, Robyn, and Charlie huddled around the coffee machine, giggling and chatting.

"You lot are all mad," Mike said with a shake of his head, a smile tugging at the corners of his mouth. "Here I am, slaving away over a hot stove, and you're out here having a party."

Sarah grinned. "Oh, come on, Mike. We're just learning the ropes. Charlie's giving us a masterclass in coffee making."

"Masterclass, huh?" Mike replied, raising an eyebrow. "Well, as long as you don't burn the place down, I suppose it's all good. Just remember, you can't run a coffee shop without a properly working oven. And that's my domain."

"Point taken," Sarah called after him, still smiling. "We do appreciate all your hard work, Mike. We couldn't do this without you."

Mike paused in the doorway, glancing back at the trio with a sly grin. "Well, at least my work is now fuelled by lots of free coffee. I guess that's one perk of having a bunch of coffee enthusiasts running the place."

Sarah laughed, feeling the warmth of camaraderie wash over her. "Consider it our way of keeping you motivated, Mike. We need our renovation finished, after all."

Robyn nodded, a twinkle in her eye. "And don't worry, we'll make sure you get the best brews. Charlie's already making us coffee connoisseurs."

Charlie chuckled, his earlier seriousness giving way to the shared mirth. "I'll make a coffee snob out of you yet, Mike. Just you wait."

Mike gave a mock groan, but his eyes were bright with amusement. "Great. As if I don't have enough to deal with, now I must contend with you lot turning me into a coffee addict."

The four of them burst into laughter, the sound filling the coffee shop with a joyful energy. It was moments like these that made the hard work and long hours worth it.

As the laughter died down, Sarah looked around at her family, feeling a deep sense of gratitude. "Seriously though, I couldn't do this without any of you. Charlie, your passion for coffee, Robyn, your creativity and enthusiasm, and Mike, your technical skills. We're a great team."

Charlie raised his coffee cup in a toast. "To *Sarah's Secrets*. May it be a place of great coffee, delicious food, and wonderful memories."

Robyn and Mike raised their mugs in agreement, and Sarah felt a lump form in her throat. This was more than just a coffee shop. It was a new chapter in all their lives, a fresh start filled with promise and potential.

"To *Sarah's Secrets*," they echoed, clinking their mugs together. The coffee shop was almost ready to open its doors and Sarah was ready to face whatever challenges lay ahead, knowing she had the best team by her side.

Chapter 3

Sarah stood outside the *Serenity Health Spa*, leaning against the window as she scrolled through her phone, checking messages and emails. The irony wasn't lost on her—here she was, outside a wellness haven meant for relaxation, but instead, she was consumed by her work, the glow of her screen reflecting in her eyes. She chuckled softly to herself, wishing she could simply put the phone down and embrace the calm that surrounded her, but her mind had other plans.

As she looked up from her screen, she spotted Robyn approaching, her vibrant presence impossible to miss. The sight of her niece's easy-going walk brought a smile to Sarah's face, a welcome distraction from the pressure she'd been feeling moments before.

"Hey, Auntie Scarah!" Robyn exclaimed, bounding over to Sarah and enveloping her in a tight hug. "Thanks for setting this up. I can't wait to relax and unwind!"

Sarah returned the hug, smiling at her niece's infectious enthusiasm. "Of course, Robyn. I think we both deserve a day of pampering," she said warmly, brushing a stray curl of Robyn's hair out of her face.

As she pulled back, Sarah gave her niece a teasing look. "You know," she said with a playful shake of her head, "maybe now that we're going to be working together, we should lose that nickname of 'Auntie Scarah.' It might not sound quite as professional, huh?"

Robyn laughed, her eyes sparkling with mischief. "Oh no, you're definitely stuck with it! I'll never let you live that down, Auntie Scarah," she teased, giving Sarah a wink.

Sarah chuckled, her heart warmed by Robyn's lighthearted response. "Well, I suppose I'll have to agree," she said, rolling her eyes dramatically but clearly amused. "But if we're sticking with it, you'd better start bringing the coffee shop some serious business, Miss Robyn!"

"Ready to dive into some serious relaxation?" Robyn asked, her eyes sparkling with excitement.

Sarah laughed, feeling the tension of the past few days melting away in Robyn's presence. "Absolutely. Let's do this."

With a shared smile, they pushed through the door of the *Serenity Health Spa* and stepped into the calm and inviting reception area. Kerry, the spa owner greeted them warmly, "Welcome to *Serenity Health Spa*," she said with a smile. "I'm glad you could join us today. If you'll just follow me, I'll get you checked in and show you around. We hope that you'll find it like a little bit of an escape from real life for the next couple of hours."

Sarah and Robyn followed as she led them down a corridor, the soft lighting casting shadows on the walls. As they passed by treatment rooms, they found it hard not to peek in, revealing tantalising glimpses of various therapies, each one promising relaxation and rejuvenation.

Finally, they reached a door labelled "Serenity Room," and the spa owner, Kerry, turned to them with a warm smile. "Here we are. This will be your sanctuary between treatments. Feel free to make yourselves at home," she said, her voice calm and inviting.

As Kerry stepped away to attend to other guests, Sarah and Robyn entered the Serenity Room, taking in the tranquil atmosphere that surrounded them. Soft music played in the background, its gentle melodies lulling their minds into a state of relaxation. The scent of lavender filled the air, instantly calming their senses as they breathed it in deeply, feeling the weight of the world start to lift from their shoulders.

"You'll have a few minutes to settle in before your first sessions," Kerry's voice drifted back to them. "When you're ready, just make your way down to the changing area, where hopefully you'll find everything, you need to get comfortable and settled."

Sarah and Robyn nodded, appreciating the time to unwind. The room was warm and soothing, the soft lighting and plush furnishings creating a cocoon-like atmosphere that invited them to let go of all their worries. The air felt thick with serenity, as if the space itself was designed to cradle them in comfort.

Without hesitation, Sarah sank down into one of the recliners, feeling the plush cushion mould to her body. She closed her eyes for a moment, allowing herself to fully absorb the quiet, peaceful energy of the room. The weight of the day seemed to evaporate as she let herself relax deeper into the chair.

"Ah, this is perfect," Sarah sighed, her voice muffled with contentment as she sunk further into the lounger. "I could get used to this."

Robyn, already feeling the stresses of daily life melting away, perched herself comfortably in the chair next to her. She smiled, her posture softening as she let out a small laugh. "Definitely. I think we're in for a treat today."

Sarah smiled as well, her eyes still shut, and she gave a small chuckle. "You know, if I start snoring, feel free to give me a shake," she said playfully, her voice thick with relaxation.

Robyn chuckled in response, clearly amused by the thought. "Don't worry, I'll make sure the snoring stays in check," she teased.

The room was so calm and soothing that Sarah could easily imagine falling asleep right then and there. She sighed again, her thoughts slowly becoming a distant hum, and for a moment, the world outside of the Serenity Room felt miles away.

Tempting as it was to simply drift off into a peaceful nap right there in the cosy recliners, both Sarah and Robyn knew that even more relaxation awaited them. The treatments they had booked were designed to melt away every ounce of tension, and they were both eager to fully immerse themselves in the experience. With a reluctant sigh, Sarah shifted slightly in her chair, feeling the plush cushions offer one last comforting embrace before she slowly sat up.

"Okay, as much as I could stay here forever, we've got more pampering ahead," Sarah said with a soft laugh, stretching her arms as she eased herself out of the chair.

Robyn, who had been sinking further into her own chair, looked at Sarah with a playful grin. "I'm not going to lie, I could probably fall asleep right here, but you're right—let's not waste the opportunity."

They shared a moment of amused reluctance before both stood, shaking off the allure of the recliners. Taking one last look around the serene room, they made their way to the door. The soothing music and lavender scent still lingered in their senses, urging them to stay a little longer, but they knew that the real relaxation was waiting for them downstairs.

As they descended the stairs to the changing rooms, they exchanged knowing glances, the anticipation of the next phase of the experience bubbling between them.

As Sarah and Robyn stepped into the changing rooms of *Serenity Health Spa*, the bright, white interior immediately enveloped them in a sense of calm. Though the white walls could have felt stark or clinical, the lighting softened the edges, giving everything a gentle, soothing glow. It was the kind of place that made you feel like you could leave everything else behind the moment you stepped inside.

In the centre of the room, a wide mirrored area reflected their images back at them, showing their relaxed expressions as they took in the space. The mirror was framed with a subtle, minimalist design that didn't detract from the serenity of the room but rather added to the overall feeling of peacefulness.

To the left and right, two small rooms beckoned with their promise of privacy, offering the comfort of a space where they could change and prepare for their treatments without distraction. The soft rustling sound of the privacy curtains as they swayed gently added to the sense of peace, and the sense of having everything needed within arm's reach felt reassuring.

Despite the pristine white walls, the space didn't feel empty. Small, thoughtful details had been added to make the room feel welcoming and lived in. Neatly arranged hairdryers, soft towels stacked in tidy piles, and delicate bottles of creams, sprays, and lotions lined the counters and shelves, each item placed with purpose. The subtle scents of essential oils mingled with the soft lavender of the Serenity Room, continuing the spa's calming atmosphere. It was clear that Kerry had anticipated every need, ensuring the changing area was equipped with everything you could possibly require—whether it was an extra hair tie, a soothing cream, or just a comfortable place to unwind before the next part of the experience.

Sarah smiled to herself as she looked around. It was obvious that Kerry had put a great deal of thought into creating a space that was both practical and peaceful, allowing guests to feel fully taken care of. It was as if she had thought of everything, from the smallest of comforts to the most practical of necessities, making it easy to settle in and feel completely at ease.

However, they weren't alone in the changing room. A woman paced back and forth in front of the changing room doors, her attention absorbed by a heated conversation she was having on her phone. Meanwhile, a man leaned nonchalantly against the dressing table, seemingly lost in his own thoughts.

"Excuse me," Sarah said politely, attempting to navigate around the pair to reach one of the changing rooms.

The woman glanced up briefly, annoyance flashing across her face before she returned her focus to her phone call. Ignoring Sarah, she continued her conversation as if she was invisible.

Robyn exchanged a puzzled glance with Sarah before deciding to intervene. "Um, excuse me," she began, her tone polite but firm. "We just need to use one of these rooms." She gestured towards the doors, hoping to catch the woman's attention.

The woman let out an impatient sigh, her annoyance evident as she reluctantly stepped aside, allowing Robyn access to the nearest changing room. However, the man remained unmoved, blocking the entrance to the room on the right.

Sarah felt a twinge of frustration rising within her but attempted to keep her composure. "Could we please just get by? We have appointments," she explained, hoping to appeal to the man's sense of courtesy.

The man glanced at Sarah as if she were a minor inconvenience, his indifference palpable. "Well, I was just going in there," he retorted, his tone dismissive. "I'm waiting for my wife."

Sarah arched an eyebrow, unimpressed by the man's attitude. "Well, we're waiting for our turn," she shot back, her patience waning thin. "I can be in and out before you know it."

After a moment of tense silence, the man finally relented, grumbling under his breath as he stepped aside, allowing Sarah to slide back the door and enter the changing room. As she moved to close the door behind her, she caught Robyn's eye, rolling hers in a silent protest at their companions. Robyn giggled, then slid her own door shut behind her.

Inside the changing room, Sarah let out a frustrated sigh, feeling the weight of the encounter lingering in the air. "Some people are so self-centred," she muttered to herself, shaking her head.

Realising that it was pretty hard to stay irritated when you're in your underwear, Sarah slipped her arms into a fluffy robe and emerged from the changing room, determined not to let the encounter dampen her spirits.

As they made their way back into the reception area, Kerry, greeted them with a warm smile. "Ready for your treatments?" she asked cheerfully.

"We are now that we're not trapped in a room with Mr and Mrs Inconsiderate", Robyn laughed.

Kerry rolled her eyes slightly at the sight of the husband and wife still lingering in the corridor. "Yeah, that one's always been a bit like that," she replied, revealing that perhaps this wasn't her first experience of the couple.

Sarah and Robyn exchanged a knowing look, sharing a silent laugh at the absurdity of the situation. "Absolutely," Sarah replied with a smile, determined to make the most of their day of pampering despite the initial hiccup.

Pushing all thoughts out of her mind and channelling the calmness of the zen-like music, Sarah followed Kerry towards the beckoning door of the treatment room.

Chapter 4

As Sarah settled onto the hydrotherapy massage bed, the soft, fluffy blanket enveloped her in warmth, providing a comforting cocoon against the world outside. She adjusted the position of the pillow beneath her head, sinking into the warm leather surface of the bed with a contented sigh. The gentle pressure of the bed beneath her seemed to melt away the tension she hadn't realized she was holding.

With a small movement, Sarah reached for the button on the machine beside her, pressing it to start the soothing flow of water. As she shifted her arm to reach, even that small action made the waterbed jiggle slightly beneath her, creating a brief ripple across the surface. She held herself still, waiting for the bed to settle down, the water calming once more as she allowed her body to sink deeper into the sensation of the warm, massaging water.

With her eyes closed, Sarah sighed in anticipation, letting go of any remaining stress, knowing that she was about to experience a level of relaxation unlike anything she had felt in a long time.

A gentle whooshing sound filled her ears as the hydrotherapy jets sprang to life, sending a ripple of warm water cascading down her back. Sarah let out a relaxed breath, allowing the tension to melt away as she surrendered herself to the moment. The stresses of the day gradually faded into the background as the rhythmic motion of the water lulled her into a state of peaceful bliss, her mind unburdened by the myriad of shop-related thoughts that had previously plagued her. For the first time in what felt like ages, she allowed herself to simply be, embracing the present moment with open arms.

Before she knew it, the gentle hum of the machine signalled the end of her session. Slowly, Sarah roused herself from her state of relaxation, stretching out her newly loosened muscles with a contented sigh. Wrapping the robe around herself, she rose from the massage bed, feeling rejuvenated and refreshed.

As she made her way out of the room, she caught sight of Robyn emerging from one of the neighbouring rooms, her expression one of pure bliss. Their eyes met, and a shared smile passed between them, each of them silently acknowledging the rejuvenating effects of their spa treatments.

Their moment didn't last long though, as their calm was interrupted by the sight of Kerry, knocking insistently on a door at the end of the corridor. Her brow furrowed in concern, Sarah watched as Kerry called out to the occupant, her voice tinged with urgency.

Curiosity piqued, Sarah approached Kerry, concern etched on her features. "Is everything ok?" she asked, her tone laced with genuine concern.

Kerry's usual cheerful demeanour had completely vanished. Her shoulders were slightly hunched, and her eyes, once bright and welcoming, now appeared distant and troubled. She had a slight frown on her face, and for the first time, Sarah noticed the tension in her posture as she glanced over her shoulder, almost as if she were trying to hide something.

Without the warm smile Sarah had grown accustomed to, Kerry turned to face her. The flicker of unease in her eyes didn't go unnoticed, and for the first time, Sarah felt a ripple of discomfort. There was something amiss, and it was clear that whatever it was, it had broken the easy, welcoming atmosphere that had surrounded the spa just moments before.

Kerry turned to face Sarah, her expression a mixture of worry and frustration. "I'm not sure," she admitted, her voice tight with anxiety. "One of our guests hasn't responded to repeated knocks, and I'm starting to get worried."

Sarah, sensing the shift in Kerry's demeanour, frowned slightly. "Is this something that happens often?" she asked, her voice gentle but concerned.

Kerry shook her head, a sigh escaping her lips as she tried to gather her thoughts. "Not usually," she replied, her eyes flicking nervously towards the door. "Sometimes people fall asleep during their treatments, and we have a little trouble rousing them. But even then, they don't usually take this long to respond." She paused, clearly unsettled. "I'm starting to get a bad feeling about it."

Robyn joined them, her curiosity evident as she glanced at the closed door. "Do you want us to help?" she offered, eager to assist however she could.

Kerry hesitated for a moment, her anxiety visibly rising as she looked at the door, then she nodded gratefully. "Yes, please. I hate to ask, but I'm afraid something might be wrong."

Her voice faltered as she spoke, and Sarah could tell that whatever was happening behind that door was starting to unsettle Kerry more than she was letting on. "Can you carry on knocking while I go and find the spare key?" Kerry added quickly, her hands fidgeting as she looked between Sarah and Robyn. "I'm not sure what's going on, but I need to make sure we have a way in, just in case."

Sarah nodded, her concern growing but wanting to keep the situation under control. "Of course. We'll keep trying."

As Kerry hurried off, disappearing down the hallway in search of the spare key, Sarah and Robyn exchanged a tense look. The stillness of the hallway around them made the air seem even heavier, and the uncertainty of the situation loomed large. Sarah resumed knocking gently, her concern now more focused on what could possibly be wrong. She kept glancing back toward Kerry's retreating figure, hoping she would be back soon with a solution.

The room seemed to hold its breath as Sarah and Robyn exchanged a look, both of them sensing the same unease in the air. Whatever was going on behind that door, it wasn't just a simple case of someone snoozing too deeply. Something was off.

The silence of the hallway was almost suffocating as they stood just feet away from the unknown behind the door. Kerry came into view, clutching a set of keys tightly in her shaking hand, her breath quick and shallow. Her face was pale, and her eyes were wide with barely contained worry.

"I've got them," Kerry said, her voice tight with urgency, her fingers fumbling slightly as she approached. She inserted the key into the lock with haste, her hands trembling as she turned it.

The door clicked open, and they all stood in the threshold for a moment, each of them holding their breath as they braced themselves for whatever they would find on the other side.

As the door creaked open, a rush of cool air swept over them, sending a shiver down Sarah's spine. The room beyond was dimly lit, the curtains drawn tightly shut, casting eerie shadows across the space. Sarah's senses were immediately assaulted by the acrid scent of burnt hair and plastic, a stark contrast to the soothing aromas of the spa.

Robyn peered over Sarah's shoulder, her eyes widening in alarm as they fell upon the scene before them. The red light bed stood in the centre of the room, its metallic frame gleaming under the faint glow of the overhead light. But it was the figure lying motionless inside that sent a chill coursing through Sarah's veins.

A woman lay sprawled on the bed, her skin tinged with an unnatural shade of red, her limbs twisted at odd angles. It was clear that something had gone horribly wrong.

Kerry gasped, her hand flying to her mouth in shock. "Oh my God," she whispered, her voice trembling with horror. "Is she…?"

As Sarah's heart pounded in her chest, she stepped cautiously into the room to stand beside Kerry, her eyes fixed on the woman's still form. With a sense of dread gripping her, she approached the bed, her breath catching in her throat. As she bent over in shock, her mind reeled with disbelief, for the face she was now staring at, lifeless and cold, was unmistakably the same woman she had bumped into in the changing rooms not more than an hour ago. A surge of horror and realisation flooded through her, sending shivers down her spine.

As Kerry stood rooted to the ground, her eyes wide with shock, Sarah's heart went out to her. She could see the fear and confusion etched on Kerry's face as she stared at the scene before them, unable to comprehend the tragedy that had unfolded in the seemingly serene surroundings of the spa.

Instinctively, Kerry stepped forward to reach out towards the woman lying on the bed, her hand trembling as she moved to check for signs of life. But before she could make contact, Sarah's voice cut through the air, sharp and commanding.

"Stop, Kerry!" Sarah exclaimed, her tone firm yet gentle. "You probably shouldn't touch anything. I know how you feel, but it's obvious that she's already gone."

Kerry recoiled at Sarah's words, her hand freezing in midair as she took a step back. The gravity of the situation seemed to dawn on her, and she nodded numbly, her movements hesitant as she withdrew from the scene.

Meanwhile, Robyn craned her neck, trying to catch a glimpse of what lay beyond Sarah's protective stance. Her curiosity was palpable, her eyes wide with a mixture of fascination and horror. But Sarah, sensing Robyn's eagerness, stepped forward, positioning herself between her niece and the tragic view before them.

"Robyn, stay back," Sarah urged, her voice gentle but firm. "You don't need to see this."

Robyn's expression fell, and although her immediate response was to try and argue, one look at her aunt's face made her hold her tongue as she reluctantly did as Sarah asked. She took a step back, her gaze flickering between Sarah and the macabre scene in the room, her mind undoubtedly racing with questions.

As the weight of the situation began to settle over them, Sarah couldn't help but feel a sense of protectiveness not only towards Robyn, but also to Kerry, who looked as if her world had just crumbled around her.

As Sarah stood considering what they needed to do next, she took a moment to gather herself. She closed her eyes briefly, willing herself to push aside the overwhelming sense of dread that threatened to consume her. Drawing a deep breath, she opened her eyes, her gaze sweeping back across the room in search of anything that might explain what had happened.

The dim lighting and soft strains of music that filled the room only served to heighten Sarah's unease, casting long shadows that danced across the walls. The room was bathed in a red glow, which under normal circumstances would probably have felt warming, a comforting embrace against the outside world's harshness.

But now, that red hue only added to the sinister atmosphere, giving everything a menacing tinge. The crimson light spilled across the furniture, transforming once familiar shapes into ominous forms, an abandoned coffee cup taking on a macabre appearance, as if it was filled with blood rather than the remains of a forgotten drink.

Sarah turned her attention back to the woman lying on the bed, a wave of nausea washed over her as the reality of the situation sank in. But as she tried to push down the initial feelings of shock, Sarah's mind whirred with questions. How had this happened? And why here, in the supposedly safe confines of the spa?

Turning to Sarah and Robyn, Kerry's expression was a mixture of fear and confusion. "I don't understand," she murmured, her voice barely above a whisper. "She was fine when I left her. How could this have happened?"

Sarah wrapped her arm around Kerry's shoulder, offering her a reassuring squeeze. "I don't know," she admitted, her own voice heavy with uncertainty. "But we'll figure it out together. Right now, let's focus on getting help."

Robyn's voice broke through Sarah's thoughts, her tone urgent. "We need to call the police."

Sarah nodded in agreement, her mind racing as she fumbled for her phone. Her hands were shaky, but she managed to dial the emergency number, pressing the phone to her ear as it rang. When the operator picked up, Sarah's voice trembled slightly, her nerves fraying. "Hello, yes… I need help. We've found someone who has died."

The operator's calm voice came through the line, asking for details. Sarah motioned for Kerry's attention, her hand moving to cover the mouthpiece of the phone. She leaned toward Kerry, her whisper urgent. "They're asking for her name."

Kerry's face drained of colour, her eyes wide with shock and fear. She gulped, her voice barely audible as she replied, "It's Terri. Terri Treharne."

As the weight of the situation sank in, Kerry's mind raced with all kinds of questions. How could this possibly have happened? Terri had been perfectly fine when she had shown her into the room. Kerry vividly recalled the polite exchange they had shared, her smile as she thanked her and closed the door behind her, hearing the lock clicking into place as she'd walked away.

As Sarah and Robyn exchanged worried glances, Kerry's mind raced, trying to piece together the events leading up to Terri's death. The realisation slowly dawned on her, like a heavy fog creeping in, that Terri hadn't been alone in the salon. Dread coiled in the pit of her stomach as she knew she would have to break the devastating news to Terri's husband.

Feeling sick at the thought, Kerry stumbled towards the Floatation Tank room where Terri's husband had been booked for a session. Her hand trembled as she reached for the door, her heart pounding in her chest. As she went to knock, the door swung open silently, revealing an empty room devoid of any trace of Terri's husband.

Shock immobilised Kerry for a moment, her mind struggling to process the implications of the empty room. A sense of helplessness washed over her, rendering her slow to react. As she backed away, hand clasped over her mouth to stifle a rising wave of nausea, Robyn's presence startled her. With a slight shriek, Kerry turned to see Robyn's concerned expression.

She leaned in, gently placing a hand on Kerry's arm. Kerry looked up at her, startled, and Robyn shushed her in a whisper. "It's ok," Robyn said quietly, sensing the storm of emotions swirling in Kerry's mind. "What's wrong?"

Kerry's eyes filled with concern, her voice shaky as she spoke. "It's Terri's husband... You know that man you met in the changing rooms earlier?" Her hands trembled slightly as she ran them through her hair. "He was supposed to be here with her. They were meant to be together today, and now I can't find him anywhere. How am I supposed to break the news to him if he's not even here? I just... I don't know what to do."

Robyn's gaze softened with understanding, and she leaned closer, her voice a comforting murmur. "We'll find him, Kerry. We'll figure this out. You're not alone in this."

Robyn placed a comforting arm on Kerry's shoulder, her touch gentle but firm as she apologized softly for the surprise. "I'm so sorry, Kerry. I know this is overwhelming." Then, without hesitation, Robyn turned and walked down the salon corridor, her eyes scanning each room carefully for any sign of Terri's missing husband. She knew they needed to locate him, especially now that things had taken such a distressing turn.

Kerry watched her go, her heart heavy with a mixture of gratitude and apprehension. As much as she appreciated Robyn's calm presence, there was still a growing knot of anxiety in her chest. She was trying to keep it together, but the weight of what was unfolding was almost unbearable.

After a few moments, Robyn quietly returned, her footsteps soft as she approached.

Despite Robyn's reassuring words, Kerry could still feel the weight of the situation pressing down on her. The fear of having to face Terri's husband, of telling him the news, seemed almost more daunting than anything else. But for the moment, all they could do was continue searching, hoping for some sign of him before the situation grew any darker.

Sarah returned to Kerry's side, her presence a steadying force in the chaos. She gently took Kerry's hand in her own, her voice soft yet firm. "I don't think we should touch anything," she said, her eyes scanning the room for any sign of change. "The police are on the way. Maybe we should go and wait for them, and then they can try and make sense of what on earth has happened here."

Kerry nodded, her shoulders slumping slightly in resignation, and let Sarah lead her toward the reception area. Her steps felt heavier now, the shock settling in as she walked away from the room that held so many unanswered questions.

As they reached the reception, Sarah caught Robyn's eye. She guided Kerry to one of the sofas and sat her down gently, then turned to Robyn, her voice low but urgent. "Robyn, maybe Kerry could do with a drink, and I think she's not the only one. Do you think you could try and find something for us all?"

Robyn gave a quick nod, understanding the weight of Sarah's words. "Of course," she said, her expression determined. With a final glance at Sarah and Kerry, Robyn made her way toward the back of the spa, hoping the kitchen would provide some sense of comfort in the middle of the turmoil.

She found the kitchen tucked behind a door, along with what looked to be a small staffroom. The scent of fresh coffee lingered in the air, and Robyn took a moment to breathe it in, grounding herself before getting to work. She grabbed a handful of what she assumed were complimentary biscuits, their packaging simple and unassuming, and added them to a tray alongside a few mugs she found near the counter. After filling the mugs with tea and coffee, she balanced the tray carefully, her movements steady despite the tension that still lingered in the air.

With a deep breath, Robyn made her way back towards the reception, the tray clinking softly with each step. When she reached Sarah and Kerry, she set the tray down on the low table in front of them. "Here you go," Robyn said gently, offering them both a smile, even though it didn't reach her eyes. "It's not much, but hopefully it helps."

Sarah nodded gratefully, picking up her mug, the warm liquid offering some comfort, though it couldn't quite ease the tightness in her chest. Kerry, too, took a sip, her eyes distant as she stared at the floor, lost in her thoughts. They were all waiting now, waiting for the police to arrive and for some answers to be revealed. The calm before the storm was heavy, but at least they were together, even if they still didn't know what would come next.

Sarah and Robyn sat side by side on the plush leather sofa in the Serenity Spa's reception area, their shoulders pressed together as they waited anxiously for the police to arrive. The air was heavy with tension, and the soothing ambiance of the spa seemed to offer little comfort in the wake of the tragedy that had unfolded.

Robyn glanced at Sarah, her expression etched with concern. "Are you ok, Auntie?" she asked softly, her voice barely above a whisper.

Sarah forced a small smile, though her eyes betrayed the worry gnawing at her insides. "I'm hanging in there," she replied, her voice tinged with uncertainty. "Just trying to process everything."

Robyn nodded understandingly, her gaze shifting to the closed door that led back to the room where the body had been discovered. "I can't believe this is happening," she murmured, her voice barely audible over the hushed murmurs of other guests in the reception area.

Sarah reached out and squeezed Robyn's hand reassuringly. "I know, sweetheart," she said, her voice gentle. "It's a lot to take in."

They lapsed into silence, each lost in their own thoughts as they waited for the police to arrive. Finally, the sound of footsteps echoed through the reception area, and Sarah and Robyn both looked up expectantly as two police officers entered the room. The lead officer, a stern-faced young man with a no-nonsense demeanour, approached them with purposeful strides.

"Sarah Meadows?" he said, his voice firm but not unkind.

Sarah nodded, her throat tight with apprehension. "Yes, that's me," she replied, her voice barely above a whisper.

The officer gave her a brief, professional nod. "I'm Detective Inspector Stanley. We're here to investigate the incident that occurred today."

Sarah exchanged a quick glance with Robyn. The weight of the moment settled on her chest as Stanley gestured toward one of his officers. "We'll need statements from both of you soon," he said, then turned to Kerry, who had been hovering nearby, arms crossed tightly over her chest. "First though, can you take me to the scene?"

Kerry swallowed hard, then nodded. "Of course. This way."

Without hesitation, he followed Kerry as she moved towards the treatment rooms, his notebook already in hand. As they passed through the reception door, Stanley's tone was measured. "How did you know the victim, Ms. James?"

Kerry shifted slightly, arms crossing over her chest. "She was a customer," she said, keeping her voice neutral. "She came in for treatments now and then." She hesitated, as if debating whether to say more. "And... I knew her from college. A long time ago."

Stanley raised an eyebrow. "You were friends?"

Kerry let out a short laugh, shaking her head. "Not exactly. We weren't close, but we moved in the same circles. There was a group of us—Rachel and Emily, who both run spas now, and Marcus, Terri's brother, and Emily's boyfriend, Matt. It was one of those friendships that was more about circumstance than choice."

Stanley noted the slight tension in her tone. "So, you didn't get along?"

Kerry exhaled. "We got along well enough. But Terri had a way of making herself the centre of things, whether she meant to or not. If she wanted something, she usually got it." She glanced away, "That caused problems sometimes."

Stanley's gaze sharpened. "What kind of problems?"

Kerry gave a small shrug. "The usual things—fallouts, shifting alliances. We were all just kids back then, but some things stuck with people more than others."

Stanley leaned forward slightly. "You mean Terri?"

Kerry's lips pressed into a tight line. "I'm just saying that not all friendships survived beyond college. Some grudges last longer than others."

Stanley made a note, filing the name away. He studied Kerry for a beat before closing his notebook. "All right, Ms. James. If you remember anything else, let me know."

The inspector's gaze swept over the hallway, taking in Kerry's unsettled expression as she led him further inside.

Sarah sat stiffly on the plush leather sofa in the reception area, Robyn beside her, their shoulders pressed together. The usual soothing ambiance—the gentle hum of soft music, the faint scent of lavender—felt artificial now, unable to dispel the tension that gripped the space.

Sarah tried to focus on her breathing, but her mind kept replaying the moment she'd seen Terri in the changing room earlier that day—the tense encounter, the clipped exchange. She had barely thought about it in the chaos that followed, but now the memory loomed large and unshakable.

From her seat, Sarah could hear Inspector Stanley's voice carrying through the open hallway.

"Where's her phone?"

Her stomach twisted.

Kerry's voice, uncertain, followed. "Her phone?"

Stanley's tone was measured, but firm. "Yes. Most people carry one. Wouldn't someone usually leave it on the side or in their robe pocket? If she had one, it should be here."

A beat of silence. Then Kerry again, sounding troubled. "I—I don't know. It wasn't with her things when we checked in the changing room lockers."

Sarah's pulse quickened. Terri had definitely had her phone. She was using it in the changing room when Sarah had walked in.

The memory sharpened, Terri standing there, a towel wrapped around her, speaking into her phone in hushed but urgent tones.

"I can't believe you still care about that night."

Sarah swallowed hard. She had barely registered the words at the time. But now? Had she missed something important? She turned her head slightly, watching Stanley from a distance as he exchanged glances with his officers.

"Then where is it?" he muttered.

Chapter 5

As Detective Inspector Stanley introduced himself, Sarah's gaze shifted to take in his appearance. Sarah couldn't help but think to herself just how incredibly young he looked. He couldn't have been more than in his early thirties, and that thought made her feel a strange mix of surprise and bemusement. *Is this really what it's come to?* she thought, the realization dawning on her. She stifled a small laugh to herself. *Isn't it a sign that you're getting old when you start to think that police officers look young?*

Her lips quirked into a wry smile, and she quickly refocused her attention on Stanley, shaking off the fleeting thought. It was a bit ridiculous, but the age gap felt so stark in the moment. She couldn't deny it though—he had the air of someone who knew what he was doing, even if he didn't look quite as seasoned as she would have expected.

His eyes were focused, and though he wore a calm, professional expression, there was a certain sense of energy in the way he moved.

Sarah noted the slight stiffness in Stanley's demeanour as he approached them, his expression carefully neutral as if he was wary of revealing too much. His eyes, a piercing shade of blue and for a moment she thought she saw a flicker of uncertainty as they met hers, but it was gone just as quickly, his calm focussed stare returning.

As Stanley continued to speak, Sarah observed him closely, noting the way he struggled to maintain eye contact and the subtle tension in his shoulders. It was clear that he was awkward in dealing with a situation like this, his discomfort evident in every word he spoke.

"Mrs. Meadows, Ms. Marsh," Stanley said, his voice clipped and professional. "I'm Detective Inspector Stanley. I'll be leading the investigation into the death of Terri Treharne."

Despite her own anxiety, Sarah felt a surge of empathy towards Stanley. She could only imagine how daunting it must be for him to engage with a group of women in such a charged environment.

Stanley's gaze shifted between the two women, as if assessing their reactions. "Can you tell me what happened?" he asked, his tone professional yet compassionate.

Sarah took a deep breath. "We were here for spa treatments," she began, her voice steady as she recounted the events leading up to the discovery of the body. "I had just finished my hydrotherapy massage, and when I came out, I saw Kerry knocking on the door of one of the treatment rooms. She seemed worried, so I went over to her to see if everything was ok. That's when we found..."

Her voice trailed off, unable to bring herself to say the words aloud. Robyn reached out and squeezed her hand in silent support.

Stanley's eyes flicked between the two women as he absorbed Sarah's account. "I see," he murmured, his voice measured. "So, everything appeared normal until this incident occurred."

Sarah nodded in agreement, her frustration evident in the furrow of her brow. "Yes, it seemed that way," she admitted, her mind drifting back to the seemingly ordinary moments before chaos ensued. "But there was one thing..."

Stanley's interest piqued as Sarah hesitated, prompting her to continue.

"Robyn and I overheard a conversation in the changing rooms," Sarah confessed, her voice tinged with uncertainty. "It wasn't anything significant, just... rude remarks exchanged between two clients. It didn't strike us as particularly unusual at the time."

Stanley's expression remained impassive, though a flicker of intrigue danced in his eyes at the mention of the overheard conversation. "I see," he murmured, making a mental note of the information. "Thank you for sharing that with me."

As the conversation turned, Stanley's focus shifted to the matter of Terri's husband. "Did either of you see the missing man?" he inquired, his tone sharpening with urgency.

Sarah and Robyn exchanged a glance before both shaking their heads in unison. "No, we haven't seen him since we left the changing room," Robyn replied, "As far as we could see, he was still waiting for his wife, for Terri."

Stanley frowned, processing this information.

"Surely if he is walking the streets in a white dressing gown and slippers, he's going to be easy to spot," Robyn asked, her tone laced with a hint of dry humour.

Stanley looked at her, clearly confused, his brow furrowing slightly. He wasn't quite sure if she was joking or if she expected a serious answer to her comment. The sarcasm seemed to be lost on him, and he paused for a moment, unsure how to respond. His gaze flicked briefly from Robyn to Sarah, as if trying to gauge the situation and figure out if he should take her words at face value.

"Well, uh…" he started, his voice trailing off awkwardly. "It seems he made it back to the changing rooms to retrieve his clothes before disappearing again." His tone was more formal now, but the slight uncertainty in his voice suggested that he wasn't entirely comfortable with Robyn's comment.

He couldn't quite put his finger on it, but there was something about Robyn—her casual air mixed with an underlying sharpness—that unnerved him. It was as if he couldn't fully decipher whether she was being serious or just testing him, and that left him in a position where he wasn't sure how to respond.

A sense of unease settled over the room as Stanley's words hung in the air, the mystery surrounding Terri's death deepening with each passing moment.

"Thank you, Mrs. Meadows," he said. "We'll need to speak with the other guests and staff members as well, but for now, if you could remain here, we may have more questions for you later."

Sarah nodded. As Stanley prepared to leave, he turned his attention to Robyn one last time. Stanley's reserved facade cracked ever so slightly as he spoke to Robyn, his tone gentler, almost hesitant.

"Ms. Marsh is there anything else you can think of that might help us?" he asked, his voice steady but with an undertone of urgency.

Robyn shook her head, her expression pensive. "No, I don't think so," she replied, uncertainly.

Just as Stanley turned away, Robyn's eyes widened as a sudden thought occurred to her. "Wait," she called out, her voice halting him mid-step. "There is one more thing. It's going to sound stupid, but the room where we found Terri... it smelled like marzipan."

Stanley looked up abruptly, his eyes locking onto hers with renewed intensity. "Marzipan, you say. Like almonds?"

"Yes," Robyn confirmed, nodding. "That's exactly what I mean."

Stanley's expression shifted, a spark of intrigue lighting up his features. "Interesting," he murmured, his tone thoughtful, as he noted it in his black pad.

Turning on his heel, Stanley strode purposefully towards the crime techs working nearby. "I know you will be, but be extra careful with the water bottle and coffee cup," he instructed them, his voice firm. "We need to test for poisons as well as fingerprints."

Sarah and Robyn watched as Stanley relayed his instructions. The mention of the marzipan smell had clearly struck a chord with the detective.

Stanley turned to them briefly, offering a reassuring nod. "Thank you, Ms. Marsh. That could be a crucial piece of information."

Robyn managed a small, tentative smile. "I hope it helps," she said, her voice soft but sincere.

"It very well might." Stanley gave a distracted nod, his mind already shifting to the next steps. "I might be back, please stay put," he said, barely finishing the sentence before turning away, eager to get back to the rest of his team.

As the minutes stretched on, Sarah and Robyn sat in the reception area, their anxiety mounting with each passing second. The tension in the air was palpable, suffocating almost, as they waited for any sign that told them what was going to happen next.

Sarah leaned in close to Robyn, her voice barely a whisper. "I can't believe this is happening," she admitted, her eyes welling with unshed tears. For the first time, she allowed the weight of everything to hit her, the emotions she'd been holding back rising to the surface. She had always prided herself on staying calm under pressure, on managing to keep a clear head when things got difficult. But now that the immediate crisis had passed, the relief mixed with the overwhelming reality of the situation, and she couldn't keep it in any longer.

Robyn squeezed her hand tighter, offering her silent support. "I know, but we'll get through this, Auntie," she whispered back, her voice filled with apprehension.

Their surroundings seemed to blur into a haze of muted colours and distant voices as Sarah's mind raced with a flurry of thoughts and emotions. She couldn't shake the feeling of disappointment that had settled over her since they first arrived at the spa, like a dark cloud looming ominously overhead, casting a shadow over what was supposed to be a relaxing occasion. Instead, it had turned into anything but relaxing, unravelling into a series of unsettling events that left her on edge and anxious.

Robyn glanced at Sarah, her eyes filled with worry. "Do you think they'll find out who did it?" she asked in a hushed tone, her voice barely above a whisper.

Sarah bit her lip, her mind still reeling from the shock of the morning's events. "I don't know," she admitted, her voice tinged with uncertainty. "But we have to trust that Inspector Stanley will do everything he can to find the truth."

As if on cue, the door from the corridor to the reception area swung open, and Stanley emerged, his expression grave as he made his way towards them. Sarah's heart skipped a beat, her pulse quickening with a surge of anxiety at the sight of him.

"Mrs. Meadows, Ms. Marsh," Stanley said, his voice sombre. "I'm afraid we're going to be here for a while yet as we check the crime scene."

Sarah felt a knot form in her stomach at his words, a sense of helplessness washing over her like a tidal wave. She exchanged a worried glance with Robyn, their shared concern mirrored in each other's eyes.

"Thank you, Inspector," Sarah said, her voice barely above a whisper. "Please let us know if there's anything we can do to help."

Stanley nodded in acknowledgment before turning to leave, his footsteps echoing softly against the tiled floor. As Sarah watched him go, a sense of unease settled over her like a heavy blanket, weighing her down with a mixture of fear and uncertainty.

Robyn reached out and squeezed Sarah's hand in silent support, offering her strength in the face of adversity.

As Sarah and Robyn sat in the reception area, the minutes stretched on, each one heavier than the last. The exhaustion from the day's events was beginning to take its toll, leaving them both feeling frazzled and drained. The air was thick with tension, the weight of the situation pressing down on them as they sat helplessly, unable to do anything but wait.

Around them, the forensic team arrived, their white suits a sharp contrast to the spa's muted tones, and the flurry of activity only served to highlight how still and inactive Sarah and Robyn felt. While the professionals moved with purpose, working quickly to assess the situation, Sarah couldn't help but observe their efficiency, the contrast between their focused movements and her own inability to act.

Meanwhile, Robyn was busy texting Charlie, updating him on everything that had unfolded. Each beep of her phone was a reminder of the world outside, a world that was still moving, even as they remained stuck in this quiet, tense limbo.

Sarah leaned forward, her eyes following Stanley as he spoke with the forensic team. She couldn't help but feel a sense of unease as she observed the exchange, wondering what evidence they might uncover.

Eventually, Stanley broke away from the group and made his way towards Sarah and Robyn. He approached them with a solemn expression, his demeanour still guarded but not as distant as before.

"Thank you for your patience. You're free to go home for now," Stanley said, his voice measured. "But I'll need to speak with you both again. Can you tell me where I can find you?"

Sarah hesitated for a moment before responding. "I'll be in *Sarah's Secrets*, it's a new coffee shop opening soon on Castle Road," she replied.

Stanley's gaze shifted to Robyn, and Sarah could sense the unspoken question in his eyes. "Will you be there as well?" he asked, his tone softer than before.

Robyn met his gaze with determination. "Yes, I'll be there," she answered.

Stanley nodded in acknowledgment before turning to leave. As Sarah and Robyn watched him go, a sense of apprehension settled over them. They knew that the investigation was far from over, and they were now involved, whether they liked it or not.

Gathering up their belongings, Sarah fished her phone out of her bag, her fingers still trembling slightly as she dialled Mike's number. She held the phone to her ear, the sound of ringing echoing in the quiet reception area.

"Hey, Mikey," Sarah said when he answered, her voice weary but tinged with relief at hearing his familiar voice.

"Hello, baby. Everything ok?" Mike's voice came through the phone, his chattiness in stark contrast to the atmosphere around her.

Sarah sighed, the events of the day weighing heavily on her. "It's been a hell of a day," she admitted, her tone heavy with exhaustion. "Far from relaxing."

Mike's voice softened over the line. "Oh, well that isn't good," he said, his tone sympathetic. "Do you want to talk about it?"

Sarah hesitated for a moment, the words catching in her throat. "Not right now," she replied, her voice strained. "I just want to come home. I'll tell you about it when I get there."

"Okay, baby, I'm still tinkering at the shop," Mike said, his voice gentle. "I'll be here when you get there."

"Thanks, Mikey," Sarah said, her voice catching slightly. "I'll see you soon."

As she ended the call, a wave of relief washed over her. If you had asked her this morning, she would have told you that the coffee shop was a source of chaos, a never-ending list of things to manage. But now, in the midst of everything that had unfolded, it seemed like her sanctuary.

The thought of retreating there, to the familiar hum of the espresso machine and the warm, comforting space she was building, filled her with a sense of calm. It was a stark contrast to the turmoil of the day, and in that moment, it felt like the one place she could truly breathe.

As they stepped out onto the street, Sarah turned to Robyn, pulling her into a tight hug. This hadn't been the day that she had planned at all, but she was still glad that she'd had Robyn by her side throughout the day. Robyn's arms wrapped around her, and Sarah squeezed her a little tighter, as if the hug would somehow make up for all the chaos they had just experienced.

"I'll see you tomorrow," Robyn said softly, pulling away with a smile. "I'll be back to help at *Sarah's Secrets*."

Sarah gave her an extra big squeeze, wanting to hold onto the moment a little longer. "Thanks, Robyn," she whispered, her voice thick with gratitude. "You've been amazing today."

With a final squeeze, Sarah stepped back and waved as Robyn started walking down the street toward her own home. Sarah watched her go, her heart warmed by the thought that, despite the difficult day, she wasn't alone. The hug had given her a sense of closure, and as Robyn disappeared from sight, Sarah turned toward the coffee shop, ready to find some peace there at last.

Just as she had expected, the act of stepping through the door of the coffee shop caused a wave of relief to wash over Sarah. The familiar sights—the polished walnut counter, the cosy seating by the window—along with the comforting smells of freshly ground coffee, offered a sense of solace amidst the turmoil of the day. It was as though the chaos of the outside world couldn't reach her here. She took a deep breath, allowing the warmth of the space to settle around her, willing herself to push aside the lingering unease that had settled in the pit of her stomach.

For a moment, Sarah closed her eyes, letting the peace of the shop fill her senses. *This is what it's all about*, she thought. The thought of one day creating this same sense of comfort for others—the feeling that this place could be a refuge from the outside world for anyone who needed it. She hoped that someday, when people walked through the door of Sarah's Secrets, they would feel what she felt now, a haven, a place to pause, to unwind, and to find a little peace amidst the noise of life.

Mike looked up from behind the counter where he was fixing shelves, a concerned expression clouding his features as he caught sight of Sarah's troubled expression. "Hello baby, you're back," he said, his voice filled with genuine concern. "Are you ok?"

Sarah forced a small smile, though her mind was still reeling from the events at the spa. "I'm fine," she replied, her voice tinged with uncertainty. "It's just been a bit of a day, that's all."

Mike looked at Sarah with concern, his brow furrowing slightly as he noticed her distressed expression. He didn't know all the details yet, but it was clear that something was weighing heavily on her. "You're home now," he said softly, his voice filled with reassurance. "Let's just get you settled in. We'll figure everything out."

As Sarah made her way behind the counter to join Mike, she let out a deep sigh, her mind still racing with everything that had happened. She absentmindedly began to sift through the pile of post that had accumulated during her absence. The act of sorting through the mail gave her a small moment of escape from the swirling thoughts of the day. The junk mail was discarded without a second thought, a trivial task that allowed her to focus on something so mundane that it almost felt like she could breathe again.

With each piece of paper she handled, she began to slowly recount the events of the day to Mike, her voice taking on a more detached, factual tone as she spoke. "It all just spiralled so fast," she began, her fingers mechanically working through the mail as she continued to narrate the details. "We got to the spa, everything seemed fine at first, but then…" She trailed off as she continued sorting, the mindless task giving her space to breathe, to retell the story without getting overwhelmed by the raw emotion that had threatened to surface earlier.

Her hands moved mechanically, sorting through the mail without really seeing it as she recounted the events of the day to Mike.

Mike listened intently, his brow furrowing as the gravity of the situation sank in. His face reddened with frustration, and he stood up straighter, the concern turning into a mix of disbelief and anger. "Are you kidding me?" he said, his voice rising slightly. "Why didn't you call me straight away? I can't believe this happened."

Sarah flinched at his reaction, her shoulders tensing. She hadn't expected him to respond this way, but she understood. "Mike, I…" She began, but he cut her off, his emotions spilling out.

"No, don't say you were trying to protect me," he interrupted, his voice rough with worry. "This is serious, Sarah. I should have been there with you."

"I'll be fine," she assured him, though her words sounded hollow even to her own ears. Lost in thought, Sarah absentmindedly picked up a letter from the pile, tearing it open without really looking. But as she glanced down at the contents, her heart skipped a beat.

"Sarah, what is it?" Mike asked, his voice tinged with concern as he caught sight of her pale face.

Sarah held out the letter to him, her voice barely above a whisper. "It's... it's a threat," she said, her voice trembling with fear. "Someone doesn't want me to open the coffee shop."

Mike's expression darkened as he read the ominous words scrawled on the paper.

*Castle Road doesn't need outsiders like you. You should have stayed away. If you open that shop, you **will** regret it. Businesses here don't survive long when they don't belong. We'll be watching. Don't make us prove how serious we are.*

Walk away – while you still can.

His jaw clenched with anger, and he reached out to gently squeeze Sarah's hand in a silent gesture of support.

"Who would do something like this?" he muttered, his voice tight with frustration. "And why now, of all times?"

Sarah shook her head, her mind racing with possibilities. "I don't know," she admitted, her voice tinged with fear. "But whoever it is, it looks like they're trying to scare me away."

Mike's grip on her hand tightened, his protective instincts already in overdrive. "Well, they picked the wrong person to mess with," he declared, his tone defiant. "No one's going to intimidate you. I'll make sure of it."

Sarah could feel his anger building, and she quickly placed a hand on his arm, gently guiding him to calm down.

"Mike, please," she said softly, her voice steady despite the turmoil inside her. "I know you want to protect me, but getting worked up like this won't help. We need to stay focused."

He paused, looking at her, still clearly riled but softening at the sight of her concerned expression. "I just—" He stopped himself, taking a deep breath. "I just hate the thought of you being scared. I want to fix this. I'll do whatever it takes."

Sarah squeezed his hand, trying to reassure him. "I know, but right now, we need to think this through carefully. I'm not going anywhere. The coffee shop, this whole dream—it's not going to be taken away from us. We'll handle this, together."

Mike exhaled slowly, his shoulders relaxing slightly, though the fire still flickered behind his eyes. "You're right," he muttered, more to himself than her. "But I still don't like it."

Despite his words, Sarah couldn't shake the feeling of unease that settled like a lead weight in her stomach. She had tried so hard to build something meaningful with the coffee shop, to make it a place of peace and connection. But now, this unknown threat loomed over her, casting a shadow over the very future she had envisioned.

She leaned against Mike for a moment, trying to steady herself. "I know it might be nothing, but it feels so personal," she said quietly, the weight of the situation pressing down on her. "And I can't help but wonder if it's just the beginning."

Despite her growing apprehension, Sarah forced herself to focus, her mind racing as she tried to piece together the puzzle before her. Who would want to harm her, and why? Was the note a warning, a threat, or something more sinister?

As she pondered these questions, a sense of determination settled over her. She may not have all the answers yet, but she refused to let fear dictate her actions. With a steely resolve, she turned to Mike, her voice steady despite the tumultuous storm raging within her.

Taking a deep breath, Sarah squared her shoulders and met Mike's gaze with determination. "We won't let anyone scare us away. I'm not giving up on my dream that easily."

Mike watched Sarah, knowing her well enough to recognise the fire in her eyes, the unyielding determination that had always driven her forward. But he also saw the fear lurking beneath the surface, a fear that threatened to undermine her resolve.

"Sarah," he began gently, "we need to take this seriously. This isn't just about the coffee shop anymore. Someone out there wants to intimidate you, and we need to know why."

Sarah nodded, her mind already racing through the possibilities. "I know. But we can't let them win, Mike. This place means too much to me—to us. We'll just have to be more vigilant."

Mike pulled her in for another hug. "We'll figure it out," he promised. "In the meantime, I think it's time to let the paranoia that you always claim that I have really come into its own. Maybe we should think about getting some security cameras just to be safe."

As they discussed their next steps, the front door of the coffee shop jingled and Charlie walked in, making a beeline for his Sarah.

"Mum!" Charlie exclaimed, her face lighting up with relief. "Are you ok? Robyn told me about everything that happened today, and I just wanted to check that you were ok with my own two eyes."

Sarah managed a small smile, grateful for her son's concern. "I'm fine, just a bit shaken. But there's something else," she said, holding up the threatening letter. "I know it's a long shot, but you don't know anything about this do you?"

Charlie's eyes widened and he shook his head as he read the note, his expression shifting from shock to anger. "Who would do something like this? This is insane!"

"We don't know yet," Mike said, his tone calm but firm. "But we're going to find out. And in the meantime, we're going to take some precautions."

Charlie nodded in agreement. "Good idea."

Taking in the concerned faces of two of her favourite men in her life, Sarah took a deep breath, feeling a renewed sense of purpose. "Thank you both. I really appreciate you both, you do know that don't you?'

Chapter 6

Later that evening, Sarah found herself alone in the quiet, dimly lit space of the coffee shop. She walked through the familiar rooms, her footsteps echoing softly on the wooden floors, the only sound breaking the silence. The gentle hum of the refrigerator in the back and the soft flicker of the overhead lights were the only signs of life in the shop that evening.

The events of the day played over and over in her mind, each new detail adding to the puzzle she was determined to solve. But as she moved through the shop, a sense of calm began to settle over her, grounding her thoughts.

As much as she loved having everyone around her—the hustle of workmen, the chatter of friends and family—it was moments like these, when she was alone in the shop, that she truly appreciated. It was during these quiet moments that she could feel the weight of the space, the way it was starting to shape itself into something that was completely hers. It was the only time she felt like she fully owned the space, where every corner, every table, every coffee bean in the jar was a product of her vision, her effort, her heart.

She paused for a moment by the counter, running her fingers along the smooth surface. The soft glow of the hanging lights cast a warm hue across the room, creating a cosy, intimate atmosphere that made her feel, for a moment, like she could breathe a little easier. The thought of someone trying to destroy it was almost too much to bear. But beyond the anger and fear was something more insidious—the creeping feeling that this threat was beginning to tarnish her dream.

For a moment, she could almost feel the joy and excitement she had once felt when imagining this space slipping away. It was as if this shadow of fear was starting to colour everything—the coffee cups, the inviting warmth of the counter, the cozy corners she had carefully designed. She had worked so hard to make this place a reflection of her hopes, her aspirations, and now, it felt like someone was trying to steal that purity away.

No, she thought, taking a deep breath as she shook her head, trying to force the dark thoughts from her mind. She wouldn't let fear take away what she had built. With a final, steadying breath, Sarah pushed the unease aside, focusing instead on the things that made this place hers. She would not let anyone take away the peace it had brought her, or the joy it would bring to others. It wasn't just a coffee shop—it was a part of her. And she wasn't about to let anyone tarnish that.

As she stood there, lost in thought, the door opened quietly, and Inspector Stanley stepped inside. "Mrs Meadows?" he called softly, his voice carrying a note of concern.

Sarah turned, offering him a tired smile. "Inspector Stanley. I think after the day that we've had, you can call me Sarah and thank you for coming. I didn't realise that you would make a personal appearance."

"Oh, it's not a problem," Stanley nodded, his expression serious. "The desk clerk told me about the note and it's not often that the same name comes up twice in one day. I thought it best to check in on you."

Sarah handed him the letter, watching as he read the threatening words. His brow furrowed, and he looked up at her with concern. "This is far from friendly, isn't it? Do you have any idea who might have sent it. Or for that matter, why someone might be upset with you?"

"No," Sarah admitted, frustration creeping into her voice. "I can't think of anyone who would want to hurt me or stop the coffee shop from opening."

Stanley nodded thoughtfully. "Well, we're obviously going to be tied up for the moment investigating the incident at the spa. But I'll take the opportunity to ask around while I'm in the area. In the meantime, I agree with your husband's suggestion to install security cameras. And please, be careful. Whoever is behind this, they seem determined to scare you."

Sarah nodded, her resolve hardening once again. "I will. And thank you, Inspector."

Stanley gave her a reassuring smile, as he moved towards the door. "We'll get to the bottom of this, Sarah. Just hang in there."

Alone once again in the empty shop, she took a final look around, turned off the lights and locked the door behind her, stepping out into the cool night air. She glanced back at the little coffee shop, feeling a surge of protectiveness and pride. This was her dream, her sanctuary, and she wasn't about to let someone ruin it before she had even started.

The next morning, Sarah was in the middle of rearranging cushions in the window seat when she heard a small knock on the window. Looking up, she smiled as she saw Amy, the owner of the ceramics shop down the street, waving at her through the glass.

As she welcomed her into the shop, Sarah took in the vision of Amy, with her barely contained mane of hair valiantly held back by a colourful headband adorned with ceramic beads that Sarah was certain Amy had crafted herself. Sarah always felt that Amy's warm smile seemed to light up the room when she arrived, her presence carrying a vibrancy and infectious joy.

Amy's outfit reflected her eccentric personality, with a flowy bohemian-style tunic covered with intricate patterns and layers of beaded necklaces that clinked softly with each step. Her hands, adorned with rings of various shapes and sizes, were rarely still, often gesturing animatedly as she spoke.

Right from the first days of getting the keys to her place, Amy's role in Sarah's venture into the world of coffee had been more than just friendly, it was pivotal. In the early days of planning and preparation for the coffee shop, Amy was a constant presence, offering invaluable advice and support. She would often drop by Sarah's shop-to-be, the smell of fresh paint still lingering in the air, to lend a hand or simply to chat over a cuppa.

Not only did Amy provide practical guidance on setting up shop and sourcing the best beans, but she also played the role of a community ambassador, introducing Sarah to the eclectic mix of locals who frequented her ceramics store. With a mischievous twinkle in her eye, Amy would provide a running commentary on each person she introduced, sharing titbits of gossip and stories that gave Sarah a deeper understanding of the vibrant community they were a part of.

In those early days, Amy had been one of the first to pop her smiley face around the door, partly out of pure nosiness, but also reaching out that hand of friendship to the new shop owner. It was clear that she wanted Sarah to feel welcomed to the street, to feel like she was a part of something special. Amy's presence had a way of making Sarah feel that the coffee shop wasn't just another business in a row of shops—it was becoming part of a wider, close-knit community. And even from their first meeting, Amy had been instrumental in giving Sarah both moral and literal support in the process of getting her place up and almost running.

Every time Sarah needed advice, whether it was about where to source her pastries or how to set up the counter in a way that invited customers to linger, Amy was there, ready with answers—or at the very least, helpful suggestions. What Sarah didn't realize at first was how much more than advice Amy was offering. Her presence was a reassurance, a quiet anchor in the whirlwind of getting the coffee shop ready. It was incredibly reassuring to know that Amy, with her wealth of knowledge and easy-going nature, was just doors away whenever Sarah needed her. The genuine sense of camaraderie Amy offered was like a warm embrace, a reminder that no matter how daunting the task, Sarah wasn't alone.

And it wasn't just about business, Amy genuinely wanted Sarah to feel at home in their neighbourhood, and her efforts didn't go unnoticed. As Sarah reflected on those early days, she couldn't help but feel grateful for Amy's warmth and generosity, which had played a significant role in making her feel welcomed and supported as she embarked on this new chapter of her life.

Amy's influence was felt every day in the shop—through the carefully curated selection of local art, the handmade mugs, and, of course, the stories she would share with Sarah.

As much as Sarah had hoped to create a space for the community, Amy had already made it clear that she was here to support her friend.

Despite the bustling nature of her ceramics shop, she always seemed to have time for a friendly chat or a spontaneous burst of laughter, her enthusiasm for her craft infectious to anyone lucky enough to encounter her. As Amy greeted Sarah with a hug, it felt as though her warmth and joy flowed through the embrace, filling Sarah with a sense of comfort and ease.

"Amy, hey!" Sarah exclaimed, pulling her down to sit beside her in the window seat. "It's so good to see you. How's everything going down at yours?"

Amy's face lit up with a wide smile as she approached Sarah, her colourful trainers padding softly against the wooden floor. "Oh, you know, same old same old," she replied with a chuckle. "Trying to keep up with all these pottery orders. The summer holidays are always crazy. Mums and dads trying to entertain their little 'darlings'... I swear, it's like a non-stop circus some days."

Sarah laughed, shaking her head in agreement. "I can't even imagine! You're braver than me. I mean, I have three boys of my own, and just thinking about the countless opportunities for smashing things is terrifying!"

Amy raised an eyebrow, grinning mischievously. "Ah, but that's what makes them *darling*—the occasional chaos is all part of the charm! But enough about me, how's my favourite coffee shop owner doing?"

Sarah laughed, gesturing for Amy to take a seat at one of the tables. "Busy, but good," she replied. "Mike and I have been working non-stop to get everything ready for the grand opening next week."

"It's going to be fine," Amy said, her tone reassuring as she placed a hand on Sarah's arm. "You've got it all planned out, and you and Mike make a great team. Just one last final push, and you'll be there."

But then her expression shifted, becoming more serious. "Hey, I heard about what happened at the *Serenity Spa*," she said, her voice softening with sympathy. "Are you ok? It must have been pretty scary."

Sarah nodded, her mind briefly flashing back to the chaos of the previous day. She wasn't surprised that the news had travelled that quickly, as gossip was one of the most sought after currencies in this street.

"Yeah, it was definitely unexpected," she admitted. "But I'm ok. Just trying to focus on getting everything sorted here."

Amy leaned in closer, her eyes curious. "Do you know anything about what actually happened?" she asked, her voice dropping to a whisper.

Sarah shook her head, her brow furrowing in thought. "I don't really know that much more than anyone else," she replied. "Just rumours and speculation, really."

Amy let out a snort of laughter, her bubbly personality shining through once again. "Well, they definitely missed the mark on the whole 'serenity' thing, didn't they?" she remarked, shaking her head. "I mean, you couldn't have a less serene experience if you tried."

But as she looked at Sarah, she noticed a subtle shift in her demeanour. Sarah's smile had faded, and her eyes seemed distant. Amy leaned in closer, her brows furrowing in concern. "Is there something else bothering you?" she asked gently. "You seem a bit down."

She instantly realized she might have been too flippant, that perhaps Sarah wasn't ready for jokes just yet. Her face softened with regret. "Sorry, you know me," Amy continued, her voice quiet with sincerity. "I'm always trying to make a joke, no matter what's going on. I honestly didn't mean to upset you."

Sarah shook her head, her voice soothing. "It's not you, Amy. Really."

But Amy wasn't convinced. She reached out, placing a hand on Sarah's arm, her concern deepening. "Come on, you don't seem like yourself at all," she said, her tone soft but insistent. "Has this really got to you? What happened... it's more than just the usual stuff, isn't it?"

Sarah hesitated, unsure whether to share her concerns, but Amy's insistence made her want to open up. "Well, it's not every day that you see a dead body, that's certainly bad enough…. but there was also this….," she began, her voice trailing off as she reached into her bag and pulled out a crumpled piece of paper.

Amy's eyes widened as she took the note from Sarah's outstretched hand. Unfolding it carefully, she squinted at the harsh words scrawled across the page, her brows knitting together in concentration. For a brief moment, something flickered across her face. But it was gone just as quickly.

"Who would send you something like this?" Amy exclaimed, her voice carefully measured despite the shock in her tone. "Do you have any idea who it might be from?"

Sarah shook her head, her heart heavy with confusion and hurt. "I have no idea," she confessed, her voice barely above a whisper. "But it's been bothering me ever since I found it."

Amy's expression softened with empathy as she reached out to comfort Sarah. "I'm so sorry, Sarah," she murmured, her voice filled with genuine concern. "I can't imagine why anyone would want to upset you, especially since you've been fitting in so well around here."

Sarah managed a weak smile, grateful for Amy's support. "Thanks, Amy," she replied, her voice wavering slightly. "It means a lot to me. Maybe I'm not fitting in as well as I had hoped, though."

Amy's concern deepened at Sarah's words, but she could sense that she didn't need any more stress at the moment. "Hey, don't worry about that now," she said reassuringly, reaching out to squeeze Sarah's hand gently. "You're doing great, and you'll find your place here in no time."

Sarah nodded, appreciating Amy's attempt to lift her spirits. "Thanks, Amy,". "Anyway, that's enough about that for the moment", she murmured gratefully. Tell me more about what's been happening at the ceramics shop. I can't wait to hear all about your latest creations."

As Amy began to animatedly describe her latest artistic endeavours, Sarah tried to focus on her friend's words. She reached into her bag to put the letter away, hoping that out of sight might mean out of mind. Her fingers brushed against the crumpled paper, and she pushed it deep into the bag, attempting to shove her worries along with it.

Just as she managed to tuck the letter out of sight, Sarah glanced down at her wrist and realized with a start that her watch was missing. She remembered taking it off during her treatment at the *Serenity Spa* and felt a twinge of annoyance at herself for forgetting it.

Making a mental note to go back to the *Serenity Spa* tomorrow to retrieve her watch, Sarah forced herself to refocus on Amy's recounting of her latest ceramic projects. Despite the nagging worries in the back of her mind, she forced herself to focus on her friend, and the escape from all her worries that her presence provided.

As their conversation flowed, the tension of the previous topic melted away, replaced by a sense of camaraderie and friendship. Sarah found herself grateful for Amy's visit, grateful for the opportunity to take a moment to connect with someone who understood the challenges of starting a new business in Southsea. she listened intently, her own excitement growing as she imagined the beautiful pieces Amy was describing. Despite the chaos of preparing for the coffee shop's opening, she couldn't help but feel inspired by Amy's creativity and dedication to her art.

"You know, Amy," Sarah said, her eyes lighting up with an idea, "I've been thinking about how to make the coffee shop stand out, and I just had the best thought. What if we used some of your ceramic pieces in the shop? Like, handmade mugs, plates, maybe even some decorative tiles?"

Amy's face lit up with delight. "Oh, Sarah, that's a brilliant idea! I'd love to make some custom pieces for you. Imagine how unique it would be—handmade crockery right from our own street!"

Sarah nodded enthusiastically. "Exactly! It would add such a personal touch, and I think customers would really appreciate the uniqueness. Plus, it's a great way to support each other's businesses. Maybe we could even sell some of your pieces in the shop?"

Amy clapped her hands together, her excitement bubbling over. "Yes, absolutely! I can just see it now—bright, colourful mugs and plates that add character to your coffee shop. We can collaborate on the designs to match the theme of *Sarah's Secrets*. This is going to be so much fun!"

Sarah smiled, feeling a renewed sense of excitement. "I can't wait to see what you come up with, Amy. This is exactly the kind of thing that makes this community so special. And it'll be something truly unique for the shop."

Amy grinned. "I'll get started right away. Let's meet up soon to brainstorm designs and colours. I want to make sure everything fits perfectly with your vision for the shop."

"Sounds like a plan," Sarah agreed, feeling a wave of optimism wash over her. "Thanks, Amy. This is going to be amazing."

As the afternoon sun streamed through the windows, casting a warm glow over the cosy interior of *Sarah's Secrets*, Sarah and Amy laughed and chatted, their bond growing stronger with each passing moment.

Eventually, as the conversation began to wind down, Amy glanced at her watch and sighed. "Well, as much as I'd love to stay and chat all day, I've got to get back to the shop," she said regretfully, pushing herself up from the table.

Sarah stood up as well, giving Amy a warm hug. "Thanks for stopping by, Amy," she said sincerely. "It was so good to catch up."

Amy returned the hug with equal warmth, her smile bright. "Anytime, Sarah," she replied. "And if you ever need a break from the coffee shop chaos, you know where to find me."

With a final wave, Amy made her way out of the coffee shop, the bell above the door jingling softly in her wake. As Sarah watched her go, she felt a sense of gratitude wash over her. Amid all the uncertainty and stress of starting her new venture, it was moments like these—moments of connection and friendship—that reminded her why she had taken the leap in the first place.

As the door shut behind Amy, Sarah took a moment to savour the warmth that her friend's visit had brought. The laughter, the lightness of their conversation—it had all filled the space with a kind of energy that made the coffee shop feel like a real place, a hub of connection and creativity, just as she had always envisioned. For a moment, the shop was her dream come true. The hum of the espresso machine, the low murmur of customers, and the quiet familiarity of the space settled around her like a blanket. She smiled softly, feeling reassured that this place was becoming exactly what she wanted it to be.

But as the door swung shut behind Amy, the atmosphere shifted in an instant. A sharp, familiar voice abruptly punctured the warmth, the joy, the fleeting sense of calm that had filled the shop.

"Mrs Meadows, I hope I'm not interrupting anything too important," came the gravelly tone of Edward Barnes, who appeared in the doorway like a dark cloud on an otherwise sunny day.

The change was almost physical, as if the energy in the room was a revolving door, with Amy's departure ushering out the cheerfulness and Edward's arrival dragging in something colder, heavier. The shop seemed to shrink a little, the lightness vanishing with each step Edward took further into the room. Sarah felt the mood shift almost like a weight pressing down on her chest as he stood there, blocking the doorframe with his imposing presence.

Where Amy had left a sense of comfort, Edward seemed to fill the space with a tension that was almost palpable. The door had hardly closed behind Amy, yet the change was undeniable. It was as if the moods revolved with the people who came in and out, and Edward's presence never failed to pull the room in a different direction. Sarah braced herself, her smile faltering as she faced him, knowing that whatever conversation was about to unfold, it wouldn't carry the same warmth that had lingered just moments before.

"Mr. Barnes, not at all. What can I do for you?" she asked, trying to keep her tone as welcoming as possible.

Edward Barnes stepped inside, his cane tapping against the wooden floor with deliberate precision. His expression was stern, his brow furrowed as if he were carrying the weight of the world on his shoulders—or at least, the weight of Castle Road.

"I've noticed that since you've started preparing to open this coffee shop, there's been a certain... increase in activity around here," he began, his tone suggesting that his visit was far from a casual drop-in.

Sarah blinked in surprise. "Activity?" she echoed, unsure of where this conversation was headed. "Well, I suppose that's to be expected with all the preparations and workmen coming in and out."

Edward's lips pressed into a thin line, his displeasure evident. "It's not the activity I'm concerned about, Mrs Meadows. It's the *kind* of people it's attracting. The workmen, the police stopping by after that incident at the *Serenity Spa*, and even some of the other shop owners have been poking their heads in. It's all very unsettling."

Sarah's heart sank a little. She had hoped her coffee shop would be a welcome addition to the community, a place where everyone could eventually feel at home. "I'm sorry to hear that, Mr. Barnes," she said earnestly. "I never intended to cause any disruption. I thought a bit of liveliness might be a good thing for all of us on the street."

Edward grunted, unimpressed. "Liveliness is one thing, but this... this is bringing in a crowd that doesn't understand the quiet dignity of this street. They loiter, they chat loudly, and some of them even wander into my shop, as if it were some sort of curiosity to gawk at instead of a place of business."

Sarah's initial reaction was to think, *Isn't that what shops were for?* But before she could voice the thought, a pang of guilt struck her. She knew Edward's antique shop was his pride and joy, a testament to decades of dedication. The thought of causing him distress over something she had worked so hard to create troubled her deeply.

Taking a breath, she softened her approach, her tone sincere. "I understand your concerns," she said, her gaze steady. "But I assure you, once the shop opens, I'll make sure it adds to the charm of Castle Road, not detracts from it. I want *Sarah's Secrets* to be a place that complements the atmosphere here, not disrupts it."

She looked at him, hoping her words would ease some of his apprehension. The last thing she wanted was for her dream to be the source of conflict in the very community she was trying to become a part of.

Edward's eyes narrowed slightly, his expression still stern. "See that it does, Mrs Meadows. This street has a history, a reputation, and I won't see it tarnished by newcomers who don't appreciate what's already here."

Sarah nodded, understanding that behind his gruff exterior was a deep-rooted fear of change. "I promise you, Mr. Barnes, I'm committed to being a positive addition to this community. I'll do everything I can to ensure that *Sarah's Secrets* respects the traditions of this street."

Edward studied her for a long moment, then gave a curt nod. "I'll hold you to that," he said, his voice carrying a note of finality. With that, he turned and made his way out of the shop, his stick tapping with a sense of deliberate purpose as the door closed behind him.

Chapter 7

Rachel Bennett stepped into the reception area of *Lotus Blossom*, her wellness centre, with the quiet confidence of a woman who had carefully constructed a life of balance and grace. The space was a sanctuary of calm, bathed in the golden glow of flickering candlelight, the air perfumed with a delicate blend of patchouli and frankincense. Soft, ethereal music drifted through the room, harmonizing with the subtle chime of wind bells that adorned the doorway.

Everything in *Lotus Blossom* had been meticulously curated to exude tranquillity, a reflection of Rachel herself. Gone was the impersonal sterility found in many wellness centres; here, rich draped tapestries in shades of deep indigo and soft lavender cascaded along the walls, creating a sense of warmth and peace. Crystals lined the windowsills, catching the fading light and casting tiny rainbows across the floor—a gentle reminder that even in the quiet, there was magic to be found.

Rachel had spent years refining her presence to mirror the calm she provided for her clients. She looked every inch the kind-hearted carer—wide blue eyes framed by softly curled hair that she'd pinned behind her ears. Though slight in stature, there was a resilience to Rachel's stance that suggested she'd seen her share of challenges. A few faint freckles dusted the bridge of her nose, and laughter lines creased at the corners of her eyes whenever she smiled—which was often. Today, she wore a flowing, bohemian-style blouse in plum that complemented the room's purple hues.

Despite the serene air she projected, Rachel knew better than anyone that peace was not something stumbled upon—it was something cultivated, shaped through discipline and resolve. There had been a time when her hazel eyes carried the weight of exhaustion, of nights spent wrestling with self-doubt, of the relentless pursuit of perfection in both her business and herself. Now, when she met the gaze of her reflection, she saw a woman who had built something real, something enduring.

A soft click from the front door drew Rachel's attention. A new visitor had arrived, stepping hesitantly into the embrace of *Lotus Blossom*. Rachel's gaze softened as she approached, her voice a soothing melody in the hushed ambiance.

"Good morning, and welcome," Rachel greeted, her voice echoing through the serene space. "How can I help you today?"

The client, a weary-looking woman with lines etched into her brow, offered a hesitant smile in return. "I have an appointment for a massage with Rachel Bennett," she replied.

Rachel's smile widened, "How lovely, that would be me. Please come on through" she said, gesturing for the woman to follow her towards the treatment rooms located down the hall. "You're in good hands, even if I do say so myself", she laughed.

As they reached the treatment room, Rachel ushered her client inside with a gentle wave of her hand. "Please make yourself comfortable," she said, her voice a soft murmur. "I'll be with you in just a moment."

With practiced precision, Rachel set about preparing the space for the upcoming massage, her movements deliberate and purposeful. She arranged the towels with care, adjusted the lighting to create a soothing ambiance, and chose a selection of aromatic oils designed to relax and uplift the senses.

As Rachel worked, her mind drifted to the events of the morning—the shocking news of Terri's death, the whispers of suspicion that lingered in the air. Despite her best efforts to remain composed, a sense of unease gnawed at the edges of her consciousness, threatening to shatter the illusion of tranquillity she had worked so hard to maintain.

She had woken up that morning with a strange feeling in the pit of her stomach, an uneasy premonition she couldn't quite place. The news had already started to spread like wildfire, but the full weight of it didn't hit until she overheard a conversation in the wellness centre's reception earlier. Two clients, sitting side by side and sipping their welcome drinks, were talking in hushed tones, their voices tinged with anxiety.

"I'm so glad we're booked in here today," one of them said, her tone low but filled with clear relief. "I mean, with what happened over at that other place... I wouldn't feel safe at all right now."

Her friend nodded vigorously. "I know, right? A woman was found dead! How awful. And they're saying it might have been something more than just an accident. I heard someone mention 'murder' earlier. I'm just glad I'm not anywhere near that place."

The words hit Rachel like a cold wave. She felt a tightening in her chest as she turned away, instinctively pulling herself together. Murder. The word echoed in her mind, and her stomach churned. She had tried to keep the spa's reputation pristine, to maintain the image of calm and healing, but now, this tragedy, and the suspicion hanging over it, threatened to disturb everything.

Leaving her client to relax with a face pack covering her face, Rachel took the opportunity to step into a small side area and reached for her phone, her fingers trembling slightly as she unlocked the screen. Her heart pounded in her chest, and she found herself dreading what she might see. She opened a local social media chat, hoping to find some semblance of clarity amidst the chaos.

As the page loaded, Rachel's heart sank when she saw the headline, "Tragedy Strikes at Local Spa, Woman Found

Dead." Her breath caught in her throat, and she hesitated before scrolling through the comments, each one filled with speculation and fear. Every message seemed to spiral further into uncertainty, with whispers of foul play, concerns about the spa's reputation, and questions that Rachel knew would only make things worse. The calm she had worked so hard to create now felt distant, slipping through her fingers like sand.

Feeling a knot form in the pit of her stomach, Rachel closed the app with a shaky exhale. The reality of Terri's death hit her like a punch to the gut, sending shockwaves of unease through her already fragile composure.

With a heavy sigh, Rachel tried to force herself to focus on her work, but despite her efforts to push the thoughts aside, the idea of Terri's lifeless body lingered in her mind.

Stepping back in the treatment area, she focussed her attention back on her client. As Rachel's skilled hands worked to knead away her client's tension, her mind wandered back to the news about Terri. But it wasn't just the unpleasant nature of the news that shook Rachel—it was how close to home it hit. She knew Terri.

While they hadn't always had a close relationship, and at times their interactions had bordered on toxic, it was all so long ago. They had their differences, sure, but hearing about her sudden death, especially in such a brutal and shocking way, was something Rachel never expected, and certainly never wanted to hear. No matter how many times they'd butted heads in the past, no matter how much their approaches to business had clashed, she never imagined that it would end like this.

Rachel felt a deep, unsettling discomfort gnawing at her. *No one ever expects this*, she thought. Even with all the bad blood between them, the idea of someone so familiar—someone she had seen around the community, someone who had shared this world with her—ending up dead in such a tragic way was jarring. It was a stark reminder of how fleeting everything could be, and how quickly things could spiral out of control. The shock of the news twisted in her stomach, her fingers briefly faltering as she worked.

But now, with Terri's life cruelly cut short, Rachel couldn't help but wonder if there was more to their turbulent relationship than met the eye. Could there be a connection between Terri's death and the simmering tensions that had defined their interactions for so long?

As the session came to an end and her client departed, Rachel felt the weight of the day's events settle upon her shoulders once more. Alone in the quiet of the treatment room, she allowed herself to finally confront the whirlwind of emotions churning within.

Tears pricked at Rachel's eyes as she grappled with the enormity of Terri's death and the implications it held for her own life and livelihood. Feeling the need to talk to someone that might share her feeling, Rachel reached for her phone, her fingers moving quickly as she composed a message.

"Have you seen the news?" she typed, her thumb hovering over the send button for a moment before finally pressing down. The message sent with a soft beep, disappearing into the digital ether as Rachel anxiously awaited a response.

In his cluttered flat on the outskirts of Southsea, in Eastney, Marcus Combes sat alone, surrounded by the remnants of a life marked by hardship and regret. The flat, tucked away at the slightly isolated end of the five-mile-long seafront, felt as much like a refuge from the world as it did a cage for his mind. The air was thick with the smell of stale coffee and the remnants of half-finished projects. A worn armchair sat in one corner, a book left open on the table next to it, but Marcus hardly noticed. His focus was elsewhere, on the view through his window.

He could see the uninterrupted stretch of water from where he sat, the grey blue of the sea blending seamlessly into the sky. Marcus stared out at the water, lost in the vastness of it, trying to come to terms with the news of his sister Terri's death. It had shaken him to his core, stirring up a whirlwind of conflicting emotions that threatened to consume him.

They hadn't been close in recent years—his relationship with Terri had always been strained, full of tension and unspoken resentments. She had lived her life with a fierce determination, always striving for more, while he had drifted, weighed down by his own choices and missed opportunities. And yet, despite the distance, hearing that she was gone left a bitter taste in his mouth.

Marcus had always known that their paths had diverged, but he never imagined it would end like this. There had been no warning, no signs of what was to come. The loss felt sudden and raw, and his mind raced through old memories, some of them filled with regret. The view outside his window, the unbroken expanse of the sea, seemed to mock his inability to find clarity. The water stretched on forever, just like the unresolved feelings he had carried for years. How could he make peace with the past now, when it felt like it had slipped away so suddenly?

He wiped his hand over his face, taking in a shaky breath, trying to steady himself. His thoughts felt like the waves outside—choppy, relentless, and difficult to navigate. There was no escaping the grief, no matter how hard he tried to distance himself from it. Staring out at the endless horizon, the isolation of Eastney seemed more profound than to him ever.

As he sat amidst the disarray of his surroundings, Marcus couldn't escape the memories that haunted him—the bitter arguments, the broken promises, the unspoken resentments that had driven a wedge between him and Terri. Their relationship had always been fraught with tension, a tangled web of love and loathing that he suspected was shared by many siblings.

Now, with Terri gone, Marcus was left adrift in a sea of guilt and grief, his heart heavy with the weight of what could have been. He had never been able to mend the rift between them, to bridge the divide that had grown wider with each passing year. And now, it was too late.

Looking around his cluttered room, Marcus saw reminders of his troubled past at every turn—the unpaid bills stacked haphazardly on the kitchen counter, the empty bottles littering the coffee table, the faded photographs gathering dust on the mantelpiece. Each one was a painful reminder of the mistakes he had made, the chances he had squandered.

But amidst the chaos of his surroundings, there was one thing that stood out—a photograph of Terri, smiling brightly at the camera, her eyes alive with laughter and mischief. It was a stark contrast to the woman he had known in recent years, a shadow of her former self consumed by bitterness and regret.

Staring at the photograph, Marcus felt a surge of guilt wash over him, a tidal wave of remorse for all the things left unsaid, all the wounds left unhealed. He had never been able to tell Terri how much she meant to him, how much he regretted the way things had turned out between them. And now, he never would.

Tears pricked at Marcus's eyes as he struggled to come to terms with the enormity of his loss. He had never been one to show his emotions, to wear his heart on his sleeve, but now, in the privacy of his own home, he allowed himself to finally confront the pain that had been simmering beneath the surface for so long.

But amidst the torrent of feelings, there was another, darker emotion lurking—an insidious guilt that gnawed at him, one that went beyond the loss of a chance to reconcile. For weeks before Terri's death, Marcus had been contemplating reaching out to her, not just to mend their fractured relationship, but also to seek her help. He was drowning in debt, his financial situation growing more desperate by the day, and he had hoped that perhaps Terri, with her relative stability, might be able to lend him a hand.

He had even drafted a letter, now crumpled and abandoned in the corner of his desk, in which he had poured out his heart, pleading for her understanding and help. But he had never found the courage to send it, his pride and the fear of rejection holding him back.

Terri's death had snatched that away from him. Or had it?

The thought crept into his mind, unbidden and unwelcome. As the only remaining family member, wasn't there a chance he might inherit something from her estate? The idea made his stomach churn with a mixture of hope and self-loathing. It was a vile thought, one that made him feel even more despicable, but in his desperation, he couldn't completely push it away.

Marcus wiped his eyes and forced himself to stand. He walked over to the desk and picked up the crumpled letter, smoothing it out with shaky hands. He read through it one last time, the words blurring as fresh tears welled up. Then, with a sigh, he let the paper fall back to the desk, his mind racing with conflicting emotions.

He hated himself for even thinking about the possibility of benefiting from Terri's death, but the reality of his situation was inescapable. The bills wouldn't stop coming, and his creditors wouldn't wait forever. He had to face the truth, no matter how painful it was.

As he stood there, staring at the letter, Marcus felt a heavy sense of dread settle over him. He knew he would have to find out what Terri had left behind, if anything. And if he did inherit something, would it ease his guilt, or only deepen it?

Chapter 8

Emily Parker sat in the third row of the seminar room at Portsmouth University, her attention wavering between the speaker at the podium and the insistent buzzing of her phone in her pocket. Her fingers curled around her phone, the edge of the device pressing into her palm. The lecture on the latest advancements in skincare technology barely registered as she struggled to focus. Giving in to distraction, she discreetly glanced down at her phone, where the message notification flashed urgently.

Terri's dead.

A muscle in her jaw tensed. She forced herself to exhale, smoothing her expression before anyone noticed. *Calm, stay calm*, she told herself. When the speaker asked a question, Emily shifted in her chair, nodding as if she were following along.

Her phone vibrated again, and she nearly dropped it.

"Are you ok?" The woman beside her frowned slightly. Emily gave a quick, taut smile and then excusing herself, she stood up and shuffled past the people seated in her row, slipping out of the seminar room and into the corridor, where she quickly rechecked her phone.

Reading the message from Rachel, a wave of shock and disbelief washed over her. Her mind instantly transported back to a vision of the three of them at college. It might have been twenty years since her training days with Rachel and Terri, but the news of Terri's death still hit her like a punch in her stomach.

Despite the chaos of her thoughts, Emily tried to maintain her outward composure, her professional facade unyielding as she made her way back to the seminar room. But as she stepped inside, she could feel the cracks beginning to show. The dim lighting of the room, though welcome, couldn't fully mask the red-rimmed eyes and blotchy skin from the tears she had fought so hard to keep in check.

As the lecture continued, Emily found it increasingly difficult to focus. The speaker's words seemed to blur together, his slides flashing before her eyes without registering. Her thoughts raced uncontrollably, her heart heavy with the weight of Rachel's message and the memories it had stirred up. Every word she read echoed in her mind, reminding her of feelings that she'd pushed down inside herself for so long.

Taking a deep breath, Emily tried her best to compose herself. She could feel the heat rising in her chest, the emotions threatening to spill over once again. But for now, all she could do was pretend to listen, to act as if she were fully present, even though every part of her mind was elsewhere.

Was it possible that Terri was really gone? Unable to resist, Emily had searched online for any mention of her old friend, and what she found was an avalanche of rumours. As she sat there, the messages and online chatter echoed in Emily's mind. Whispers of a police investigation, shock at Terri's sudden death, and unsettling rumours that only seemed to grow the more she read.

Some hinted as suspicious circumstances, others at a missing husband the police were eager to find. There were mentions of pressure, arguments, and tension- though no one seemed to know the full story. And then came the darker speculation, the ones Emily barely dared to consider. Words like *murder* and *foul play* were surfacing more often, tangled n gossip about rivalries and betrayals. The truth was uncertain, but one thing was clear: Terri's death wasn't as straight forward as it first seemed.

Emily tried to push the thoughts away, but they clung to her mind like an unwelcome fog. What could have happened to Terri? Was there really more to her death than just an unfortunate accident? The whispers swirling around town suddenly felt more ominous, more sinister, and Emily couldn't shake the feeling that there more to the story than anyone was letting on.

As the seminar ended and the other attendees began to filter out of the room, Emily remained seated, her mind a whirlwind of conflicting emotions. She knew she needed to reach out to Rachel, to offer her support and find out more about what had happened. But as she stared at her phone, her thumb hovering over the reply button, Emily couldn't shake the feeling that the truth behind Terri's death might be far more complicated—and far more dangerous—than she ever could have imagined.

Arriving at *Parker Dermatology*, Emily was greeted by the familiar hustle and bustle of her clinic. The usual sounds of phones ringing, patients chatting, and staff moving about their day filled the space but beneath it all, Emily couldn't shake the strange dissonance. It was as if the world around her had somehow continued, completely unaware of the storm that had just hit her own life.

She was stunned by how normal everything felt. The clinic, usually a place of calm efficiency, hadn't changed. Yet to Emily, it seemed surreal. How could her colleagues be so casual? How could the world keep turning when Terri was dead?

Her interactions with the staff were cordial, but there was an awkwardness to them that hadn't been there before. An unspoken understanding lingered in the way some of them looked at her. The hushed voices when they thought she wasn't listening. The quick, stolen glances exchanged between colleagues. It was as if they had all agreed to continue with their routine, burying the weight of it beneath their daily tasks.

Emily felt a growing sense of isolation creeping in. The sense of normality around her felt jarring, like an affront to the chaos churning inside her. How could they all go on like this? How could anyone pretend that nothing had happened. She carried those questions with her throughout the day, their answers always just out of reach.

Out in the clinic, the whispers had already started spreading. Throughout the day, Emily found herself fielding questions from concerned clients, offering reassurances while suppressing the storm within.

One client, a middle-aged woman, hesitated before speaking. "I heard about what happened... over at that other spa," she said, her voice low, as though not wanting to speak too loudly. "Terri Treharne, right? It's just... awful. Do you think it'll affect the local businesses? Will it be safe to keep coming around here?"

For a moment, Emily's heart skipped a beat. She saw it then, the unspoken fear in the woman's eyes. Her heart skipped a beat, but she quickly composed herself, flashing the client a reassuring smile. "I understand your concern," she said smoothly, her voice calm and steady. "But I assure you, the clinic is as safe as it's ever been. The situation is being handled, and we're all continuing with our usual routines. You have nothing to worry about."

Her words were soothing, though inside, she was anything but calm. The thought of someone dying so suddenly, so violently, was still too raw, and it gnawed at her even as she spoke. But she couldn't let it slip. She had to keep the façade intact.

The woman nodded, still looking uncertain but comforted by Emily's words. As she left, Emily let out a slow breath, regaining her composure. The questions, the worries, the rumours, she would have to manage them all. She had to stay strong even if inside, she felt anything but.

As the day wore on and the clinic began to empty out, Emily found herself alone in her office. She sat in silence, staring at nothing, her mind racing with questions and doubts. But beneath the weight of her concerns about Terri's death, another pressing matter clawed at her consciousness.

She reached for her phone, hesitating for a moment before scrolling through her contacts. There it was, buried among the names of acquaintances and former colleagues. Emily's thumb hovered over the screen, the memories of their shared history flooding back to her.

It had been so many years since she'd last spoken to Terri's brother, yet there was something unresolved between them, a conversation that needed to be had, especially now, in the wake of Terri's passing.

With a deep breath, Emily pressed the call button, bracing herself against the reception that might be at the other end of the line.

Marcus fumbled for his phone in his pocket, his fingers brushing against the worn fabric of his jeans. Pulling it out, he glanced at the screen, his stomach sinking when he saw the name flashing there. It was a name he had not expected to see today, or frankly, anytime soon. The very sight of it sent a chill through him, his grip tightening around the phone as a wave of unease washed over him.

His heart beat a little faster as the phone continued to ring, instantly on edge. He knew this was someone he couldn't avoid, someone whose call might bring up a whole mess of things he wasn't sure he was ready to face. But the call was already in progress, and the only option now was to answer.

He cleared his throat, trying to mask the tremor in his voice. "Hello?" he said, forcing his tone to remain even, despite the growing wariness building within him.

"Marcus, it's Emily," she said. "I know it's been a while, but I think we need to talk."

He paused, then sighed. "Yeah, I figured you might call. Where will I find you?"

"I'm at my clinic. Can you come by? I think it would be better if we spoke in person."

"Sure, I'll be there in a bit," Marcus replied, hanging up the phone in resignation.

When Marcus arrived at the clinic, it was just as the last of Emily's colleagues were shutting up and clearing out for the day. The low murmur of their goodbyes and the sound of coats being grabbed from hooks filled the air. Emily could feel the curious glances directed her way as she stepped out to meet him, and though she tried to ignore them, the weight of their gaze was undeniable.

With a quick glance over her shoulder, Emily ushered Marcus into the salon, the space still humming with the remnants of the day's energy. "Come on," she said, trying to keep her voice steady, "Let's head to my office."

As they walked, Emily was keenly aware of the hushed whispers that filled the space behind them. Her colleagues—now gathered in small groups, ready to leave for the evening—watched them closely, their glances sharp and filled with questions she didn't have answers for. She kept her focus on the path ahead, resisting the urge to look back, though she could feel the weight of their silent speculation pressing against her shoulders.

The salon's warmth and movement soon faded as they stepped into the corridor leading to her office. It was stark in contrast—clean lines, pale walls, and sharp fluorescent lighting that cast a cold glow on the polished floor. The faint scent of antiseptic still clung to the air, a reminder of the clinical precision Emily brought to her work. Each footstep echoed slightly in the stillness, emphasizing the quiet distance from the lively front of the building.

When they reached her office, she opened the door and motioned for Marcus to enter first, her hand lingering on the doorframe as she hesitated for a moment, feeling the weight of everyone's eyes on her back. The soft click of the door closing behind her provided a small, almost welcome sense of privacy.

Inside, the atmosphere shifted. Unlike the sterile corridor, Emily's office held a softer, more personal touch. The lighting was lower, casting gentle shadows against the deep oak desk, its surface meticulously organized but not without traces of personality—an old leather notebook with dog-eared pages, a framed photo of a cat tucked discreetly to the side, a single orchid in a sleek ceramic pot. The faint scent of something warmer, lingered in the air, a contrast to the antiseptic sharpness beyond the door.

Marcus looked around, his expression betraying that he felt like an outsider in this setting. The balance of precision and something deeply personal unsettled him—it was as if he had stepped into a space that was both part of Emily and yet carefully guarded from the outside world.

Emily stood for a moment in the doorway, watching him as he took in the surroundings, her own unease bubbling under the surface. Here, in this space where she allowed herself the smallest hint of vulnerability, she felt the conversation ahead settle heavily between them.

"It's been a long time since we last met," he said, taking a seat opposite Emily.

"Too long, some might say," Emily agreed, offering a small, sad smile. "How have you been holding up?"

Marcus shrugged. "As well as can be expected, I guess. Terri's death has been... difficult."

Emily nodded, sensing the weight of his words. "I can't imagine how hard this must be for you. I know you and Terri had a complicated relationship."

"That's putting it mildly," Marcus replied with a bitter half laugh. "I know that you're not supposed to speak ill of the dead.... but she always had this way of making everything about her."

Emily listened, the familiar ache of her own resentment surfacing. "It must have been frustrating."

"It was," Marcus admitted, his eyes narrowing slightly. "There were times I wanted to... I don't know, bring her down a peg or two. Make her see she wasn't the centre of the universe."

Emily leaned forward, her heart pounding. "Marcus, did you ever... talk to anyone about those feelings? I mean, besides me?"

Marcus looked at her sharply, then sighed, his anger dissipating. "No just you, Emily. You were always there when I needed to vent, when I felt like I was going to explode."

Emily's mind raced. "Did you ever think about actually doing something to make her feel that way? Something drastic?"

The atmosphere in the room was thick with unspoken words, but Emily could see the tension building in his expression.

"Are you being serious?" Marcus asked, his voice low, the disbelief clear in his tone. "How could you even ask me something like that?"

He shook his head, his brows furrowing in frustration as if he were trying to make sense of the question. The silence between them hung heavy as he processed her words. "I wanted to, sometimes," he continued, his voice softening slightly. "But no, I never did anything. It was just talk. Why are you asking this now?"

"Do you think people ever really change?" Emily asked.

Marcus glance up at her. "That depends. Why?"

She shrugged, but the movement was too controlled, too measured. "Just thinking. Some people...they get away with things for too long. Makes you wonder if they ever stop to consider the consequences."

Marcus frowned. "You sound like you have someone in mind."

Emily gave a faint, strained laugh. "No one in particular. Just a thought. Do you ever think that some people deserve what's coming to them?"

There was a flicker of something in Marcus's eyes. Suspicion? Or curiosity? Emily couldn't tell.

The tension, once focused solely on the circumstances surrounding Terri's death, now shifted to something deeper. Emily could see the internal struggle in his eyes as he wrestled with his emotions, and she felt the sharp sting of the question she had posed. Despite her need to understand, she could see that it had touched a nerve.

Marcus exhaled sharply, shaking his head again, almost as if trying to rid himself of the question itself. His eyes remained locked on hers, his defiance clear, but there was something else beneath it—a flicker of vulnerability that Emily had never expected to see.

Emily hesitated, choosing her words carefully. "I think someone did. And they might have been influenced by our conversations."

Marcus stared at her, a mix of confusion and realization dawning in his eyes. "Emily, are you saying...?"

"I'm saying we need to be honest about everything, Marcus. The police are going to be digging, and they'll find out about our past, our conversations. We need to be prepared."

Marcus slumped in his chair, Emily's words playing in his head.

"Do you ever think that some people deserve what's coming to them?"

The question had lodged itself in his mind like a splinter. He could feel it festering, growing.

He had wanted Terri to fail, sure. To see what it was like to be the one struggling, the one scraping by. But did he want her dead?

Emily's gaze was steady, calculated. "Marcus, if you know something—if there's something bothering you—keeping it in won't help."

He clenched his fists. "Terri wasn't a saint."

"No, she wasn't," Emily agreed. "But that doesn't mean she had to…" She trailed off, but her eyes said the rest.

Had to die.

Marcus looked away, his chest tightening.

He had spent so long being bitter, resenting her success, that he'd never let himself feel the weight of her absence. She was gone. And he hadn't done anything to stop it. "I never wanted it to go this far. I just... I wanted her to understand what it felt like" he whispered.

Emily nodded, her own feelings of regret and responsibility gnawing at her.

"I have to go," he muttered, pushing himself up from the chair.

Emily didn't try to stop him. She simply watched, her expression unreadable.

Chapter 9

The morning at *Sarah's Secrets* was just beginning to settle into its usual rhythm when the bell above the door jingled cheerfully, announcing an unexpected visitor. Sarah, who was preparing a freshly brewed pot of coffee for the workmen, turned to see Detective Inspector Stanley stepping inside, his presence commanding attention as he scanned the cosy interior with a discerning eye.

"Oh hello!" Sarah greeted him with a surprised look, setting down the coffee pot she had been holding. "I didn't expect to see you here."

Stanley's expression was serious as he approached the counter, his gaze fixed on Sarah. "I am continuing my investigations by speaking with Kerry James again and I thought that while I was just round the corner, I would take the opportunity to come and talk to you about the incident."

Sarah signalled to Inspector Stanley as she moved around the counter. "Please, take a seat," she said, gesturing toward one of the newly positioned tables. "It's not exactly the most polished setup yet, but we're getting there."

Stanley glanced around the shop, taking in the scene of organized chaos with a raised eyebrow. "I can see that. Looks like you've got a lot on your plate."

Sarah gave a small laugh, trying to ease the tension. "Yeah, we're still finding our footing. I'm sorry about the mess." She quickly finished pouring a freshly brewed cup of coffee and brought it over to him, carefully placing it in front of him on the table.

Stanley took a sip, nodding in silent appreciation of the welcome caffeine hit.

Sarah set her own cup down on the table and pulled up a chair across from him, nervously waiting to see what he was going to ask. "I'm sure you're busy. What can I do for you, Inspector?"

Hidden away in the kitchen, Robyn had been sorting through supplies, but at the sound of Stanley's deep, unmistakable voice in the coffee shop, she paused mid-task. She tried to keep her movements casual, as if absorbed in her task, but her focus was entirely on the conversation. She strained to catch every word, wanting to know what exactly was being said, and hoping to get a better idea of where this investigation was headed.

Deciding she couldn't just leave Sarah to handle this alone, Robyn sidled around to the back of the counter, pretending to organize a few things but with the real intention of getting a better ear on the conversation unfolding between Sarah and the Inspector. She leaned slightly over the counter, her eyes catching glimpses of Stanley as he spoke. A wave of suspicion washed over her, her protective instincts kicking into overdrive. She had always been fiercely loyal to her aunt Sarah, and the idea of anyone questioning her or her actions filled Robyn with a sense of unease.

Stanley set his cup down carefully and leaned forward slightly, his eyes steady. "We're still trying to piece everything together. I know you have a lot on your mind, but I need to ask a few questions about Terri—about the situation before her death."

Her heart has skipped a beat at his words. "It was such a horrible accident, are you any closer to knowing how it happened?" she asked, her mind racing to recall any additional details that she might possibly be able to share.

Stanley shook his head slightly. "Not an accident, Sarah," he clarified, his voice low. "We're treating it as a murder."

Sarah's heart pounded in her chest as she set the coffee pot down. The words "murder" echoed in her mind, making the small, cosy coffee shop feel suddenly ominous. She struggled to find her voice.

"Murder? In Southsea? This can't be real…"

Stanley nodded his head slowly, "I'm afraid it is. Based on the initial assessment of the scene, it appears that Terri Treharne may have been alone in the red light room at the time of her death. The door was locked from the inside, which suggests no intruder interrupted her."

Sarah's mind raced, trying to piece together what little she knew of Terri's last moments. "But if the door was locked from the inside, how can you be sure it wasn't an accident?"

"That's what we're trying to determine. We've interviewed several people and collected evidence, but we're still piecing together the full picture."

"But who would want to hurt Terri?" Sarah asked.

Stanley continued, "The preliminary report has come back. The only fingerprints on the coffee cup were Terri's, although the water bottle also had her husband's fingerprints. Our initial thoughts are that someone could have tampered with the equipment, causing her death intentionally."

"Oh, so it definitely wasn't poisoning?" Sarah asked, trying to mask the tension in her voice, but the thought of her own wild assumptions made her uneasy. Sarah's mind raced back to the unsettling moment when Robyn had first mentioned the faint, sweet smell of marzipan lingering in the air near the scene. She had been quick to jump to conclusions, her thoughts spiralling as the smell seemed so out of place. *Could it be cyanide?* she had wondered. *It has a distinct almond-like scent, right?* The idea of the deadly poison lingering in the spa had felt terrifyingly plausible, especially with all the uncertainty surrounding Terri's sudden death.

Stanley slightly scoffed, a knowing look in his eyes. "No, it wasn't cyanide, as you might have suspected," he said, his tone a little more amused than he intended. "In fact, a lot of people can't even detect the smell of cyanide. It's not as easy to detect as the TV detectives might suggest. You'd be surprised how many people would miss it altogether."

Sarah felt a slight flush creep up her neck at his comment. *Of course, I should've known better*, she thought, feeling the weight of her own quick judgments. She had read about cyanide in novels and, perhaps in her haste to make sense of the situation, had fixated on the idea of it being the cause of death.

Stanley continued, his expression now more serious. "Anyway, that wasn't what killed Terri," he said, his voice firm. "The cause of death appears to be electrocution, the result of someone tampering with the red light therapy bed."

Robyn's eyes widened in shock. "Electrocution?" she echoed, forgetting for a moment that she wasn't meant to be part of the conversation. Both Sarah and Stanley turned toward her, their eyes locking on her as they realized she had been listening in.

Robyn's face flushed pink, realizing too late that she'd drawn attention to herself. Her cheeks burned with embarrassment as she awkwardly straightened up from behind the counter, trying to act as though she had just been tidying up. "I—I didn't mean to interrupt," she stammered, a nervous laugh escaping her lips. "Just... didn't realize the cause of death was... that."

Sarah gave her a pointed look, a mixture of amusement and exasperation. "Robyn," she said, her tone gentle but firm, "maybe you should be helping with the coffee instead of listening in."

Stanley, though clearly caught off guard, raised an eyebrow, his expression softening just slightly. "No harm done," he said with a hint of a smile, though he couldn't quite hide his amusement. "I suppose if you're here, you might as well join us for the conversation."

Robyn's blush deepened, but she nodded awkwardly, trying to regain her composure. "Right, of course," she mumbled, stepping back slightly as if to give them space to continue. Still, she couldn't shake the curiosity swirling inside her, her mind racing with the implications of what she had just heard.

"That's the assumption that we're working on," Stanley confirmed, his tone grim. "It's not an accident. Someone knew what they were doing. and it looks like they deliberately altered the equipment to cause a fatal electrical discharge. It wasn't immediately obvious, but the forensic team found signs of tampering."

Sarah's mind raced as she tried to make sense of this new information. "Who could have done such a thing?" she wondered aloud, her voice tinged with disbelief. The thought of someone intentionally causing harm in her space, a place meant for healing and relaxation, felt almost impossible to wrap her head around.

"We're still investigating that," Stanley replied, his tone grave as he leaned forward slightly. "We're looking into who had access to the equipment and who might have had a motive. It's possible someone tried to make it look like an accident, but the specific targeting of the red light therapy bed suggests it was premeditated."

Robyn, who had been standing quietly, suddenly spoke up, her curiosity and concern clearly showing. "But how do you know Terri was the intended victim?" she asked, her brow furrowing. "Couldn't anyone using the bed have been hurt?"

Stanley met her gaze, his expression thoughtful. "I checked with Kerry," he said, his voice steady. "There had only been one other booking for the bed that morning, and that person was a no-show. So, we know Terri was the only one who used it. We can't rule out that Terri wasn't the intended victim, but for now, we're treating it as if she was."

Robyn's face clouded with confusion, and she shifted uncomfortably. "What about Terri's husband? Does he have any idea who might have wanted to harm her?"

"We're still trying to locate him," Stanley said, a hint of frustration in his voice. "He disappeared shortly after the incident, which complicates things."

"Do you think he's in danger too?" Sarah asked, her concern deepening.

"It's a possibility," Stanley admitted. "Until we find him, we can't be sure."

As the gravity of the situation settled over them, Sarah and Robyn felt the weight of uncertainty pressing down harder than ever. The spa, once a sanctuary of relaxation, had become the epicentre of a dark and complex mystery.

"Thank you for the update, Inspector," Sarah said, her voice steady despite the turmoil inside her.

Stanley nodded, his expression resolute. "If either of you remembers anything else, no matter how insignificant it might seem, please let me know."

"I'm afraid I can't tell you much more about Terri," Sarah admitted, her voice tinged with regret. "I only knew what I saw of her, that day at the spa. But there was something... off about that phone call. The woman sounded panicked, as if she was in some kind of trouble."

Stanley leaned forward, his eyes intent as he listened to Sarah's account. "Did you recognise the voice? Or hear anything that might give us a clue as to what was happening?"

Sarah shook her head, her brow furrowing in concentration. "I couldn't tell who she was talking to, or what they were talking about," she confessed. "But it definitely seemed urgent, like something was about to happen."

Sarah bit her lip, thinking hard. She hadn't really known Terri well at all, their only interaction being a strange encounter in the changing room of the spa. At the time, she hadn't thought much of it—just a brief, awkward moment that she chalked up to an entitled attitude. It had seemed like one of those things she could easily brush off, nothing more than a minor irritation. Terri had been distant, almost aloof, and Sarah had felt a mild frustration at her, but she had never thought to pay closer attention to the interaction.

She had brushed off the oddness of their brief interaction as nothing more than a fleeting inconvenience. But what if it had been more than that? What if there had been more to Terri's behaviour—something she missed because she didn't know to look deeper?

"Inspector, this is terrifying. Do you think the murderer could still be here, in Southsea?"

"We're considering all possibilities. It's important that everyone remains vigilant and reports any suspicious activity."

As Stanley made a note of Sarah's statement, she couldn't shake the feeling that she was now entangled in something far more sinister than she had ever imagined. As her gaze drifted across the once-charming, now chaotic coffee shop, she couldn't help but wonder just how deep the secrets of Southsea ran.

Sarah's instinct, whenever faced with a problem, was to try to fix it. It was a trait she had inherited from her parents, both of whom had been problem-solvers. Her father, a former military officer, had always been someone people turned to in times of trouble. Her mother, equally practical, had managed their family with efficiency, always knowing the right course of action. Watching them both had shaped Sarah's own approach to life—whenever there was a challenge, she tackled it head-on, determined to find a solution. It was in her nature to be the one who took charge.

Her love for murder mysteries and crime novels over the years had only reinforced this mindset. Hours spent reading about detectives unravelling complicated webs of deception had given her, perhaps, a false sense of what was realistic. She had always seen herself as someone who could be like those fictional detectives, able to piece together clues and solve the case before the last page turned. But this was real life. The stakes were much higher, and the consequences far more dangerous than anything she had ever read about in a book.

As she tried to piece together the puzzle of Terri's death, a heavy sense of dread crept over her. This wasn't a mystery she could solve with a few casual observations or by diving into her usual list of actions. This was a murder investigation. The knowledge that she wasn't equipped for this kind of situation—emotionally, legally, or practically—was a sobering realization. She knew she was in over her head, yet part of her still itched to dive deeper, to solve the problem herself.

But the danger was real. The more she considered it, the more she recognized the risks. If she didn't take a step back, if she let her instincts push her too far, she could find herself in a dangerous situation. This wasn't just a story—this was a real-life tragedy, and the consequences of misjudging it could be far worse than she imagined.

"Sarah, are you sure you're ok?" Robyn's voice cut through her thoughts, grounding her in the present. Her concern was clear, her eyes searching Sarah's face for any signs of distress.

Sarah took a deep breath, trying to steady herself. She nodded slowly, knowing Robyn could see through her attempts to stay composed. "I'm fine," she said, her voice more strained than she intended. "It's just... overwhelming. I'm so used to fixing things, to being in control. But this... this is something else entirely."

It wasn't just the fear of the unknown, it was the weight of the situation pressing on her. For the first time in a long time, Sarah wasn't sure she could fix it. And that, more than anything, was what scared her the most.

Robyn reached out, squeezing her hand reassuringly. "You don't have to do this alone. Let the police handle the investigation." she said, nodding towards the Inspector. "That's their job. Your job is to stay safe and get this coffee shop ready for opening."

Sarah smiled weakly, appreciating her words but still feeling the weight of her own instincts pulling her in the opposite direction. "I know," she said softly. "But it's hard to just sit back and do nothing." But the nagging feeling that she could somehow help, that she could piece together the fragments of this mystery, lingered in the back of her mind.

Deep down, Sarah knew that the real challenge lay ahead. She would have to balance her natural inclination to solve problems with the need to stay safe and let the professionals do their work. It was a delicate line to walk, but she was determined to find a way.

Looking over at Robyn, Sarah noticed the subtle shift in her niece's demeanour. Whatever her initial suspicions might have been about the Inspector, it was clear that Stanley's protective attitude toward Sarah was beginning to win her over slightly. Robyn's usual guarded expression had softened, and though she still wasn't entirely convinced, Sarah could see a hint of trust starting to form in her eyes.

As Detective Inspector Stanley stood up to leave, he gave Sarah and Robyn a final, measured look. He had come here to ask questions, to gather facts, and yet somehow, he found himself offering reassurances instead. How had that happened? He wasn't usually one to explain himself, certainly not to people under scrutiny, and yet something about this place, or these two, had drawn him in.

Shaking off the thought, he straightened his coat. "I'm sure I'll be speaking with both of you again in the near future," he said, his voice carrying the weight of the ongoing investigation. The words hung in the air, a reminder that this was far from over.

Sarah nodded, offering him a tight but polite smile. "Of course, Inspector. Thank you for your time." She gestured to the door as he made his way out.

Robyn, still a bit hesitant, gave a small nod. "Goodbye, Inspector," she added, her tone more reserved than Sarah's, but respectful, nonetheless.

Stanley gave them both a brief nod before he stepped toward the door. As it swung open, the cool air from outside swept in briefly, before the door clicked shut behind him.

The two women stood in silence for a moment, the weight of what had just transpired settling heavily between them. Sarah's thoughts were swirling with the implications of Stanley's visit, the ongoing investigation, and the uncertainty that had taken root in her heart.

Robyn, sensing her aunt's unease, leaned her head against Sarah's shoulder in silent support. It was a small gesture, but it was enough to offer Sarah some comfort. Together, they watched the door for a moment longer, as if hoping to find some sense of closure in Stanley's departure, but the looming reality of the investigation was still there, hanging in the air like a storm waiting to break.

Chapter 10

As Sarah unloaded her car, she balanced a stack of folders on top of a box filled with coffee shop equipment. Struggling to close the car door with no free hands, she noticed two shopkeepers further up the street eyeing her. Their watchful gazes followed her every move. A she bumped the car door shut with her hip, she couldn't help but hear their murmured conversation, catching fragments of their words as she made her way from the car to the front of the shop.

"Did you hear? She was at the spa that day, and now the police are here," one of them said, her voice laced with curiosity and suspicion.

The other shopkeeper leaned in, lowering her voice even further, though Sarah could still hear the edge of excitement in her tone. "Maybe she's involved? I mean, who knows? What if we have a killer amongst us?"

The first shopkeeper nodded, glancing nervously down the street. "Yeah, the whole situation has put everyone on edge. I mean, a murder right here in our small town. It's unsettling."

"And now she just walks around like nothing happened, as if to taunt us," the second added, a hint of disdain in his voice. "Makes you question what really happened that day at the spa."

"Exactly," the first agreed. "And with the police coming by more often, it just adds to the tension. Everyone's watching their backs now, wondering if they're next."

The weight of their stares felt heavy as Sarah awkwardly manoeuvred the bulky box and folders. She could hear the low murmur of conversation behind her, their whispers growing more audible with each step she took.

Sarah's steps faltered, a sudden chill running down her spine. She didn't want to acknowledge the growing unease, but their words were hard to ignore. The implications of what they were saying settled like a weight in her stomach. Despite her best efforts to ignore it, the sense of being judged was palpable.

She set the box down momentarily to adjust her grip, taking a deep breath. Then, bending to retrieve it, with a determined push she steadied the load in her arms and continued towards *Sarah's Secrets*, trying to focus on the day ahead rather than the murmurings and suspicions swirling around her.

Trying hard not to be upset by what she was hearing, Sarah walked into her shop, her mind racing. Was it the frequent visits from Inspector Stanley over the last couple of days that made them whisper, or was there something more personal at play? As she thought back to the threatening note she had received, a sense of unease settled over her, casting a shadow on her normally upbeat disposition.

She entered the warmth of the shop which should have been soothing, but today it did little to lift her spirits. She tried to shake off the feeling, telling herself she was being paranoid. But the thought gnawed at her—maybe not everyone was happy to have her here on Castle Road.

As Sarah carefully settled the box and folders down on the counter, the weight of the task momentarily made her pause. She rubbed her tired hands, glancing down at the cluttered paperwork she'd been carrying around all morning. Just as she was about to focus on organizing the mess, she noticed a familiar figure approaching through the shop's door.

Amy walked in, clutching a stack of discount vouchers in hand, her bright smile immediately catching Sarah's eye. She looked like she was in good spirits, as always, and Sarah couldn't help but feel a small lift at the sight of her.

"Hey, Sarah!" Amy greeted cheerfully, her voice warm as she crossed the room to the counter. "Got these for you." Amy set the vouchers down in front of Sarah. "Thought it might help drum up some more business."

Sarah glanced over the top of the boxes, momentarily distracted by Amy's thoughtful gesture. She straightened up, a grateful smile crossing her face. "Thanks, Amy. That's really thoughtful of you."

Amy immediately picked up on the subtle shift in Sarah's usually cheerful mood. Although they hadn't known each other for very long, Amy had become quite good at reading Sarah, and right now, she could tell that something was off. She set the stack of vouchers down and leaned forward slightly, concern flickering in her eyes. "Everything ok?" she asked, her voice soft but filled with genuine worry.

Sarah sighed heavily, running a hand through her hair as she leaned against the counter, her gaze momentarily drifting toward the window. "I don't know, Amy. Lately, it feels like everyone's watching me, whispering behind my back. I can't tell if it's because of the police visits or something more personal. And what with that note... it's been playing on my mind."

Amy's expression softened with understanding. "I can see how that would get to you. But you know what? People love to gossip, especially in a small town like this. It doesn't necessarily mean anything bad."

Sarah nodded, appreciating Amy's attempt to reassure her. "I know, but it's hard not to let it get to me. I just want this place to be a success and to feel like I belong here."

Amy reached out and squeezed Sarah's hand. "You do belong here, Sarah. And your coffee shop is going to be amazing. You know what it is like, not everyone likes change. But people will come around. Just give it time."

Sarah smiled, feeling a bit of the weight lift from her shoulders. "Thanks, Amy. I needed that."

Amy grinned. "Anytime. Now, let's get these vouchers sorted. I'm sure they'll bring in some new faces."

As they worked together, arranging the vouchers and chatting about lighter topics, Sarah felt her mood slowly improve. She knew she couldn't let the whispers and glances get to her. She had worked too hard to let anything or anyone derail her dream.

"I remember when I first opened up shop here," Amy said, a nostalgic smile creeping across her face. "Feels like ages ago, but those early days are still fresh in my mind. It wasn't easy, you know? The stares, the whispers—it's a small town, and news travels fast."

Sarah nodded, understanding the weight of Amy's experience. "It's comforting to know you've been through this too," she admitted, stacking another pile of vouchers.

Amy reached out, placing a reassuring hand on Sarah's shoulder. "You'll get through this, just like I did. But remember, it's ok to feel a bit uncomfortable. It's all part of the process. This discomfort—it means you're pushing boundaries, making something new here."

Sarah absorbed Amy's words, feeling a mix of reassurance and unease. She appreciated the support, yet the thought of facing ongoing scrutiny was daunting.

Inspector Stanley sat at his desk, staring out the window of his new office, the early morning light filtering through the glass. The view was unremarkable, a patch of grey sky and a few scattered buildings that had grown familiar over the past few weeks. He couldn't help but compare it to his old station, the one on Highland Road, where he'd worked for the last few years. The Old Police Station had been built in 1932, with its towering brick façade and the heavy, historic feel of the place. It had its flaws, of course, but it had character. The kind of place where you could feel the weight of history in the air, where the walls almost seemed to whisper secrets. But now, with the station being turned into flats and the move to Winston Churchill Avenue, Stanley couldn't help but feel like he was losing a part of the old Southsea he'd known. This new station, closer to the shops and conveniences, made grabbing lunch a lot easier, but it didn't have the same atmosphere—the same sense of purpose.

He let out a frustrated sigh and pushed away from the window, trying to shake off the nostalgic thoughts that were distracting him. *Pull yourself together, Stanley,* he thought. *You've got a case to solve.*

The investigation into Terri's murder wasn't progressing as quickly as he would have liked. The case seemed to be running in circles, with a missing husband and no real suspects to speak of. There were too many questions, not enough answers.

Stanley glanced down at his notes. He had already interviewed Kerry a couple of times, but nothing had come from those conversations that could move the case forward. One name kept coming up, though—Megan, the spa's assistant. He had tried to catch up with her earlier, but she had been out of the office when he'd arrived. Now, with the case stagnating, it was time to chase up on her missing statement.

He grabbed his coat, the weight of the unanswered questions pressing on his shoulders. He needed something more concrete, something from Megan that could either move the investigation forward or at least give him a new lead to follow. He headed for the door, mentally preparing himself for another round of questioning, but this time with a clearer goal in mind.

It had taken longer than expected, but he wasn't about to let anything slip through the cracks now. He had to speak with Megan. The clock was ticking, and the more time he spent with the same few leads, the less progress he was making.

He arrived at *Serenity Spa*, where the tranquil atmosphere stood in stark contrast to the tension that had been building around the investigation. The soft scent of lavender filled the air as he walked through the serene treatment rooms, each space meticulously arranged for relaxation. It was hard to reconcile the calm of the surroundings with the dark events that had unfolded here just days earlier.

Not immediately finding anyone at the reception desk, Stanley popped his head through the door leading to the corridor, off which all the treatment rooms opened. He called out a quick "Hello?" hoping to catch someone's attention. When there was no immediate response, he stepped into the corridor, his footsteps echoing on the wooden floor as he walked down the narrow passage. The sound of his shoes on the floor was the only noise in the quiet spa, further amplifying the eerie stillness in the air.

He moved down the corridor with purpose, glancing into the open doorways of the treatment rooms, until he finally found Megan. She was alone, folding towels in one of the empty rooms. She looked up in surprise when Stanley entered, her eyes widening slightly.

"Inspector," she said, setting the towels down and brushing her hands together nervously. "I didn't expect you to be back again."

Stanley gave a polite nod, his gaze focused on her. "I've been meaning to catch up with you," he said, his tone calm but insistent. "I need to ask you a few more questions about the day of the incident."

Megan hesitated for a moment, then set down the towels and nodded. "Of course. What would you like to know?"

Stanley paused, his mind racing with the pieces of information Megan had provided. The mention of Kerry's stress, the lawsuit, and the secretive phone calls all seemed like threads that might be worth pulling. But he wasn't ready to let his guard down just yet. He had one more question to ask, one that had been gnawing at him ever since the investigation started.

"Can you tell me anything about Terri's husband, Robert?" Stanley asked, his tone more direct now, watching Megan closely for any sign of hesitation.

Megan shifted uncomfortably, clearly unsure about how to answer. She bit her lip, glancing away before speaking. "I don't think I can be of much help with that," she said slowly. "The last time I saw him, he was walking into the Floatation Tank room. He had his phone in hand, texting away. I remember thinking at the time that if he wanted to fully enjoy the experience, he was going to have to separate himself from that phone. But I haven't seen him since then."

Stanley's brow furrowed. "You didn't see him come out?"

Megan shook her head. "No, not after that. He never came back out of the room, as far as I know. I was busy with some other things and didn't notice if he left."

Stanley leaned back slightly, turning the information over in his mind. "That's interesting," he murmured to himself. "I wonder if I can locate him using his phone, given how attached he seems to it."

He jotted down a quick reminder to himself in his notebook. *Check phone records—could be a lead on his whereabouts.* He looked up at Megan again. "Thank you, Megan. This is helpful. If you remember anything else, no matter how small, don't hesitate to let me know."

Megan nodded, her expression still tense. "I will, Inspector. I just want this all to be over."

Stanley gave her a reassuring smile, though he knew that for everyone involved, this was far from over. As he walked back along the corridor of the spa, he couldn't shake the feeling that Kerry's behaviour, while explainable on the surface, might still hold clues to the deeper mystery of Terri's death.

Emily let herself into her house, the familiar click of the door behind her marking her return. She flicked on the lights as she moved through the hallway, closing the curtains and dimming the house to a more intimate setting. As she entered the kitchen, she opened the fridge, the light inside casting a glow on the empty shelves. She stared into it for a moment, hoping for something more than the usual collection of leftovers and unappetizing takeaway containers. But, as expected, there was nothing that would spark her interest or satisfy her hunger.

Sighing, Emily closed the fridge door, the sound of it sealing echoing too loudly in the quiet house. Just then, she heard the familiar padding of little feet across the floor. Before she could react, a small, fluffy white cat appeared, weaving its way around her ankles in a pattern she knew well.

"Oh, hello Cinnamon," Emily muttered, forcing a smile despite herself. "I see you haven't made dinner for us for the 100th day in a row." She bent down to scratch the cat behind the ears, but her smile was fleeting, quickly replaced by the tightness in her chest. "Guess that's still my job, huh?"

Cinnamon purred louder, as if to answer, but Emily barely registered it. Her mind kept returning to the same thoughts, swirling around uncontrollably. Terri's death, Marcus, the interview. She opened a cupboard and grabbed a can of cat food, then quickly threw together a microwaved dinner for herself, barely paying attention to the motion of her hands as they worked. Her mind was consumed by a constant loop of images and thoughts—Marcus' tense, unpredictable nature, the frustration he'd felt toward his sister, and now, the reality of her being gone.

Once the plate was made, Emily set it down in front of Cinnamon, who wasted no time in digging in, then she collapsed onto the sofa, her own plate of food left untouched for a moment. She reached for the half-open bottle of wine, pouring herself a generous glass. The cool liquid slid down her throat, but it didn't help ease the gnawing sensation in her stomach, the weight pressing on her chest.

Marcus had been volatile in the past, and today, when she spoke to him, it was as if all that anger was still lurking just beneath the surface. He'd been nothing but difficult, evasive, and unpredictable, making it impossible to know if he had any involvement in his sister's death. But as much as she tried to shake the thoughts, she couldn't escape the gnawing feeling that he might know more than he was letting on. The memory of how frustrated he had been with Terri, how he'd clashed with her so often, now seemed like a warning sign she hadn't seen at the time.

Terri was gone. Emily kept repeating it in her head, but it didn't seem real. The sharp edges of her emotions felt too jumbled, and the more she tried to focus, the more her thoughts scattered. Marcus' outbursts, the way he'd stormed around the place with his angry words, it was all starting to make sense in a way she didn't want it to. Had he done something in that fit of rage? Her mind kept returning to the unspoken animosity between them. She couldn't help but wonder if the frustration and resentment he'd held for his sister had finally pushed him too far.

She took another sip of wine, hoping it would numb the thoughts that refused to quiet, but it didn't. All she could think of was Marcus and Terri—the past, the present, and the dark, unfinished threads hanging between them. The case wasn't just a professional matter anymore. It was personal, too close to her own experience. She closed her eyes for a moment, trying to breathe through the dizziness in her head, but the overwhelming feeling of frustration remained.

With a sharp breath, she opened her eyes again, trying to refocus, but it felt like her thoughts were tangled, too heavy to unravel. She glanced down at Cinnamon, who was now finishing her meal. At least the cat was content. Emily just wished she could say the same for herself.

Chapter 11

Sarah stood outside the *Serenity Spa*, her hand hesitating just inches from the chrome handles of the door. A shiver ran down her spine as memories of the day she last left the spa resurfaced. Taking a deep breath, she pulled the door open and stepped inside.

The familiar scent of lavender filled the air, but it did little to ease the knot of anxiety in her stomach. She approached the reception desk, where Kerry was sitting. It was clear just looking at Kerry that the last few days had really taken their toll. Where she would normally look fresh-faced and cheerful, now she had dark circles under her eyes, a sign of sleepless nights. Her hair, usually pulled back into a neat, perky blonde ponytail, now hung loosely and looked as though it hadn't seen a brush for days. She appeared as if the weight of everything had drained her of the usual vitality that once radiated from her. The upbeat, confident woman Sarah had known was nowhere to be found—replaced by someone clearly overwhelmed, struggling to hold everything together.

Kerry didn't seem to notice Sarah at first, her focus on the papers spread across her desk. But then she sensed a presence and looked up, her eyes widening in recognition. "Oh, Sarah," she said, her face strained but attempting a smile. "I didn't see you come in."

"Hello Kerry," Sarah replied gently. "How are you holding up?"

Kerry sighed, her expression growing more sombre. "Not very well to be honest. I still can't quite believe what happened." She shook her head as if trying to shake off the lingering disbelief.

"I know this isn't a priority right now," Sarah said, her tone gentle and understanding, "and I don't want to intrude on your day. But in all the panic the other day, I realized I left my watch here. Have you by any chance come across it?"

Kerry gave a slight nod, her eyes showing a flicker of recognition. "Let me check for you." She opened the drawer of her desk where she usually kept lost items, but after a quick glance, she sighed. "I don't see anything in here, unfortunately."

As she moved her arms over the papers in front of her, Sarah's eyes caught a glimpse of the ledgers and figures. They looked like a set of accounts. Kerry quickly shifted her arms, covering the papers, a flash of unease passing across her face.

Not wanting to push too far, Sarah gave her a warm smile. "No problem. Would you mind if I just take a quick look in the hydrotherapy room to see if I can find it? It's probably just sitting somewhere in there."

Kerry seemed to relax at the suggestion, offering a quick nod. "Of course, help yourself," she said, her voice carrying the faintest hint of relief that Sarah wasn't lingering over something that clearly seemed to weigh on her.

Sarah gave her a reassuring smile. "I won't interrupt you much longer. I imagine you must have a lot on your plate. Have you heard anything more from the police yet?"

Kerry shook her head, her face betraying the stress she was under. "It's been a challenging few days, to say the least. The police haven't told me much yet, only that they are sure the death is suspicious."

Sarah's brows furrowed in concern. "That sounds serious. Do they have any leads?" she asked, her voice laced with a mixture of curiosity and worry.

As she spoke, Sarah couldn't help but weigh the situation in her mind. Kerry's response, or lack of details, seemed to confirm the conversation Sarah had had with Stanley earlier. Either the Inspector had told her more than he had let on to Kerry, or Kerry was playing down just how bad the police's view of the situation was. Sarah felt a subtle unease settle in her stomach as she considered the two possibilities. She could sense that Kerry wasn't being completely forthcoming, and the vague answer felt like a carefully chosen understatement.

Kerry shifted uncomfortably, folding her arms slightly as she met Sarah's gaze. "As far as I know, there aren't any new leads," she said, her voice heavy with frustration. "I've told the police everything I can." She paused for a moment, her eyes flickering toward the papers she had been covering up earlier, but she quickly returned her attention to Sarah. "It's just... it's hard not knowing what's really going on."

Sarah nodded slowly, her mind still processing Kerry's words. The absence of new leads made everything feel even more uncertain, and it seemed as though Kerry was either hiding something or simply wasn't fully in the loop. Either way, Sarah couldn't shake the feeling that there was more to this than what was being said.

Kerry sighed heavily, glancing back down at the paperwork under her elbow before meeting Sarah's eyes again. "It's the last thing I need right now," she said, her voice tinged with frustration. Then, realising how callous that sounded, she quickly added, "I mean, it's just... it's terrible what happened. I can't believe it. I keep thinking, 'Why here? Why now?'"

Sarah nodded sympathetically. "I understand. It must be overwhelming dealing with all this on top of running the spa."

Kerry's expression softened, her eyes reflecting the depth of her weariness. "It really is. The spa was already struggling, and now this... It's like the universe is conspiring against me."

Sarah placed a comforting hand on Kerry's arm, offering what little reassurance she could. Kerry gave a tired smile, appreciating the gesture.

Wanting to understand why Kerry was so miserable, Sarah casually asked, "If you don't mind me asking, what's been going on with the spa? Why are you struggling?"

Kerry sighed, her shoulders slumping slightly. "Oh, it's not that bad. It's just... well, even in a small seaside town like this, there's a lot of competition. You're always looking for ways to stay ahead, to keep your clients coming back. The market's changed, and it's been tough to keep up with all the new trends, not to mention the constant pressure to keep the quality up while managing costs. It feels like you have to work twice as hard just to stay in the same place sometimes."

Sarah nodded, understanding all too well the pressures of running a business. "I can imagine. It must be hard to keep that balance."

Kerry sighed again, rubbing her temples. "It's a lot. And with everything going on right now, I don't know if I can handle much more."

"If you need anything, don't hesitate to ask. I know it's not much, but I'm here for you."

"Thank you, Sarah. That means a lot," Kerry replied, her voice sincere. "And I really appreciate you coming by. It's nice to know there are still kind people around." She paused for a moment, her eyes momentarily lowering as if she were lost in thought. Then she added, "It's good to see that there are some people who aren't too scared to set foot in the place. With everything that's happened, I wasn't sure if people would still come."

Sarah gave a reassuring smile, trying to ease the tension in Kerry's voice. "Of course, Kerry. It's not your fault, is it?" she said, her tone gentle but firm, offering a sense of solidarity.

Kerry's eyes flicked up to meet hers, a strange expression crossing her face—one Sarah couldn't quite read. It lingered for only a second before Kerry quickly looked away, as if she had caught herself. The brief shift didn't go unnoticed, but Sarah didn't comment on it.

Kerry cleared her throat, the moment passing as quickly as it had come. "Go on through and see if you can find your watch, Sarah. It's no trouble." Her voice was softer now, her usual guardedness returning as she gestured toward the hydrotherapy room.

Sarah nodded, still unsure of the flicker she'd seen in Kerry's eyes but choosing not to dwell on it. She smiled politely and walked toward the treatment area, feeling the weight of the situation settle back onto her shoulders. There were still too many unanswered questions, and something about Kerry's reaction had only made her more determined to get to the bottom of it all.

Sarah pushed through the door to the treatment rooms, retracing her steps back to where she'd been earlier. Her heart beat a little faster as she looked around, her eyes scanning the space. She remembered leaving her watch on the bench before heading into the spa, but when she looked there now, it wasn't in sight. Frowning, she crouched down and peered behind the bench, half-expecting to find it buried somewhere behind the furniture. Sure enough, there it was, tucked at the back, having clearly fallen down when she had taken her robe off. She bent down to retrieve it, the metal of the watch cool against her fingers.

Slipping the watch back onto her wrist, she heard footsteps approaching. Looking up, Sarah saw a pair of feet walking past the open door. She recognized them immediately from the brightly decorated crocs she'd seen before—Megan. Something in Sarah's gut told her this was an opportunity she couldn't pass up. Maybe she could ask her more about the spa, about the strange tension she had sensed earlier.

Without wasting a moment, she stepped into the hallway, following Megan at a careful distance. She watched as Megan disappeared around the corner into what appeared to be a staff room. Sarah hesitated outside the staffroom door, listening for a moment before gently knocking. When there was no immediate response, she pushed it open slightly, peeking inside.

Megan sat at a small table, a tissue clenched tightly in her hands, her posture tense. She looked up sharply, her red-rimmed eyes widening slightly before she quickly composed herself.

Sarah stepped inside, offering a small, reassuring smile. "Megan, isn't it?"

Megan sniffed, nodding slowly. "Yeah."

Sarah kept her tone light. "We met the other day when I was here." She hesitated, not wanting to dwell on the circumstances of their previous meeting—it felt too raw. "I just wanted to check in."

Megan's eyes flickered toward the door before she let out a soft, humourless laugh. "You're the second person to try talking to me about this today… you and that inspector."

Sarah took a careful step forward, noting the way Megan's fingers twisted around the tissue, how her shoulders were rigid with barely contained tension.

"You may as well sit down," Megan muttered. "But I don't think I've got anything that I can tell you."

Sarah lowered herself onto the chair across from her, watching as Megan nervously picked at the tissue in her hands.

"I know this must be really difficult for you," Sarah said gently. "Terri's death… it's shaken a lot of people."

Megan let out a shaky breath. "It just started out as a normal day… with normal clients. Why did it have to end up like this?"

Sarah let the silence stretch between them for a moment before she leaned forward slightly, keeping her voice low. "Was Terri just one of those 'normal' clients, then?"

Megan gave a dry, almost bitter laugh, shaking her head. "Depends on what you mean by normal."

Sarah kept her expression neutral. "How do you mean?"

Megan sighed, gripping the tissue tighter. "She was in here all the time these last few months, but she wasn't like most people. She had… *expectations*. Always wanted things just right, never satisfied, always pushing for more."

Sarah nodded, waiting.

Megan exhaled sharply. "It wasn't just the treatments. She had a way of making you feel like you were always getting something wrong. Like no matter what you did, it was never enough."

Sarah thought back to her own brief encounter with Terri. The woman had exuded confidence—almost arrogance—but she could see now how that same presence could feel intimidating to those around her.

"I can imagine that must have been exhausting," Sarah said.

Megan gave a small nod, her shoulders slumping as if she was finally releasing some of the frustration she had been holding in. "It wasn't just that," she murmured. "There was something off. She got into it with Kerry a few times. And lately, Kerry's been... different."

Sarah tilted her head. "Different how?"

Megan hesitated. Then, lowering her voice, she said, "I don't think she's telling the whole truth about Terri."

Sarah's heart skipped a beat. "What do you mean?"

Megan's eyes darted toward the door again, as if making sure no one was listening. "Kerry and Terri had some kind of history. I don't know the details, but I know there was tension. Then suddenly, Terri's in here all the time? Acting like she owns the place? Kerry was *never* comfortable around her."

Sarah's mind churned, piecing it together. "You think Kerry was hiding something?"

Megan swallowed hard. "I think she was *scared*."

A chill ran through Sarah. *Of what?* Before she could ask, Megan's hands twitched, her grip on the tissue tightening further. Sarah caught the movement, her instincts flaring. Megan's nervous energy had shifted—this wasn't just about Kerry. Sarah leaned back slightly, softening her tone. "Is everything else ok?"

Megan jumped slightly, her fingers tightening around the tissue. "Oh! Yeah, just... someone left a towel in the wrong locker."

Sarah raised an eyebrow. The lie was obvious.

"People forget things all the time," Sarah said lightly, her gaze watching Megan closely. "Phones, wallets, jewellery..." She let the sentence linger.

Megan's fingers twitched. Her breathing changed—just for a moment.

"Y-yeah," Megan said quickly. "But not, like... *murder evidence* or anything."

Sarah's eyes narrowed. "Who said anything about murder evidence?"

Megan's throat bobbed as she swallowed hard. "No one. I mean—it's just... people talk, you know?"

Sarah nodded slowly, her mind racing. Megan was hiding something.

"Thanks again, Megan," Sarah said softly. "I'll leave you to take a moment."

With one last glance toward Megan, Sarah turned and made her way back to the reception area, her mind racing. As she walked through the spa's calm corridors, she felt an uncomfortable knot forming in her stomach. She wanted to confront Kerry, to ask her directly about what she knew, but she wasn't sure how to approach it without making it seem like she was prying or accusing her. The last thing she wanted was to alienate Kerry or make her feel defensive—especially if there was something important that she wasn't saying.

When Sarah reached the reception area, she found Kerry behind the counter, going through some papers. She had a slight frown on her face, looking lost in thought, but she looked up as Sarah approached.

"Hey, Kerry," Sarah began, her voice casual but thoughtful. "I bumped into Megan just now. She told me a little bit about how Terri had become a more regular visitor recently. I didn't realize how much she'd been coming by, to be honest." Sarah paused, gauging Kerry's reaction. "Megan kind of gave the impression that Terri wasn't exactly the easiest customer to deal with."

Kerry's expression shifted for a moment, almost imperceptibly. She placed the papers down and met Sarah's gaze, her shoulders slumping a bit as if considering how much to reveal. "Well... maybe I did know her a little more than I let on," she admitted, her voice quiet. "We were friends once, in a previous life, you could say. A long time ago." She looked away briefly, as though the memory was one she hadn't expected to resurface.

Sarah paused, surprised by Kerry's admission. "You were friends? What happened?"

Kerry sighed, her gaze distant as she recalled the past. "We were close once, but we had a falling out a number of years ago. Terri was always competitive, always looking for an edge. It was exhausting trying to keep up, and eventually, our friendship just...turned into something else."

Sarah frowned. "If you two weren't friends anymore, why would she be a client here? Why stay in touch at all?"

A flicker of something, resentment, maybe even shame, passed over Kerry's face. She hesitated, then looked down at her hands. "Terri had a way of getting into people's business. She knew things about me...about my financial situation."

Understanding dawned, but Sarah pressed on. "And she used it against you?"

Kerry swallowed hard, blinking back tears. "She didn't need to threaten me outright...she just made it clear that she could make things difficult if she wanted to. She expected favours, free services, special treatment...and I couldn't afford to say no."

Sarah felt a chill creep over her. "So, she was extorting you."

Kerry let out a shaky breath. "Terri never had to say it in so many words. But she knew exactly what she was doing. And it's not the first time she's been unkind to people we studied with. Terri had a habit of using people's weaknesses against them."

Sarah's mind raced with the implications. "Kerry, this is important. We need to figure out if anyone else from your past had similar experiences with Terri. Maybe one of them reached a breaking point."

Kerry wiped her tears and looked at Sarah with a mix of gratitude and despair. "You're right. There were others she bullied and manipulated. I could probably write you a long list of names."

Sarah nodded. "Well, it might come to that. The more we know, the better we can understand what happened. And Kerry, you need to tell Inspector Stanley everything. The financial irregularities, the extortion, your history with Terri—it all matters."

Kerry took a deep breath and stood, her resolve hardening. "I will. I owe it to Terri, to the spa, and to myself to come clean."

Chapter 12

Sarah felt like her head was spinning with confusing bits of information, all swirling around with no clear answers. It was as though her mind couldn't make sense of the pieces of the puzzle she was trying to put together. She knew she needed a break, a moment away from everything that had been weighing on her. The stress of the investigation, the conversation with Kerry, and the pressure of it all—it was becoming too much.

She glanced over at Missy, who was sitting expectantly at her side, her tail wagging in anticipation. Missy was never far away from wherever Sarah was, her constant companion. And while it was a lovely demonstration of the dog's loyalty, it often resulted in Sarah muttering under her breath as she tried not to trip over the eager Labrador's constantly shifting movements. On this occasion though, it was exactly the distraction Sarah needed. Missy's energy, her enthusiasm for the simple act of walking, was a welcome break from the swirl of thoughts that had been clouding Sarah's mind.

The thought of being by the water, away from the noise in her head, seemed like the perfect solution. Mike always said that if Sarah was feeling fed up or out of sorts, she needed to be taken within a stone's throw of the sea, and somehow, the sound of the waves and the salt in the air always made her feel better. It was as though the sea had a way of washing away her worries, if only for a while. Today, more than ever, Sarah needed that escape.

As Sarah stood up and reached for her headphones and lead, Missy's ears perked up, and in an instant, she sprang to her feet, tail wagging even faster. She trotted over to Sarah, her eyes bright and eager. It was as if she knew exactly what the action meant, time for a walk. Missy stood by her side, practically bouncing with excitement, ready to head out the door.

"Ok, girl," Sarah said, smiling as she clipped Missy's lead on. "You may as well benefit from my need to escape for a bit." With that, she opened the door and stepped outside, ready to clear her mind with a long walk along the seafront.

As Sarah strolled along the seafront, the salty breeze had exactly the effect she was hoping for, already helping to ease some of the tension in her shoulders as she walked. Missy happily bounded ahead, eager to sniff the sand and chase at seagulls. But despite the familiarity of the picturesque setting of Old Portsmouth, Sarah's mind was still anything but serene.

As she walked through the arches onto the Hot Walls beach, Sarah's thoughts swirled with the weight of her suspicions. She couldn't shake the feeling that Kerry might be involved in Terri's death, and the thought left a bitter taste in her mouth.

With a heavy heart, Sarah reached into her pocket and pulled out a tennis ball, tossing it towards the edge of the water. Missy bounded after it, splashing into the shallow waves with joyous abandon. Watching her dog play, Sarah tried to focus on the simple pleasure of the moment, but her mind kept drifting back to the investigation.

Each time she threw the ball, Sarah's thoughts grew more tangled, her worries mounting with each toss. She couldn't ignore the evidence she had uncovered, but the idea of accusing Kerry—a woman she had grown to like and respect—filled her with a sense of dread.

Sarah knew she still felt a need to find justice for Terri, but she also understood the gravity of accusing someone without concrete proof. The burden of responsibility weighed heavily on her conscience as she grappled with the moral implications of her amateur investigation.

Lost in thought, Sarah threw the ball again and again, the rhythmic motion of the action offering a small measure of solace amidst the turmoil of her thoughts. She knew she needed to tread carefully, to gather more evidence before making any accusations.

As Missy bounded back towards her, the tennis ball clenched in her teeth, Sarah forced a smile, pushing aside her doubts for the moment. She may not have all the answers yet, but she was determined to keep digging until she uncovered the truth.

It was lunchtime, and Sarah sat at the kitchen table, her hands wrapped around a mug of coffee, the warmth doing little to ease the restlessness twisting in her stomach. Across from her, Mike cradled his own cup, watching her with quiet concern. Normally, this was her favourite part of the day, a quiet moment shared with Mike before the afternoon pulled them in different directions. But today, the storm in her mind wouldn't settle.

Mike took a sip of his coffee, then set the mug down with a soft thud. "You've been fidgety all morning," he said, studying her. "Want to talk about it?"

Sarah exhaled, tracing the rim of her cup with one finger. "It's just... everything that happened. I can't stop thinking about it."

Mike leaned back in his chair, expression unreadable. "Remind me again how it's your problem? Shouldn't you be leaving this to the police?"

"I know," Sarah admitted, lifting her gaze to meet his. "But I was there, Mike. I saw everything unfold. And you know how many mysteries I've read—it's like living in a real Agatha Christie novel, and I feel like I need to do something."

Mike shook his head, a faint sigh escaping him. "It's not a book, Sarah. It's real life. And I don't want you getting caught up in something that could end badly."

His fingers curled around hers, his touch grounding her for a moment. She saw the worry etched in his face, felt the weight of it in the way he held her hand.

"I get it," she said softly. "But I can't just sit back and do nothing."

Mike was quiet for a beat, then squeezed her hand gently before reaching for his coffee again. "Just remember, you're not Miss Marple. You're Sarah Meadows, my wife. And I need you to stay safe."

Sarah smiled back, feeling a little lighter with his support. "I hope I've got a few more years in me yet until I'd classify as Miss Marple, but I get the point."

Mike took another sip of coffee, then glanced toward the fridge. "By the way, we're nearly out of milk. Remind me to grab some later."

Sarah huffed a quiet laugh, shaking her head. "Sure. Priorities."

He smirked. "Hey, even detectives need their coffee."

She smiled, feeling a little lighter with his support. But as she sat there, the weight of the mystery still lingered, pressing at the edges of her thoughts. She just hoped she could find the truth without putting herself, or anyone else for that matter, in danger.

Inspector Stanley sat at his desk, surrounded by a sea of papers and case files. His eyes flicked from one piece of evidence to another, trying to weave together the various strands of the investigation. There was so much to consider—Robert Treharne's strange behaviour, the potential complications with Kerry's insurance claims, and, of course, the overriding mystery of Terri's murder. Every lead seemed to raise more questions than answers.

He rubbed his forehead, trying to concentrate. It was hard to make sense of everything at once. He needed a breakthrough, something concrete that could tie the pieces together.

The ping of an email interrupted his thoughts. Stanley clicked open the message, hoping it would be the breakthrough he was looking for. As the data from Robert Treharne's phone records appeared on his screen, a small, satisfied smile tugged at the corners of his mouth. This was exactly what he had been hoping for. His hunch to look at Robert's phone had paid off.

Trawling through Robert's text messages, Stanley could see a secret that Terri had clearly never been privy to. There were numerous messages exchanged with someone named Vanessa. The tone of their conversations was unmistakably intimate, and Stanley's eyes narrowed as he scrolled through more of the messages. The urgency in their exchanges suggested that this wasn't just a fleeting affair—it seemed much more serious. Stanley started piecing together the timeline, and it became clear why Robert had disappeared from the spa as soon as his wife's back was turned. His secret relationship with Vanessa was something he'd been hiding for a long time.

The messages between Robert and Vanessa didn't just hint at infidelity, they revealed a deeper connection. As Stanley read on, it became clear that Vanessa wasn't just a brief fling. She appeared to be someone Robert had been hiding in plain sight, someone he had been seeing for a significant amount of time. The thought that Robert had been living a double life felt more like a certainty. Stanley leaned back in his chair, tapping his fingers thoughtfully on the desk.

The connection between Robert, Vanessa, and Terri was becoming clearer, and the significance of Robert's disappearance wasn't just an attempt to avoid confrontation. It looked like he had been running from something much worse—his own guilt, perhaps, or the fear that Terri's murder was somehow tied to his actions.

Stanley's mind shifted back to the other angle of the case, Kerry. The more he thought about it, the more he realized that Kerry had become one of his prime suspects. She had been hiding something, and her behaviour had been suspicious from the start. The way she had reacted to Terri's death, her anxiety about the insurance policy—it all pointed to her possibly being involved in something bigger than just a business rivalry.

He turned his attention back to the information on his desk. There were two key leads to follow up on now, Kerry's potential role in the insurance issues, and who exactly

Vanessa was. He already knew that Kerry had some serious explaining to do, and given the weight of her involvement, she should be his next priority.

With that in mind, Stanley made a mental note to follow up with Vanessa as soon as possible. He couldn't ignore the connection she had with Robert, but at least now he had a clearer sense of what he was walking into. He couldn't let his focus drift too far, though, Kerry was the one who seemed to be directly tied to the situation, and if she was hiding anything, it was time for him to bring it into the light.

Stanley took a deep breath, feeling the weight of the case pressing down on him. He had his next steps planned. Now it was time to face Kerry and start unravelling the truth.

Back at her house, Sarah stood in front of the open fridge, staring mindlessly at its uninspiring contents. The fridge was nearly empty—just a few jars of condiments, some wilted vegetables, and a couple of half-empty containers. She sighed, closing the door and leaning back against it. What to make for dinner?

She glanced at the clock on the wall, realizing the afternoon was already slipping by. She could always stop by the deli just around the corner from *Sarah's Secrets* when she headed back there. Emma had worked there for years, and maybe, just maybe, she would have some something that could inspire her for dinner this evening. Her mind was still buzzing with thoughts from earlier, and the conversation with Mike hadn't fully distracted her. A quick trip to the deli could be just the thing to break up the tension, and maybe even give her a fresh perspective on the situation.

"All right," she muttered to herself, "I'll figure it out later. But for now, a quick stop at the deli wouldn't hurt." With that, she grabbed her bag and headed out the door, hoping that a chat with Emma would provide a welcome distraction.

Chapter 13

"Hey, Emma," Sarah greeted, flashing a smile as she made her way to the counter.

Emma looked up from the counter, a surprised but warm smile crossing her face. "Sarah! What brings you in today?"

Sarah leaned slightly against the counter, thinking of the sparse selection of items in her fridge as she spoke. "Well, mostly the lack of any nice food at home," she began with a small laugh. "But also, I was wondering if you've ever seen someone called Terri Treharne come through here? I know pretty much everyone ends up coming through this shop at some point, and you know everyone, so I thought I'd check with you."

Emma paused for a moment, her brow furrowing slightly as she thought. "Terri Treharne..." she repeated, trying to place the name. "Not really knew her, knew her. But yeah, she's been in the shop before. I think she came in a few times, mostly for the usual things—some deli meats, bread, maybe a bit of cheese. Nothing out of the ordinary, just like most of our regulars."

Sarah nodded, absorbing the information. "Do you remember when the last time she was in? Or if she came in with her husband?"

Emma leaned back slightly, trying to recall. "Hmm, she was in maybe a couple of weeks ago. Around the time everything started getting a bit busier with the opening of the shop. I think her husband was with her a few times, but I didn't pay much attention. They were just picking up supplies like anyone else. Nothing unusual about them. Although, come to think of it, he was in a few times on his own. I don't think I ever caught his name, but he seemed a little... off. Not the type to chat much. Just came in, grabbed his things, and left. Terri was a bit more, well, vocal, always making sure everything was perfect."

Sarah nodded, taking in the information. "Anything else you can remember? Even something small could help."

Emma paused, her fingers idly tracing the edge of the counter. "Actually, now that you mention it... there was this one time when Terri came in, and she was ranting about something. I didn't catch all the details, but it seemed like she was upset about business. She wasn't talking to me—she was talking to Vanessa. But she was really worked up about something, her voice raised. I don't know exactly what she was saying, though."

Sarah raised an eyebrow, intrigued. "Vanessa, huh? Do you think Vanessa would know what it was about?"

Emma hesitated. "Maybe. She's usually around, but she's called in sick the last couple of days. You could always come back and talk to her when she's back at work. But, mind you, I'm not sure how receptive she'll be."

Sarah leaned in slightly, curious. "Why's that?"

Emma gave a small shrug, her eyes flicking to the phone in her hand as she glanced between customers. "Well, Vanessa's just been a little quiet lately. Or maybe distracted. She's barely looked up from her phone when customers come in—kind of keeps to herself. It's not like her, honestly."

Sarah nodded, processing this new piece of information. "Thanks, Emma. I appreciate you letting me know. I'll keep that in mind and see if I can catch her when she's back."

"Thinking back to Terri, from what I've seen, she could be prickly with people as well," Emma said.

Sarah's curiosity piqued, and she leaned in slightly. "What do you mean?"

Emma hesitated for a moment, then continued, her voice lower, as if sharing a secret. "I saw her sniping at someone out in the street recently. And I've heard the odd complaint about her from other customers who've been in the deli, too."

Sarah raised an eyebrow, intrigued. "What kind of people would that be?"

Emma shrugged slightly. "Well, I don't think she was very popular among the spa and health community. She had a few run-ins with them. The way she carried herself, always trying to one-up others—it rubbed a lot of people the wrong way."

Sarah's thoughts began to swirl. "Any in particular?" she asked, already guessing where Emma might be going with this.

Emma gave a small, almost reluctant nod. "Well, maybe you want to check in with Rachel. She runs *Lotus Blossom*. They've had history for years—back when they were at college together, even. I wouldn't be surprised if there's still some bad blood between them."

"Rachel, huh?" Sarah said thoughtfully. "Do you know where I can find her?"

"Her spa's just a few roads away from here," Emma replied, her voice dipping into a more cautionary tone. "But be careful, Sarah. Rachel can be quite... prickly herself. She's not someone who's easy to approach."

Sarah nodded, taking in the new lead. "Thanks, Emma. I really appreciate it."

As she left the deli, her mind was already working through the next steps. Terri's aggressive nature and her ongoing rivalries were starting to form a clearer picture. Rachel from *Lotus Blossom* could be key to understanding the dynamics between the spas in the area, and Sarah was more certain than ever that the puzzle pieces were beginning to align. But there was something in Emma's words that stuck with Sarah—*prickly* wasn't just a word to describe someone who was a little hard to get along with. It suggested something deeper, a person who might hold grudges and let them fester. It seemed like Rachel was just the person Sarah needed to speak to next.

Thinking that she might as well put this new information straight into action, Sarah decided to head towards *Lotus Blossom*. It was just around the corner, after all, and she figured there was no time like the present to follow up on the latest nugget of information. The idea of waiting until later felt too much like procrastination—she was already here, so she may as well act on it.

As she walked down the quiet street, Sarah couldn't help but notice the ethereal glow of the *Lotus Blossom Wellness Centre*. Unlike the stark modernity she had anticipated, the building exuded a welcoming, almost mystical charm. Strands of fairy lights draped across the entrance cast soft shadows against a deep plum painted exterior. A carved wooden sign, its lettering hand-painted in shimmering gold, swung gently in the breeze, inviting her into the sanctuary beyond.

Stepping into the reception, Sarah was immediately enveloped by a sense of calm - not the rigid, clinical serenity of a luxury spa, but something warmer, richer. The air was filled with the faint hint of incense curling from an amethyst dish at the front desk, while clusters of carefully arranged rose quartz shimmered in the afternoon sun, casting reflections that danced across the walls.

She let herself take it all in, the energy of the space washing over her. It was a far cry from the sleek professionalism of the *Serenity Spa*. This was clearly a retreat for the soul, a place where time seemed to slow down, and the outside world felt miles away.

Just as she was about to take a step forward, she came face to face with the woman at the desk. She greeted Sarah with a slow, knowing smile. "Welcome to *Lotus Blossom*. How can I help you?"

Sarah blinked for a moment, realizing that, despite having just come from the deli with her new-found information, she hadn't quite come up with a solid excuse for why she was here, let alone one that would explain the probing questions she had in mind. She hadn't expected to be thrown into conversation so quickly, and now that she was here, the words didn't seem to come easily.

As she stood there, looking at the woman, her mind quickly flashed back to that moment in the mirror this morning when she'd noticed a new line around her eyes. It was like every time she looked, there was another small change, another mark of time. She could only imagine that when the woman at the desk looked at Sarah, she probably had no hesitation in thinking Sarah was exactly the type who needed a treatment to turn back the clock.

Then it hit her. She smiled, deciding to embrace the situation. "Well," she began, trying to sound casual, "I'm looking for something to make me feel refreshed. I think I'm in need of a little help."

The woman raised an eyebrow slightly, still smiling, but Sarah caught the flicker of amusement in her eyes. "Of course," she said smoothly, gesturing toward a cozy seating area to the side of the reception desk. "We like to say that we help you be the very best you that you already are, but I'm sure we can find something that'll make you feel rejuvenated."

She gestured Sarah toward a pair of plush armchairs nestled beside a low carved wooden table, a neatly arranged stack of brochures resting on its surface. Rachel settled into one of the chairs with practiced ease, crossing her legs and resting her hands lightly in her lap. She had the air of someone who had given this talk a hundred times before.

"So, I'm Rachel" she continued, her tone effortlessly welcoming, "and here at Lotus Blossom we offer a range of treatments, depending on what you're looking for. Relaxation? Skincare? Maybe something a little more restorative?" She picked up one of the brochures and passed it to Sarah, her smile never faltering.

Sarah took it with a polite nod, though she barely glanced at the glossy images of serene models wrapped in fluffy towels. She wasn't here for a spa day, she was here to talk. Settling back into the chair, she kept her expression casual, hoping the conversation would shift into something more revealing.

"That all sounds wonderful," she said, glancing up at Rachel. "I imagine you must get all kinds of people coming through here."

Rachel gave a small, knowing smile. "Oh, you'd be surprised. Everyone needs a little escape now and then."

"I actually work just down the road, close to a different spa," Sarah said casually, as if the words had slipped out. "Though, I'm not sure I'd go there at the moment, not with all the recent... troubles they've been having."

Rachel's posture stiffened almost imperceptibly, but Sarah caught the flicker of something guarded in her expression. It was subtle, but it was there. She had struck a nerve. "Oh, I'm sorry, I didn't mean to bring that up," she quickly apologized, adding, "Did you know Terri?"

Rachel's eyes narrowed slightly, her poised expression faltering for a moment. "I did know her," she admitted, though the words were careful, almost reluctant.

"In that case, I'm very sorry for your loss," Sarah said, her voice softening as she tried to seem sincere. "What was she like? I've heard a few comments about her over the last few days."

Rachel let out a slow breath, brushing a stray rose gold curl from her face as she considered her words. She adjusted her stance slightly, her fingers tightening around the cloth she had been using to wipe the counter. Her eyes flicked to the side before settling back on Sarah. "I can't say I've heard much lately. Just the usual."

Sarah kept her tone light, nonchalant. "But Terri... she seemed like someone who didn't back down easily."

Rachel gave a small, tight smile. "Yes, she had a way of making herself heard, that's for sure."

"Did you two get along?"

Rachel hesitated just a fraction too long before answering. "We managed well enough. She had strong opinions. Liked things done her way."

There was something careful about the way she spoke, as if measuring each word before letting it out. Sarah recognized the guarded tone—it wasn't outright avoidance, but it wasn't openness either.

"I can imagine that made things... complicated sometimes," Sarah said, watching Rachel closely.

Rachel let out a small breath, her fingers resuming their slow swipe over the counter. "Terri knew how to handle herself. Not everyone liked that." She glanced toward the door, as if checking for someone. "But, you know, these things... they have a way of catching up with people."

The words sent a ripple of intrigue through Sarah, but she kept her expression neutral. Instead, she gave a polite nod and pushed back from her seat.

Rachel gave a small, polite smile as Sarah turned to leave. "No problem. And if you're ever in need of some... rejuvenation, here's a list of our treatments," she said, handing over a glossy booklet. "Now that you've met me, you'll know where to come."

As Sarah walked out of *Lotus Blossom*, she couldn't help but feel a sense of satisfaction that she'd acted on Emma's hint. She had hoped that speaking with Rachel would provide some insight into Terri's life, and in many ways, it had. But as she thought over the conversation, Sarah realized that all she was really doing was building up a picture of a woman who seemed to tread on toes wherever she went.

Terri had been ambitious, aggressive, and relentless in her pursuit of success—and it wasn't hard to see how she had made enemies along the way. While Sarah would never, for a moment, suggest that Terri deserved what had happened to her, she couldn't help but wonder if, just maybe, she had pushed someone too far with one of her infamous rants. It was becoming clearer that Terri's competitive streak and sharp words might have pushed someone to the edge.

The thought lingered with Sarah as she walked down the street, her mind swirling with questions. The pieces of the puzzle were starting to fall into place, but they were still jagged, incomplete. She knew that there was more to uncover, and perhaps Terri's aggressive attitude had played a bigger role in her demise than anyone had initially realized. As she mulled over the possibilities, Sarah couldn't help but feel a sense of unease. Was it possible that Terri's downfall had been something she had inadvertently brought upon herself?

Stanley stared at his desk, realizing with a start that he'd been sitting there for hours, the clock ticking past without him even noticing. His stomach grumbled loudly, a sharp reminder that he probably needed to get up and grab something to eat soon. But the pile of notes in front of him, the never-ending list of questions, and the nagging feeling that he was missing something crucial kept him rooted to his seat.

He picked up his coffee cup, taking a long gulp, but immediately choked slightly on the stone-cold mouthful. The once-warm coffee now tasted like cardboard, a stark reminder of just how long he'd been immersed in the case.

His thoughts drifted back to Kerry, her nervousness, the cryptic phone calls she'd been making, and, after a quick look at her financial records, the suspicious increase in her insurance. Everything seemed to point to someone trying to cover something up. But was it connected to Terri's murder, or was Kerry simply overwhelmed by the constant pressures of running a struggling business? Stanley set the coffee cup back down with a sigh, the weight of it all pressing down on him. He ran his fingers through his hair, trying to focus. There were too many variables—too many potential motives, too many distractions. He needed to narrow it down.

Stanley's mind shifted to the lawsuit Megan had mentioned. He'd heard about disgruntled clients before, and often, they became a dangerous liability, willing to make any accusation to discredit a business, especially one already teetering on the edge. Was there a possibility that someone had used the lawsuit as leverage, or worse, that they were using it to target Kerry personally? If this client had a vendetta, it could have led to a more desperate action.

He picked up his phone and dialled the health inspector's office, his thoughts focused. He needed to find out more about the upcoming health inspection, which could be the final blow for the struggling spa. The spa's future was hanging in the balance, and if they failed the inspection, it would be financial ruin for Kerry. Maybe she was taking desperate measures to ensure everything went smoothly, even if it meant cutting corners or covering up problems that no one was supposed to know about.

"Inspector Stanley here," he said when the phone call was answered. "I need information on the upcoming health inspection for *Serenity Spa*."

The health official on the other end of the line confirmed the inspection was indeed scheduled for next week and mentioned that Kerry had been in contact, voicing concerns about some procedural details. Stanley scribbled down the information, the official's words sinking in. Kerry's stress level was clearly escalating, but was it enough to push her to do something drastic?

He hung up the phone and leaned back in his chair, tapping his pen against the desk thoughtfully. Insurance was often a safety net for business owners, but an increase in coverage right before a major crisis, like a health inspection or a potential lawsuit, raised red flags. Had she been planning something to protect herself? Or was this simply a precaution?

Stanley's thoughts were a swirling mess of possibilities. He needed to talk to Kerry more than ever now. The more he looked at the evidence, the more it seemed like she was either hiding something—or she was simply caught in the wrong place at the wrong time. Stanley took a deep breath, his resolve hardening. He would need to confront Kerry again, but this time, he'd be asking the tough questions. There was too much at stake to let this slide.

Chapter 14

As Inspector Stanley walked into the *Serenity Spa*, he couldn't help but notice the tense atmosphere. It wasn't unusual for him to walk into a place and sense an undercurrent of unease. But there was something about this place, with its calming décor and soft lighting, that made the tension feel out of place, almost jarring. It wasn't a sensation he was unfamiliar with, though. Rarely did he show up somewhere and *not* feel it. It was a part of the job, a side effect of constantly being on alert. But occasionally, he wished he could walk into a situation and not feel like he was stepping into a simmering pot of anxiety and secrets.

Stanley paused just inside the door, taking in the quiet. The usual soothing hum of spa music was there, but it felt like background noise, barely noticeable against the weight of the silence. He made his way to the reception desk, where Kerry sat hunched over, her face a mixture of exhaustion and strain. Her eyes were red and puffy from lack of sleep, a clear sign of how much stress she was under. He'd seen it before—

when people were carrying a heavy burden, it showed, no matter how much they tried to hide it.

"Inspector," Kerry said wearily as she looked up, her voice a little more strained than usual. "What can I do for you today?"

Stanley took a breath, his gaze flickering around the spa before he focused on her. "I need to talk to you about a few things." He knew this wasn't going to be an easy conversation, but it was a necessary one.

"Kerry, I have to ask you about the recent increase in your insurance coverage for the spa. Can you explain why you decided to raise the amount so significantly just a few weeks before the incident?"

Kerry's eyes widened in surprise. "I... I didn't think it was relevant. Business has been tough, and I thought it was a prudent decision to protect my investment in case something happened."

Stanley studied her face, looking for any sign of deceit. "It's quite a coincidence, don't you think? The increase in coverage, and then an incident resulting in a death shortly after?"

Kerry's face paled. "You don't think... No, Inspector, I would never do anything to harm anyone. This spa is my life. I raised the insurance because I was worried about the future, but I had no idea something like this would happen."

Stanley leaned forward, his gaze intense. "Then help me understand, Kerry. Is there anything else you're not telling me? Any detail, no matter how small, could be crucial."

Kerry shook her head, tears welling up in her eyes. "I swear, Inspector, I'm telling you everything. I've been trying to keep this place afloat, and now with this tragedy, I don't know what to do."

Stanley softened slightly, sensing her genuine distress. "All right, Kerry. We'll continue our investigation. But remember, if there's anything you're hiding, it will come to light, eventually. The best thing you can do is to be completely honest with us."

Kerry nodded, wiping away a tear. "I understand, Inspector. I just want to find out what happened, too. She might not have been my favourite person, but Terri didn't deserve this."

"I just don't understand how it could have happened," Kerry said, her voice tinged with frustration. "The red light bed had been serviced recently by a reputable firm. They sent someone out to ensure everything was in perfect working order."

Inspector Stanley nodded, his expression thoughtful. "Do you have any records of this service? I'd like to verify it."

"Of course," Kerry replied, reaching into a drawer and pulling out a neatly filed service report. "Here it is. The technician's name was Greg Stevens, and he was here about a week ago."

Stanley took the report, scanning it carefully. "I'll need to check with the company to confirm this."

Stanley turned his back on Kerry, stepping a few paces away to make a quick call on his mobile. After a few moments on hold, he was connected to someone who quickly confirmed that Greg Stevens, a well-respected technician, had indeed carried out the scheduled service for the red light bed. As far as they were concerned, everything had been in perfect working order, with no indication of any problems during or after the service.

"Thank you," Stanley said, his voice polite but curt as he ended the call. He slipped his phone back into his pocket and turned back toward Kerry, who was still standing nearby, watching him closely.

"Greg Stevens serviced the bed, and as far as the service company is concerned, everything was functioning normally," he told her, his tone neutral. "No issues found."

As Stanley was wondering if he was going to have to write off the red light bed as an inexplicable anomaly, his frustration rising as the case seemed to hit another dead end, Megan, who had been quietly working nearby, spoke up.

"Wait a minute," she said, her voice cutting through the silence.

Stanley turned to her, confusion furrowing his brow. "Yes, what is it?" he asked, trying to piece together in his head what could have gone wrong. According to everyone that he'd spoken to until this point suggested that everything had been fine just days ago.

Megan paused, clearly thinking back to something she hadn't mentioned earlier. "Well, I don't know if it's important, erm, but the company sent another person around to finish the paperwork after Greg left," she added, her voice carrying a hint of uncertainty.

Stanley's mind quickly shifted gears. "Another technician?" he asked, his tone sharpening. "Why wasn't it all finished with Greg's visit?"

Megan nodded firmly. "He said he was there to complete the service record and asked me to sign a form. I thought it was odd, but he seemed professional enough."

Stanley stood up, his mind racing. "And did you give him the completed form?" he asked quickly, feeling the urgency of the situation.

Megan shook her head. "No, I didn't. He just left it on the desk and disappeared without taking it. I assumed he was in a hurry, but now that I think about it, it was a bit strange. Why wouldn't he just take the form with him?"

Stanley's eyes narrowed as he processed this new information. This technician had shown up, completed part of the work, left the paperwork behind, and vanished. It was all starting to feel off.

Stanley nodded, already thinking ahead. "It's worth checking. If we can get footage of him, it could help us confirm what happened that day."

"What did this person look like?" Stanley asked, leaning forward to stare at Megan.

She furrowed her brow, trying to recall the details. "He was a youngish man, probably in his late twenties or early thirties. He was wearing the uniform of the servicing company."

Stanley's eyes narrowed. "Can you describe the uniform?"

Megan nodded. "He had on a grey shirt and black trousers, but now that I think about it, his shirt didn't have the company logo on it. Everything else was the same, though."

Kerry's face turned pale as she processed Megan's words. "Are you sure, Megan? I don't remember anyone else coming to ask about paperwork."

Megan nodded firmly. "I'm positive. He said he was there to complete the service record and asked me to sign a form. I thought it was odd, but he seemed professional enough."

"Kerry," Stanley turned to her, his voice becoming more direct, "do you have any security cameras here? Anything that might have caught the technician's movements that day?"

Kerry nodded slowly, her expression thoughtful. "Yes, we have a camera at the back door, but it points down the road. It might have caught him walking by, but I'm not sure if it'll give us a clear shot of him entering or leaving the spa."

Stanley stood up, his mind racing. "Kerry, I need you to gather any security footage you might have from that day. Megan, can you recall exactly when this second visit happened?"

Megan bit her lip, thinking hard. "It was a couple of days after Greg Stevens was here. Late morning, I think. Maybe around 11 AM."

"Thank you, Megan," Stanley said, turning to Kerry. "We need to find out who this impostor was and what he did to the red light bed."

Kerry nodded, already moving to access the security system. "I'll get the footage for you right away, Inspector."

Kerry sat down at the computer at the reception desk, her fingers moving quickly over the keyboard as she logged into the program that controlled the security footage. Stanley watched intently, his mind racing. If the footage could show him who had been at the spa, this second "technician," who had tampered with the equipment, it could explain the accident—and perhaps the murder. But who was he, and what was his motive?

Kerry clicked a few more buttons, bringing up the footage from the back door camera. She scrolled through the timeline until she reached the time frame Megan had mentioned—late afternoon. Stanley's eyes fixed on the screen, his focus sharp.

The security footage finally loaded, showing the spa's entrance and service areas. They watched intently as the timestamp ticked closer to the time Megan had mentioned. Sure enough, a young man in a grey shirt and black pants entered the spa, carrying a clipboard. He moved with a casual confidence, his face partially obscured by a baseball cap.

"There he is," Megan said, pointing to the screen. "That's the guy."

Stanley paused the footage, zooming in on the man's face. Though the cap obscured part of his features, there was enough for them to get a clearer look.

"Do you recognise him?" Stanley asked, glancing at Kerry and Megan.

They both shook their heads. "No," Kerry said. "He doesn't look familiar to me."

"Me neither," Megan added.

"Can you zoom in on him?" Stanley asked, his voice tight with anticipation.

Kerry shook her head, her fingers hovering over the keyboard. "Sorry, it's a really basic camera. No zoom function—just a fixed angle," she explained, her expression apologetic as she glanced at Stanley. "We never really needed anything more detailed."

Stanley let out a quiet sigh, leaning in closer to the screen. Even though the image was grainy and not ideal, the figure was still discernible. He squinted at the screen, trying to make out any distinguishing features. The man's movements were cautious, as if he didn't want to be noticed, and he glanced quickly around before entering the spa.

"We'll have to make do with what we've got," Stanley muttered, tapping his finger on the desk in frustration. "Let's see where he goes next."

Kerry nodded and continued playing the footage, while Stanley kept his eyes fixed on the screen, hoping that any small detail might stand out. Despite the limitations of the camera, he could still feel a sense of unease. Something about this whole situation was starting to feel more complicated than it had seemed at first.

Stanley let out a quiet sigh, leaning in closer to the screen. He squinted at the screen, trying to make out any distinguishing features.

The figure paused at the door, fumbling briefly with something in his hands before entering the building. Stanley's mind raced. Was this the technician who had visited to finish the paperwork—or was it someone else altogether?

The figure's face was still mostly obscured, but something about the way he moved struck Stanley as odd. He couldn't put his finger on it yet, but there was something about the whole scenario that didn't sit right. If this man had been involved in tampering with the Red-Light bed, then he had to have a reason. And what's more—why would he leave the paperwork behind?

As the footage continued, Stanley felt the tension grow. They were closer to an answer—but the bigger questions were still swirling in his head: who was this man, and what did he have to do with the mystery that was quickly becoming much darker than anyone had imagined?

Stanley took a deep breath. "We'll need to see if we can enhance this footage and run it through our facial recognition system. In the meantime, we'll question the service company to see if they know anything about this impostor. This could be the break we need to figure out what really happened to Terri."

Stanley sat behind the reception desk at *Serenity Spa*, the quiet hum of the fluorescent lights doing little to drown out the whirlwind of thoughts racing through his mind. The footage he had just reviewed had raised more questions than answers. He rubbed a hand over his face, feeling the weight of the case settling more heavily on his shoulders.

This wasn't just a random accident, everything about this felt calculated, deliberate. The timing of the technician's visit, the way it aligned so perfectly with Terri's presence at the spa—it all pointed to someone who had precise knowledge of the spa's schedule. Stanley could feel the tension mounting, his thoughts tangled in the details.

He needed a quiet space to process what he had just seen. Kerry, noticing his discomfort, offered him the staff room, and he accepted with a tired nod. He followed her down the narrow hallway and entered the small, cluttered room. It was modest, with a couch that looked like it had seen better days and a table strewn with papers and cleaning supplies. The hum of the refrigerator in the corner seemed to amplify the silence, but Stanley welcomed it.

He sank onto the small sofa, rubbing his fingers into his eyes, trying to clear his mind. He pulled out his notebook and flicked through the pages, trying to organize the jumble of facts that had been swirling in his head all day.

The technician's visit, the timing, Terri's possible connection to the spa's rivals—it all felt interconnected. But something didn't add up. If the timing of the technician's visit was tied to Terri's death, how could they have known when she would be at the spa? It seemed too precise, too deliberate.

A more troubling thought occurred to him. What if Terri wasn't the intended victim? What if the killer hadn't cared who was there, just that someone would be in the wrong place at the wrong time? Was it possible that this had been an elaborate attempt to sabotage Kerry's business—something that had backfired disastrously?

Stanley stopped, staring at the page in front of him. The idea of a business rivalry turning deadly seemed far-fetched, but in a town as tight knit as this, where everyone knew everyone else's business, it wasn't out of the realm of possibility. Still, he couldn't shake the feeling that there was something more to this. Something more than just a petty grudge or business competition.

His thoughts swirled around the possibilities as the quiet hum of the staff room filled the air. He mulled over everything he had learned so far—how the technician's visit seemed so perfectly timed to Terri's death. It made him uneasy, like there was a piece of the puzzle he was missing. How could anyone have known when she would be there? Or perhaps, as the thought lingered, it wasn't about Terri at all. What if it was just a random opportunity to sabotage Kerry's spa, and Terri had simply been in the wrong place at the wrong time?

After a moment of quiet contemplation, Stanley pushed himself up from the couch. He stepped to the door and poked his head out, his gaze scanning the hallway. He spotted Kerry near the reception desk and walked over to her, wanting to clarify one thing—something that had been bothering him.

"Kerry, you mentioned Terri had visited a couple of times in the past few months, but you wouldn't call her a regular?" Stanley asked, hoping to gather more clarity on the situation.

Kerry glanced up and nodded. "That's right, Inspector. She had been in a few times, but not enough for her to have a set schedule or preferences. I wouldn't say she was a regular, at least not in the traditional sense."

Before Stanley could respond, Megan, who had been quietly listening nearby, stepped in. "No, not regular enough that I would remember when her appointment was." She shrugged slightly, her expression thoughtful. "But then, she wasn't that good at remembering her appointment time either."

Stanley raised an eyebrow. "What do you mean by that, Megan?"

Megan hesitated for a moment before continuing. "Well, a few days before her appointment, she called up saying that it had completely escaped her mind when she was next due in and asked if I could remind her. It's not unusual, clients forget their appointments all the time. I didn't think anything of it until now. Why, is it important?"

Stanley leaned forward, his expression intense. "I'd say it's very important. Think about it—how did the killer know exactly when Terri would be here? This wasn't a crime of opportunity, it was planned. Someone needed to know her exact schedule."

Kerry's eyes widened as she started to grasp the implication. "You think that call wasn't from Terri?"

"Exactly," Stanley said, his voice steady. "I don't think you were talking to Terri—I think you were talking to the killer. They needed to be sure of her appointment time so their plan would go off without a hitch. And really, who would be suspicious of a client calling up?"

Megan's face paled. "But... if that's true, then the killer must have known her well enough to imitate her, or at least had access to her personal information."

Stanley nodded. "That's what we're trying to figure out. Did anything about the call stand out to you? Background noise, hesitations—anything that seemed off?"

Megan shook her head. "No, nothing out of the ordinary. The call was quick, just a simple request for the appointment time."

Stanley rubbed his chin thoughtfully. "All right. This gives us a new angle to investigate. We'll need to check phone records—if the call didn't come from Terri's number, we might have a lead on the person who made it."

He paused, then glanced between Kerry and Megan, his expression hardening. "And that brings me to something else. Terri's phone."

Kerry frowned. "What about it?"

Stanley's gaze locked onto Megan. "It wasn't with her things. It's missing."

Megan stiffened, her shoulders going rigid.

Stanley continued, his tone measured but firm. "Terri was seen using her phone earlier that day, but when we searched, it was gone. That means someone took it—either to hide something incriminating, or to get rid of evidence that could lead us to the killer." He let the words settle, then added, "Megan, do you know where Terri's phone is?"

Megan swallowed hard. "I—I don't…"

Stanley didn't look away. "Megan."

Her hands curled into fists at her sides, her breathing uneven.

Kerry shot Megan a confused glance. "Wait, what's going on?"

Megan's voice wavered. "I— I found it," she finally admitted, guilt flashing across her face. "In the laundry bin. The day she… you know." She let out a shaky breath. "I didn't think it was important! I thought she just forgot it."

Stanley's jaw tightened. "And what did you do with it?"

Megan winced. "I wiped it." Her voice was barely above a whisper now. "I factory reset it and… I was going to sell it."

Silence stretched between them. Stanley exhaled sharply, rubbing his temple. So, this wasn't the work of the murderer.

All the time he'd spent chasing the missing phone, thinking it held the key to cracking the case—It was nothing. Just an opportunistic mistake by a spa assistant who had panicked. The phone had never been the missing piece. It was never going to lead them to the killer.

Walking back to his car, Stanley paused outside the shop, the quiet hum of the city surrounding him. Without really considering why, his feet led him closer to *Sarah's Secrets*. It was just around the corner from where he was standing, and something nudged at him to pop in for a quick visit. He hadn't meant to, but the thought of speaking with Sarah, and perhaps Robyn if she was around, seemed like a natural next step.

The murder investigation was still on his mind, of course, but he figured it couldn't hurt to have a brief conversation with Sarah. Maybe she had noticed something that could help. And if Robyn just happened to be there, maybe she could shed some light on things as well. After all, the more information he could gather from the people around Terri, the better.

He adjusted his coat and walked towards the door, unsure why he felt so drawn to the shop, but deciding to trust his instincts for now.

Stanley had barely stepped into the coffee shop when the scent of freshly brewed coffee hit him, and it was almost like a jolt to his senses. He hadn't realized how much he needed a proper cup of coffee until now and it was a stark reminder of his earlier encounter with the cold, stale, miserable version. The thought of that flat, lifeless drink crept into his mind as he stepped further into *Sarah's Secrets*.

The shop felt like a haven after the tension he'd just left behind. The seriousness of the case, the weight of his thoughts, and the endless hours at his desk had left him feeling drained. Now, as he stood in the doorway, the warm lighting and the gentle clink of cups on the counter made him feel, if only for a moment, like he could breathe again.

He spotted Sarah behind the counter, her focus on preparing drinks, and for the first time in hours, he allowed himself a small, almost imperceptible sigh of relief. It was just the change of pace he needed, even if only for a few minutes.

"Sarah," he said as he walked up to the counter. "I hope I'm not interrupting, but I was hoping to grab a cup of coffee." He offered a faint smile, his eyes scanning the drinks menu. As he approached the counter, Missy bounded over, her tail wagging enthusiastically. Stanley's stoic facade softened almost imperceptibly as he bent down to stroke her.

"Hey there, girl," he murmured, scratching behind her ears. Missy leaned into his touch, her tail wagging even more furiously.

Sarah looked up from the espresso machine and smiled. "She likes you," she said, watching the exchange with amusement.

"I've always wanted a dog," he confessed, as he continued to pet her. "But I work too many hours. I don't think it would be fair to leave someone at home and lonely while I'm working."

As Sarah watched Stanley pet Missy, her mind briefly wandered, and a question popped out before she had a chance to stop it. "Does that extend to not having a person at home to go home to?" she asked, her voice a little quieter than usual, realizing just as the words left her mouth that it was a very personal question to ask.

Stanley paused, his hand stilling for a moment before he shook his head. "No, it doesn't," he replied simply, his tone closing off the topic without elaboration. Sarah immediately regretted asking, feeling a slight awkwardness settle in the space between them. She quickly moved on, trying to fill the silence.

Sarah raised an eyebrow in surprise, hearing the honesty in his words. "I didn't know you were an animal person," she said, walking around the counter to join them, her curiosity piqued. "Seems like Missy's made quite an impression on you."

Stanley chuckled lightly, looking down at Missy, who was still wagging her tail contentedly. "I suspect she's got a way of doing that."

Stanley straightened up, giving Missy one last pat. "Animals are... uncomplicated," he said, a hint of wistfulness in his tone. "They don't play mind games."

Sarah chuckled. "You could always get a cat. They pretty much take care of themselves. We've got one of them as well, but she's a miserable old lady now and not quite a friendly as Missy here."

He shook his head. "I'm more of a dog person. I like their loyalty. But it's just not practical with my job."

Missy sat down at his feet, looking up at him with adoring eyes. Sarah watched the scene unfold, noting the unexpected gentleness in Stanley's interaction with her dog. It was a side of him she hadn't seen before, and it made him seem more human, more relatable.

"Well, if you ever need a dog fix, Missy is always here," Sarah offered, smiling.

Stanley nodded, a small, genuine smile tugging at the corners of his mouth. "I might just take you up on that," he said, his tone lighter than usual. But as he took a breath and straightened his jacket, his expression shifted back to its businesslike seriousness.

There was a moment of quiet, and Sarah couldn't help but feel that, for all his tough exterior, there was a more human side to Stanley that he didn't often let others see.

"Any updates on that letter you received? The poison pen one?" he asked, changing the subject back to the reason that he'd wanted to stop by.

Sarah shook her head, her lips pressed together in frustration. "Thankfully, no more letters. But I still haven't figured out where it came from or who would send something like that," she said, her voice tinged with unease. "It's been a weird feeling, knowing someone's out there, watching, trying to intimidate me without even showing their face."

Stanley's eyes softened slightly, though his focus remained on the details of the investigation. "Keep me posted if you get anything else. We'll make sure you're not left in the dark." He glanced down at the counter briefly before meeting her eyes again.

Sarah gave a small nod, grateful for his offer. "For now, we keep pushing forward, right?" she said, her voice steady as she got back to the topic at hand. Stanley's gaze lingered on her for a moment, sensing her determination, and he nodded in silent agreement.

Before she could dwell further on her thoughts, Sarah's concern for Terri's husband bubbled to the surface. "Inspector, have you been able to find Terri's missing husband?" she inquired, her voice tinged with worry.

Stanley's expression hardened slightly, a flicker of suspicion crossing his features. "Oh, yes," he replied, his voice tinged with disdain. "From what I've gathered, Robert Treharne claimed he received an urgent phone call that required him to leave immediately. But to be honest, his story didn't sit well with me. The whole thing seemed a little too rehearsed. I don't trust him, Sarah. It feels like he was trying to cover something up."

He paused, narrowing his eyes as he spoke again. "From what I can tell, Robert didn't just leave to take a phone call. It seems more likely that he took the opportunity to sneak off and see a woman while his wife was occupied. I haven't been able to catch up with him yet, but once I locate this woman—Vanessa, I think her name is—I'll be able to get a clearer picture of his alibi. If he has one, that is."

Sarah listened intently, her mind already ticking over the new lead. "Ah, I might be able to help you there," she said after a pause, a thoughtful look crossing her face. "Funny enough, I had a chat with my friend at the deli the other day. She mentioned that her colleague, a woman named Vanessa, was seen talking to Terri's husband. It sounds like you might be able to get some answers there, if you wanted to pop in."

Stanley's face brightened slightly at the prospect of moving forward. "That's good to hear. If Vanessa can confirm she was with Robert, or even if she can provide any other details, it could clear things up—or give me something to work with. I appreciate the tip, Sarah." He leaned back slightly, the wheels in his mind already turning.

Just then, the door to the kitchen swung open, and Robyn emerged carrying a tray filled with crockery. She placed it down on the counter, her eyes meeting Stanley's, before they both quickly looked away. The air between them crackled with an unspoken tension.

"Inspector," Robyn greeted, her voice tinged with a mix of shyness and curiosity.

"Robyn," Stanley replied, nodding slightly. He cleared his throat, glancing at Missy, who had shifted her attention to Robyn now, wagging her tail.

Sarah, sensing an opportunity perhaps for a bit of matchmaking, seized the opportunity. "Oh, I just remembered, I need to check something in the storeroom," she said, her tone overly casual. "Robyn, could you keep Inspector Stanley company for a moment? And Missy too, of course."

Robyn looked startled, but she nodded. "Sure, Auntie Sarah."

With that, Sarah disappeared into the back, leaving Stanley, Robyn, and Missy alone in the coffee shop.

Stanley, feeling slightly out of his element, shifted on his feet. "So, how are things here at the shop?" he asked, attempting to make small talk.

Robyn smiled nervously, tucking a strand of hair behind her ear. "Busy, but good. We've had a lot of interest from local people, so hopefully it's going to be a successful opening."

Stanley took in her words with a quiet nod, but something about the conversation didn't sit right with him. It seemed like a contradiction to the conversation he'd just been having with Sarah about unwelcome notes, and the tension that lingered in Sarah's voice when she had mentioned it earlier. He chose not to bring it up, unsure if Sarah had discussed it with Robyn yet. The last thing he wanted was to stir up more trouble by asking Robyn about something she might not even know about.

He nodded, forcing a small smile. "That's good to hear."

The awkward silence between them stretched a little longer than he'd intended. Missy, as if sensing the unease, moved closer to Robyn and nudged her hand, prompting her to pet her. Robyn obliged, grateful for the distraction.

"So, um, Inspector," Robyn started, trying to bridge the gap. "Do you have any pets?"

Stanley shook his head. "No, but I was just telling your aunt that I've always liked dogs. They're... loyal." He glanced at Missy, who was now happily receiving attention from Robyn.

"Missy is a sweetheart," Robyn said, smiling down at the dog. "She has a way of making everyone feel at ease."

Stanley looked at Robyn, noticing the genuine affection in her eyes. "She certainly does," he agreed.

Chapter 15

Charlie and Robyn stood in the cosy, sunlit shop, surrounded by the comforting aroma of freshly brewed coffee and the tantalizing scent of baking cupcakes. The new coffee shop, their family's dream, was nearly ready for its grand opening, but there was still much to do.

For the first time in weeks, the shop felt uncharacteristically quiet. Gone were the workmen and contractors bustling around, finalizing everything for the big day. The noise of drills and hammers had given way to the soft hum of the coffee machine and the occasional chatter of people as they walked past the shop. It was just the two of them, standing together in the heart of the space that had become their shared project, their future.

As they exchanged glances, both Charlie and Robyn couldn't help but feel a sense of ownership. Sure, it was Sarah's dream opportunity, her vision that had pulled everything together, but when it was just them in the shop, it felt different. It felt like theirs too. The thought that they were about to step into something this big, something that they could grow and mould between them, was exhilarating. They didn't just work here—they were becoming a part of something they could call their own.

"Can you believe we're about to run this place?" Charlie asked, looking around, his eyes filled with excitement. "Just the two of us."

Robyn chuckled softly, leaning against the counter. "Well, three if you count your mum, but yes, I know what you mean. It feels a little surreal. I mean, most people our age would probably be worried about rent and living costs, not opening a coffee shop."

Charlie nodded, the weight of it settling in. "I know, right? This is huge. Not many people get to do something like this, especially not at our age. But we have something here. It's a little scary, but also... amazing."

"Exactly," Robyn said, her smile growing as she looked around at the shop. "It's not just your mum's business—it's ours too. We've got our hands in this, and we get to shape it into whatever we want."

The quiet hum of the shop felt peaceful yet charged with possibility. They could already see the faces of future customers, the buzz of conversations, and the laughter filling the air. This wasn't just about serving coffee, it was about creating a space, a home away from home, where people would connect, unwind, and enjoy what *Sarah's Secrets* had to offer.

"I think we're ready for this," Robyn said, her voice full of conviction.

"We definitely are," Charlie agreed, looking around once more with a growing sense of pride. "We're going to make it work. And maybe, just maybe, we'll get to watch it become something bigger than we ever imagined."

Charlie was in the kitchen, his sleeves rolled up as he expertly measured ingredients for his latest batch of experimental cupcakes. His movements were fluid and practiced, a testament to his years of experience as a barista and baker. The small kitchen was cosy, but it was just right for what they needed. After all, he wasn't going to be preparing a la carte meals back here—this was all about the sweet stuff, from cakes to pastries and, of course, those decadent cupcakes that he hoped would become a feature of the shop.

The kitchen had taken some time to get just the way he wanted it. It hadn't been easy, stripping it out and setting everything up from scratch. But now, as he looked around at the tidy worktops, the neatly arranged baking tools, and the pristine oven, Charlie couldn't help but smile. This was his perfect little space—his creative hub. It was where he could lose himself, experimenting with new flavours and recipes, without the pressure of a busy kitchen environment. He had all the space he needed to bake to his heart's content.

As he mixed the batter, Charlie glanced up from his work, watching Robyn for a moment. She was behind the counter, her focus on arranging the glass jars of coffee beans, teas, and an array of colourful syrups that added to the shop's quirky charm.

Charlie wiped his hands on a towel and stepped out from the kitchen, walking across the small but warm space that had already started to feel like home. He leaned against the counter, watching Robyn carefully.

"How's it going out there? Everything looking good?" he asked, his voice warm but with an undertone of curiosity. He knew Robyn was always meticulous about keeping everything just right, and he appreciated her attention to detail.

Robyn smiled, though a hint of nervousness flickered in her eyes. "Yeah, I think so. I want to make sure it's all just right for Auntie Sarah, after all, she knows just what she wants this place to feel like."

Charlie chuckled, nodding in agreement. "Absolutely. She's always had an eye for the little things. But that's why this place is going to be amazing."

Robyn's smile widened, but she bit her lip. "I just hope we don't let her down. She's put so much into this."

Charlie paused, wiping his hands on a towel. "We won't. We've got this. Besides, you're a pro at dealing with people, thanks to your bar experience. And I know my way around a kitchen. We make a great team."

Robyn laughed, her tension easing slightly. "You're right. I just keep thinking about all the things that could go wrong. She's putting so much faith in us."

Charlie walked over to her, placing a reassuring hand on her shoulder. "Hey, it's normal to feel that way. But remember, this is a family business. I know how much Mum wants this to work. And we've got each other's backs."

Robyn nodded, taking a deep breath. "Thanks, Charlie. I needed that."

"Anytime," Charlie replied, giving her a warm smile before returning to his cupcakes. He carefully spooned the batter into the tins, humming softly to himself. "So, what do you think of these new cupcake flavours? I've got a couple of experimental ones I'm trying out."

Robyn raised an eyebrow, intrigued. "Experimental, eh? What flavours are we talking about?"

Charlie grinned, a mischievous glint in his eye. "How about lavender honey and matcha white chocolate?"

Robyn's eyes widened. "Erm wow, those sound amazing! I can't wait to try them."

"Let's hope they turn out as good as they sound," Charlie said, sliding the tray into the oven. "We'll know in about twenty minutes."

Robyn leaned against the counter, watching Charlie as he adjusted the oven settings. "Must be nice to be putting all of your training to good use." she remarked, her tone light but genuinely curious.

Charlie glanced at her, a chuckle escaping his lips. "Yeah, it is. I spent years learning all these techniques and flavour combinations. It's about time I used them for more than just fattening up the family at Sunday dinners."

Robyn laughed, shaking her head. "I don't think anyone in the family is complaining. Your Sunday roasts are legendary."

Charlie's grin widened. "True, but there's something special about creating for a wider audience. Seeing strangers enjoy something you've made from scratch—it's a different satisfaction."

Robyn nodded thoughtfully. "I can imagine. Plus, it's great for business. Unique flavours like these are sure to bring in more customers."

"Exactly," Charlie said, wiping his hands on a towel. "It's all about standing out, giving people a reason to come back. And honestly, it's just fun. I love experimenting, seeing what works and what doesn't."

Robyn watched him for a moment, admiring his passion. "You know, you're really good at this. Not just the baking, but the whole creating something new part. It's inspiring."

Charlie's cheeks flushed slightly at the compliment. "Thanks, Robyn. That means a lot coming from you. And hey, maybe one day I'll have a whole line of experimental desserts that everyone raves about."

"I don't doubt it for a second," Robyn said, with a smile. "So, what's the story behind these particular flavours? Lavender honey and matcha-what did-you-say? Those aren't exactly your run-of-the-mill choices."

Charlie leaned against the counter, crossing his arms. "Well, a trip to Provence inspired the lavender honey. The lavender fields there were incredible, and I've always wanted to capture that essence in a dessert. As for the matcha white chocolate, that came from a friend who's obsessed with matcha. She challenged me to create something unique with it, and white chocolate seemed like the perfect pairing."

Robyn nodded, impressed. "I love how personal each flavour is. It adds another layer to the story".

"Exactly," Charlie said, his eyes shining with enthusiasm. "Food is more than just sustenance. It's about memories, emotions, and connections. That's what I try to bring into everything I make."

"Well," Robyn said, reaching for a towel to help clean up. "I can't wait to see how these cupcakes turn out. I have a feeling they're going to be a hit."

"Fingers crossed," Charlie said, glancing at the oven with anticipation. "But either way, it's the process that counts. The experimenting, the tasting, the tweaking. It's all part of the fun."

As Charlie made his way back to the kitchen, he heard footsteps behind him. Robyn had followed him into the kitchen, where he was moving his used bowls and utensils into the sink to be cleaned. She raised an eyebrow as she looked down at his hands, which were adorned with bright pink marigold gloves.

Charlie glanced up at her with a grin, his eyes twinkling with mischief. "Don't ask," he said, clearly amused by the sceptical look she was giving him.

Robyn chuckled, shaking her head, but she didn't push it. "You know, I've never seen anyone look so serious in pink gloves," she teased, leaning against the counter.

Charlie shrugged as he pulled off the gloves, tossing them aside. "What can I say? I have a reputation to uphold," he said with a wink, before turning back to his cupcakes.

Then, with a curious smile, he added, "What about you, Robyn? We've all missed you while you were away studying to be a teacher, but now you're back here. And I get the impression that you have different ideas in your head."

Robyn hesitated for a moment, the question catching her slightly off guard. She leaned against the counter, her expression thoughtful. "Yeah, I guess I have. Teaching might be right for me one day, but right now, it just doesn't feel like the right fit. I need something different."

Charlie nodded, encouraging her to continue. "What changed?"

Robyn sighed, folding her arms. "I think it's more about what I need at this moment in my life. Teaching is amazing, but it can be really isolating in its own way. I was feeling...disconnected, I suppose. I need something where I am surrounded by the love of my family."

She smiled softly, looking around the cosy, bustling space of *Sarah's Secrets*. "And I couldn't think of anything nicer than being here, in this adventure that we're just starting. It feels like home. Plus, there's something incredibly fulfilling about seeing people smile over a cup of coffee or a delicious treat. It's immediate, and it's heartwarming."

Charlie's eyes sparkled with understanding. "I get that. There's something special about working with family and seeing the direct impact of what you do. Plus, you've always been amazing with people."

Robyn laughed, a hint of self-deprecation in her tone. "I hope so. I mean, I'm still figuring things out, but being here feels right. Maybe I'll go back to teaching someday, but for now, this is where I want to be."

Charlie reached out, giving her shoulder a reassuring squeeze. "Well, we're lucky to have you. And I'm sure that Mum feels the same way."

Robyn smiled, feeling a warm sense of belonging. "Aw thanks, Charlie. It means a lot. And hey, I get to see you work your magic with these cupcakes, so that's a bonus."

Charlie chuckled, turning back to the oven. "Speaking of which, let's check on these babies. Moment of truth."

The timer on the oven beeped, and Charlie quickly donned an oven mitt, opening the door to reveal the cupcakes. A fragrant wave of lavender and honey filled the air, mingling with the earthy scent of matcha.

"Perfectly baked, if I say so myself," Charlie said, carefully lifting the tray out and setting it on the counter. He grabbed a toothpick, poking it into one of the cupcakes.

Robyn leaned in, inhaling the delightful aroma. "They smell incredible. Can we try them now?"

Charlie carefully set the warm cupcakes down on the cooling rack, the aroma filling the kitchen as the golden-brown tops glistened in the light. Robyn's hands hovered eagerly around the freshly baked treats, her eyes locked on them like a kid in a candy store.

"Patience," Charlie teased, flicking at her outstretched hands playfully with his tea towel. "They need to cool first. But soon, I promise."

Robyn pouted but stepped back with a sigh, resigned to waiting. Charlie chuckled to himself as he wiped his hands and turned to look at the cupcakes, his mind wandering to something else.

The two of them had been discussing it for weeks now, trying to settle on the right atmosphere for the shop. "I still think we should go with some classic rock," Charlie said, his voice light but insistent, revisiting one of their familiar debates about the shop's music. "It has energy, and it's a great way to keep everyone motivated. We need something that gets the vibe right, but also makes people feel welcome."

Robyn rolled her eyes, placing a tray of recently dried mugs back onto the shelf below the counter. "Classic rock? Are you serious? How are people supposed to relax with that blaring in the background? We need something more soothing, like jazz or acoustic."

Charlie laughed. "Jazz? Acoustic? Come on, Robyn, that's going to put everyone to sleep. We need something with a bit more life to it."

Robyn crossed her arms, a playful smile on her face. "Okay, Mr. DJ, let's think about this. We want people to feel comfortable and relaxed, not like they've walked into a rock concert."

Charlie sighed, realising she had a point. "All right, maybe our tastes are a bit too... shouty for a coffee shop. But we don't have any customers yet, so how about we compromise? We'll play our music while we set up and switch to something more easy listening once the paying guests start coming in."

Robyn's eyes lit up. "Deal! Until then, we're going to rock this place."

With that, Charlie turned up the volume on the stereo, and the two of them laughed and danced as they went about their tasks. Charlie air-guitared with a broom while Robyn sang into a spatula, their playful antics bringing a sense of joy and camaraderie to the morning routine.

The music echoed through the empty shop, and for a little while, it was their private concert, until finally Robyn flopped down into a chair. It was time to sample Charlie's creations. He handed Robyn one of the lavender honey treats. She took a bite, her eyes widening with delight. "Oh my god, Charlie, this is amazing!"

Charlie beamed, taking a bite of his own cupcake. "Glad you like it," he said, his voice full of pride. "Now let's see how the matcha white chocolate ones turned out."

Robyn nodded, her mouth still full of the rich cupcake, and she smiled, savouring the flavour. "These are amazing, Charlie. It's such a shame the shop isn't opening tomorrow because I know these would be snapped up in no time."

Charlie raised an eyebrow, a glint of amusement in his eyes. "Well, we can always do a little test run," he said, setting his cupcake down and turning to face Robyn. "Mum was saying we should get everyone round for an afternoon before the big day—just family and a few friends. Nothing formal, just a chance to ease into things."

Robyn paused, considering the idea. A few days ago, she wouldn't have hesitated to throw herself into preparations, but after everything that had happened, her energy felt drained. Still, the thought of a warm, familiar gathering sounded comforting.

"I think that's a great idea," she said, her smile a little softer. "It'll be nice to have everyone together before things get hectic. I can message the family group chat now and see who's around."

Charlie grinned, pleased that she was getting involved. "Perfect. No pressure, just a chance to test out the coffee, let Mum boss us around, and make sure everything's working as it should."

Robyn huffed a small laugh, already scrolling through her contacts. "And what about James? Will he be able to make it back from university?" She knew Charlie's boyfriend had a hectic schedule, but James had always been enthusiastic about their coffee shop dream.

Charlie's expression brightened at the mention of James. "I think he'd love to come. He's been ridiculously supportive, even with all his studies. I've probably talked his ear off about blends and brewing techniques."

Robyn smirked. "Well, he is studying chemistry—maybe he can design some kind of scientific perfect brew for us."

Charlie chuckled. "I'll ask him. He'd probably love the challenge." Then, his smile faded slightly as he glanced at Robyn. "Hey... how are you doing?" His voice was gentler now, his teasing edge replaced with quiet concern.

Robyn hesitated, fingers still resting on her phone. She knew exactly what he was referring to. She hadn't wanted to dwell on it, not when there was so much else to focus on, but the image of what she'd seen still lingered at the edges of her thoughts. "I'm ok," she said finally, but even to her own ears, it didn't sound entirely convincing.

Charlie nudged her playfully. "I figured I'd keep you busy with coffee and cake. Distraction therapy."

Robyn let out a small, genuine laugh. "I appreciate it."

"Good," Charlie said, satisfied. "And, hey, what better way to lift the mood than a party? Well... a very tame, coffee-themed one."

Robyn smiled, nodding. "Yeah. It'll be good to have everyone together."

Just as she sent the message out, the bell above the door jingled, and Sarah walked in, looking slightly frazzled but pleased. She saw the cupcakes on the counter, and her face instantly lit up. "Wow, those look fantastic! How did the new flavours turn out?"

Robyn and Charlie exchanged a grin, the moment of heaviness passing. "They're a hit," Robyn said. "You've got to try them, Sarah."

Sarah eagerly reached for a cupcake, her eyes widening with delight as she took a bite. "These are incredible! Great job, you two," she exclaimed, her voice filled with appreciation.

Charlie wiped his hands on a towel, smiling at Sarah.

Sarah laughed, shaking her head playfully. "I'm loving your creative exploits for the shop, but these practice bakes are doing nothing for my ever-expanding waistline!" She took another bite. "I swear, every time I walk in here, I am presented with something delicious—and it's not just the customers' satisfaction that will grow!"

"It's all for the good of the business, right?" Robyn teased, glancing over at Sarah with a wink.

Sarah nodded, still grinning. "And it's great to have you both here. This place wouldn't be the same without you." She looked around, taking in the cozy atmosphere that Charlie and Robyn had helped build, the feeling of warmth that was already filling *Sarah's Secrets*. "You've made this place even better than I imagined."

Robyn felt a surge of warmth at Sarah's words. She looked around the inviting, bustling coffee shop, filled with laughter, and felt a little of her unease ease. Maybe keeping busy really was the best way forward.

Chapter 16

Detective Inspector Stanley stood awkwardly in the sleek, minimalist reception area of *Parker Dermatology*, a list of local spa owners clenched in his hand. He had narrowed down the list to just those who had been colleagues of Terri Treharne, crossing off several names as dead ends. The final name on the list was Emily Parker, and now, here he was, standing in an immaculately modern space, waiting to speak with her.

Stanley's eyes skimmed the sleek room—the soft lighting, neatly framed certificates, and spotless surfaces. His fingers drummed against his notepad, betraying his unease. Stanley shifted his weight from one foot to the other, feeling conspicuously out of place in his suit amidst the pristine surroundings.

The receptionist glanced at him again, her polite smile barely hiding the curiosity in her eyes. Stanley cleared his throat, trying to maintain his usual air of authority, though his discomfort was growing.

Finally, the door to the treatment rooms opened, and Dr Emily Parker emerged. Stanley's eyes flicked to her immediately, taking in her athletic figure, the way she moved with ease—confident, yet restrained. Her short, elegantly styled pixie haircut framed her sharp features, which seemed both serene and impenetrable. There was an undeniable air of professionalism about her, but also a quiet strength that Stanley couldn't quite place.

Her attire was simple yet polished, her fitted blouse and dark trousers conveying someone who took their work seriously. As she approached, her posture straight, her hands neatly clasped in front of her, Stanley couldn't help but notice how composed she was, exuding an aura of calm control. It wasn't the stiff formality of someone eager to please, more the quiet confidence of someone accustomed to command.

"Detective Inspector Stanley, I presume?" she asked, her tone measured but polite, with no hint of hesitation.

Stanley gave a small nod, mentally preparing himself for the conversation ahead, but still assessing her—curious about how someone like her might fit into this web of connections he was trying to untangle.

"Yes, Ms. Parker. Thank you for seeing me on such short notice," Stanley replied, extending a hand, which Emily shook briefly before stepping back.

"Of course. Please, follow me," she said, her voice polite but controlled as she led him toward the back of the office. As they passed the reception desk, Emily could feel the receptionist's gaze practically boring into her. The woman was trying to appear disinterested, but Stanley could tell she was straining to look casual, obviously curious about why a police inspector was visiting.

Not wanting to fuel the town's gossip mill any further, Emily glanced over her shoulder, offering the receptionist a tight, professional smile, and then turned back to Stanley. "Perhaps it's better if we talk privately. Would you mind coming into my office?" she asked, her tone suggesting that it was more for her own comfort than his.

Stanley nodded, sensing her unease. He followed her into a small office tucked away at the back, the door clicking shut behind them. The room was sparsely decorated, with sleek furniture and a desk that bore the weight of numerous medical journals and patient files. The faint scent of antiseptic lingered in the air, mingling with the smell of the carefully arranged skincare products on the shelves.

Emily motioned for Stanley to take a seat across from her, and he did so, feeling more aware of the privacy of the situation. As he pulled out his notepad, he glanced up at Emily, noticing the subtle tension in her posture. He cleared his throat, sensing that this conversation was going to require more finesse than he had initially expected.

"I'm following up on some information regarding Terri Treharne. I understand you studied together?"

Emily's eyes flickered with a hint of something— annoyance, perhaps? —before she nodded. "Yes, we were in the same program. But that was many years ago. I haven't seen Terri since then."

Stanley's pen hovered over his notepad, his gaze fixed on her. "Have you had any contact with her at all? Emails, social media, anything?"

Emily shook her head, her posture stiffening. "No, Inspector. Like I said, it's been a long time. I was as shocked as anyone to hear about her death."

Stanley's pen remained poised, his eyes narrowing slightly. "So, no contact in any form?"

Emily's expression didn't waver, though her fingers twitched ever so slightly. "None, Inspector. It's been years since our paths crossed."

Stanley paused, pen hovering over his notepad. 'So, you've really had no reason to think about her until now?' His tone was light, almost conversational, but his sharp gaze betrayed the question's weight.

A brief hesitation—barely a heartbeat—before Emily replied, her voice steady. "No reason at all. Like I said, her death came as a complete shock to me." She maintained eye contact, but there was a slight tightness around her mouth, a minute crack in her composed façade.

Stanley's pen danced across the paper once more. "I see. Well, thank you for your time, Emily. If you do remember anything, even the smallest detail, please let us know."

Emily nodded, her shoulders relaxing slightly. "Of course, Inspector. I'll let you know if anything comes to mind." She offered a tight smile, but her eyes remained guarded as she watched him leave.

Stanley studied her, sensing the wall she had built between them. "I understand this is difficult, but any information you can provide could be helpful. Even the smallest detail might be significant."

Emily's lips pressed into a thin line. "I wish I could help, but there's really nothing more I can tell you."

Stanley sighed inwardly, recognizing the futility of pressing further. "All right, Dr Parker. Thank you for your time."

Emily stood, her polite smile returning. "Of course. I hope you find what you're looking for."

As Stanley exited *Parker Dermatology*, he couldn't shake the feeling of isolation and frustration. The townspeople's guarded responses and suspicion were wearing on him, and Emily Parker's standoffishness had only deepened his sense of being an outsider. He glanced back at the gleaming facade of the treatment centre, feeling dejected by his lack of progress.

As he walked to his car, Stanley's thoughts churned. He glanced back at the treatment centre's gleaming facade, something nagging at him—a detail he couldn't quite place. He made a mental note to take another look at Emily Parker's file. But for now, all he had was a growing list of questions and a deepening sense of unease.

Inspector Stanley sat in the car for a moment, his forehead resting against the steering wheel. He closed his eyes, trying to summon some inspiration, some direction for what to do next. The case felt like it was slipping through his fingers, each lead more frustrating than the last. He sighed, leaning back in his seat, and as his eyes glanced down, he saw the post-it note attached to the front of a folder on the passenger seat. The word Vanessa scrawled across it in bold, black ink.

Staring at it, Stanley felt a spark of clarity. It had been nagging at him, the connection between Robert Treharne and this woman. It was time to see if he could join at least one piece of this puzzle. His instincts were telling him that this might be the breakthrough he needed. He started the engine, shifted into gear, and drove towards Vanessa's house, his mind racing with possibilities.

When Stanley arrived, he lingered for a moment outside the car, scanning the quiet street. The curtains of a nearby house twitched—someone was watching. He walked up to Vanessa's door and knocked, the sound sharp against the stillness. Inside, he heard faint movement, followed by silence. He waited a beat before raising his hand to knock again, but just as his knuckles were about to meet the wood, the door creaked open a few inches.

A young woman stood partially hidden behind it, her body angled as if debating whether to let him see further into the house. Her face was pale, bare of makeup, with the kind of features that might have been striking if not for the wary look in her eyes. Blond hair was hastily gathered up into a scrunchie at the nape of her neck.

"Can I help you?" she asked, her voice cautious.

Stanley took a step forward, keeping his expression neutral but firm. "I'm Inspector Stanley. I need to ask you a few questions about how you know Robert Treharne."

Vanessa's grip on the door tightened slightly, her knuckles paling. She glanced over her shoulder, the movement quick and furtive, as if she were checking for an escape route—or a witness. Her lips pressed into a thin line before she spoke, her words carefully measured. "I... I don't know what you mean," she replied, her voice a little too defensive. "Robert's just a friend. We've known each other for a while."

Stanley watched her closely, sensing the guarded nature of her response. He wasn't getting anywhere with her yet, but he couldn't shake the feeling that she was holding something back. As he pressed for more answers, his eyes flicked toward the background of the small flat through the partially open door. Something moved—just a shadow, but it was enough to catch his attention. It was a figure, someone walking across the room.

"Is that Robert?" Stanley asked, his voice sharp as his suspicions flared.

Vanessa froze, her face going pale for a moment before she quickly tried to cover up her nervousness. "I don't know what you're talking about," she said, but her voice trembled slightly.

"Vanessa," Stanley pressed, his tone firm now, "don't lie to me. I saw him. I know it's him."

The door creaked wider, and Robert Treharne emerged from the shadows. His clothes were rumpled, his hair unkempt, and his face drawn with exhaustion. His eyes darted between Stanley and Vanessa, like a trapped animal weighing its options.

"All right, all right," Robert said, his voice hoarse as he took a step forward. "I've been holed up here, all right? I didn't want anyone to know."

Stanley's brows furrowed. "Why? Why have you been hiding here?"

Robert looked at the ground for a moment, gathering his thoughts. "The day of the murder... as soon as Terri closed the door behind her, I snuck away from the spa. I went straight down to the deli to see Vanessa. She was the only person I could talk to, the only person who didn't judge me. I heard what happened, and when I found out she was dead..." He trailed off, his voice shaking.

Stanley narrowed his eyes, his tone growing colder. "And what does that have to do with you hiding here?"

"I didn't want to come forward," Robert admitted, his face hardening. "When I heard what had happened, I realized just how bad it would look for me. I had already been caught sneaking around, but if they found out I was with Vanessa when Terri died, it would look like I had something to do with it. I panicked, and I stayed hidden."

Stanley absorbed Robert's words, his mind racing as he pieced everything together. "You thought if you stayed out of sight, no one would make the connection. But you still haven't told me the truth about what happened that day. Why were you at the spa with Terri in the first place? And what exactly did you do after she left?"

Robert's eyes darted to the floor, a sense of guilt hanging over him. "I didn't want to be there that day," he said quietly. "But I had to go. Terri insisted. She was always so controlling, always pushing me. I had a fight with her before she left, but I didn't do anything... It just happened, Inspector. I didn't want her to die. I didn't want this."

Stanley watched Robert, listening carefully, but he knew this was only the beginning. There were still more questions, more pieces to the puzzle that weren't fitting together. But Robert's confession was a start—a messy, tangled start. Stanley knew he would have to dig deeper to uncover the truth.

Marcus stood in his small, dimly lit kitchen, the flickering light above casting shadows across the piles of clutter. His hands trembled as they rested on the counter, still holding the half-empty whiskey bottle he'd poured himself earlier. His eyes drifted to the scattered papers on the table—unopened bills, overdue notices, and gambling slips that seemed to mock him, reflecting the mess his life had become. He glanced briefly at the photographs of his late sister Terri, her smiling face frozen in time, and a wave of bitterness washed over him.

Terri had always been the one with the plan, the one who had it all together. She was the one everyone turned to, the one who was successful. While he had spent years watching from the sidelines, spiralling further into debt, she had always remained just out of his reach, out of his grasp. Now that she was gone, he didn't have to keep pretending that he was anything like her, that he could ever measure up to her.

But with her gone came another problem, no money. Terri had been his safety net, his lifeline. And without her, the debts piled up even higher. The relief he had felt at her passing was quickly replaced by the crushing weight of reality.

Marcus took another swig from the bottle, trying to shake the tension and the growing sense of dread that had settled into his chest. The knock on the door startled him, his stomach churning with anxiety. He wasn't ready for this—he never was. The thought of facing another person, especially someone like Evan, was the last thing he wanted.

He opened the door, and his eyes narrowed when he saw Evan Walker standing there, his expression cold and calculating. Marcus stepped aside without a word. He knew this wasn't going to be a friendly chat.

Evan walked into the flat, his tall frame filling the doorway before he closed the door behind him with a quiet click. "Marcus," he said, his voice low and full of intent. "Still ignoring the calls, huh?"

Marcus straightened up, trying to appear calm, even though his insides were twisted in knots. "What do you want?"

Evan cracked a grim smile, his eyes scanning the cluttered room. "You're a hard man to track down. But I've been patient. Now, it's time for you to pay up."

Marcus felt his stomach twist further, and his fists clenched involuntarily. "I've told you—I'm working on it."

Working on it?' Evan's voice cut through the room, sharp as a blade. He wandered to the table, plucking a gambling slip with two fingers as if it were trash. 'This?' He waved the paper mockingly. 'This is what you've been working on? Debts piling up, money disappearing... and your sister's gone. You think that changes anything? It doesn't, Marcus. It's time to pay."

A chill ran through Marcus as Evan's words cut through him like ice. The realization hit him hard, Evan wasn't just here for small talk. This was about the money he owed, the money that was slipping through his fingers and out of his control.

"I... I can't," Marcus said, his voice shaking slightly. "I don't have anything left."

Evan's eyes hardened, and the coldness in his gaze seemed to freeze Marcus in place. "You'll find a way. And if you don't, well... let's just say, you'll regret it. It's in your best interest."

With that, Evan turned and walked out without another word. Marcus stood frozen, his mind racing with the weight of Evan's threat. His thoughts shifted to Terri, and suddenly, it was as if she was still in the room, still pulling the strings, even from beyond the grave. She had been the one who had dragged him into this mess, the one who had coerced him into doing her bidding. Now, with her gone, it felt like her death hadn't freed him at all. Instead, it had only left him trapped, even more deeply than before.

As Marcus sank into the chair at the table, his hands ran through his hair in frustration. There was no way out now, not without paying what he owed. His eyes fell on the photograph of Terri, the woman who had dominated his life, both in life and death. He didn't want to think about the way she had always looked down on him, the way she had manipulated him into doing things he hadn't wanted to do.

But now, with her gone, he could finally breathe. Or so he thought. The truth was her death had only left him with more questions. And as he stared at her frozen smile, he wondered just how far he was willing to go to get what he needed. How far would he push, and what would he sacrifice to get out of the mess she'd left behind?

A flashback hit him like a wave. He remembered the night Terri had coerced him into helping her with her underhanded plan. The conversation played out in his mind, each word still fresh, still etched in his memory.

In the dimly lit living room of his flat, Marcus had poured another drink as he paced nervously. "Terri, I don't get why you're asking me to do this," he'd said, frustration rising in his voice. "Why can't you lodge these complaints yourself?"

Terri sighed, her smile thinning into something sharper. 'If I do it, it's obvious. Rachel will sniff me out in a second, and that's bad for both of us.' She leaned closer, her tone softening, almost conspiratorial. "You, though... you're under the radar. No one will see it coming."

Marcus had stopped pacing and looked at her, his face filled with uncertainty. "But why me?"

Terri's gaze had softened slightly, though there was still that edge of calculation in her eyes. "Look, Marcus, I know things haven't been easy for you. You've had a rough go of it, and I get that. But this is a way for you to make some money, to get back on your feet. I'll pay you well for your help. All you have to do is lodge a few complaints, make a bit of noise. It's not that big of a deal."

Marcus had frowned, taking another swig from the bottle. "But what if it backfires? What if it makes things worse?"

Terri had shaken her head, her voice firm and convincing. "It won't. Trust me. Rachel's planning permission will be denied, and she'll be out of options. It's a win-win for both of us. You get some cash, and I get what I want."

Marcus had hesitated, but with his desperation for money, the temptation had been too great. "All right," he'd said finally, his voice resigned. "I'll do it. But you better come through with the money, Terri. I'm trusting you here."

Terri's smile had been one of triumph, and Marcus had known in that moment that this wasn't just a simple favour. She had something bigger planned, something he hadn't fully understood. "You won't regret it, Marcus," she'd promised, her eyes gleaming. "I'll take care of everything."

Now, as Marcus stared at the photograph of his sister, his fists clenched. He had been coerced, manipulated—and now she was gone, leaving him with nothing but the weight of the consequences. The money, the debts, the desperate need for answers—it all pressed down on him. He didn't know how far he was willing to go, but he knew one thing for certain, he needed to find a way out.

Meanwhile, across town, Inspector Stanley was deep in his investigation. The enhanced security footage from *Serenity Spa* had given him more to consider. A young man in a cap had appeared on the tape, but it was still too blurry to identify. Stanley stared at the screen, trying to make out any details that could provide a clue.

Stanley squinted at the grainy footage. The man in the cap lingered at the entrance, hesitating before slipping inside. Something about the way he moved—furtive, deliberate—

itched at Stanley's instincts. He leaned closer. "Who the hell are you?"

⁕

The late afternoon sun cast long shadows across the cluttered floor of Amy's ceramics studio. Shelves lined with unfinished pots and vibrant glazes added a chaotic charm to the small space. Amy herself was in the back corner, her usually bubbly demeanour replaced by a tense, hurried energy. She wore an oversized shirt splattered with clay, pedal pushers, and her signature colourful trainers, but there was nothing playful about the look in her eyes.

Amy's hands trembled as she fed a stack of papers into the shredder, the machine's harsh whir slicing through the silent studio. Her eyes darted to the door, heart pounding with every grind of the blades, as if the sound might summon someone—or something.

A draft from an open window ruffled the edges of the remaining documents, and Amy hurried to gather them, her movements clumsy and frantic. As she pushed the next sheet into the shredder, the distinct texture and colour caught her eye, causing her to hesitate for a split second. The paper bore an uncanny resemblance to the one Sarah had shown her, the one with the malicious note that had unsettled the entire neighbourhood.

Amy's heart pounded in her chest, she couldn't afford to stop. Her fingers twitched as she resumed her task, the shredder mercilessly devouring the potentially incriminating evidence.

Just then, the door of the shop opened, and Amy jumped, nearly dropping the remaining papers. She quickly stuffed them into a drawer and wiped her hands on her shirt, trying to appear casual as she stepped out to greet her unexpected visitor.

"Hey, Amy! Just thought I'd drop by and see how you're doing." Sarah's cheerful voice filled the studio, contrasting with the tension Amy felt.

"A-ah, Sarah! Hi!" Amy stammered, plastering a shaky smile on her face. "I wasn't expecting you. How's the coffee shop coming along?"

Sarah's keen eyes scanned the studio, taking in the unusually disorganised state of the normally tidy workspace. "It's coming along, bit by bit. Are you ok? You seem a bit... on edge."

Amy laughed nervously, her eyes flicking towards the drawer where the papers were hidden. "Oh, you know how it is. Just a lot going on. I'm sure you can relate."

Sarah nodded slowly, her eyes drifting to the disorganized shelves. "I suppose so," she said, her tone softer now, almost curious. "I was hoping that you might have found something out about the note situation for me. But you've been quiet about it, haven't you? You're usually the first to share your theories."

Amy forced a laugh, too loud. 'Oh, I've been... busy. You

know how it is.' Her fingers tightened on the edge of her shirt, betraying the calm she tried to project.

Amy's stomach twisted in knots. "No, I haven't heard anything new. But I'm sure it's just some prankster trying to stir up trouble," she said, hoping her voice sounded more confident than she felt.

Sarah sighed, leaning against a table covered in brushes and clay tools. "Yeah, maybe you're right. It's just unsettling, you know?"

Amy nodded vigorously. "Absolutely. But we can't let it get to us. We've got to stay focused on our dreams, right?"

Sarah smiled, though there was a hint of concern in her eyes. "Right. Thanks, Amy. I'll let you get back to whatever you were doing."

Amy watched as Sarah turned to leave, a wave of relief washing over her. But as soon as the door closed behind her friend, the tension returned. She hurried back to the drawer, pulling out the remaining papers and feeding them into the shredder with renewed urgency. She couldn't afford any slip-ups.

As the last sheet vanished into the shredder, Amy slumped against the wall, breathless. She had kept the secret safe—for now. But when she glanced at the shredder bin, a corner of paper jutted out, unshredded, the words *'I know what you did'* glaring back at her. Amy's blood ran cold.

Chapter 17

Inspector Stanley pushed open the door of the coffee shop, setting off a cheerful ding from the bell above. Sarah glanced up from behind the counter. The room buzzed with chatter and laughter as Mike finished last-minute electrical work. Robyn leaned against the counter, chatting with a friend. Though not officially open, the shop already felt alive with energy.

Sarah couldn't help but think that the gentle chiming of the bell was going to get on her nerves very quickly once paying customers started coming and going. One of the workmen leaving set it off again, and she laughed to herself. Mike caught her eye as she gave an involuntary wince and it reminded her of their conversation the previous evening, when he had been laughing about how noise-phobic she was and questioning how she was going to cope with the constant bustle of the coffee shop.

Stanley took a seat at the counter, looking a bit more relaxed than usual. "Morning, Sarah," he greeted her, his eyes scanning the lively atmosphere of the shop. "It looks like you've got a good crowd here already."

Sarah chuckled, sliding a cup of coffee towards him. "Yeah, it's funny how that works out. I haven't even officially opened, and it feels like we're running at full capacity."

Stanley raised an eyebrow, a hint of amusement in his eyes. "Good practice, then. You'll be ready for the grand opening."

Sarah nodded, leaning against the counter. "Exactly. So, how did your visit to *Parker Dermatology* go?"

Stanley sighed, taking a cautious sip before responding. "Not great, I'm afraid. Dr Parker was very standoffish. She barely said anything beyond the basics and seemed determined to keep her distance. I couldn't get much out of her."

Sarah frowned, thinking it over. "Maybe she'd open up to someone she's more familiar with. Middle-aged women are more her kind of thing."

Stanley raised an eyebrow. "You think you could get her to talk?"

Sarah nodded thoughtfully. "I could pay her a visit. Pretend I'm there to see if she can do anything about these frown lines, I've developed over the years from trying to solve problems back in the corporate world."

Stanley chuckled softly, an unexpected glint of warmth in his eyes. "You don't look all that old to me, Sarah."

Sarah grinned, leaning in conspiratorially. "Well, you know, Emily looks stony-faced, but that could be down to the amount of Botox she's had."

Stanley frowned, his brows knitting together in confusion. "Botox? Is that why she looked so... inexpressive? I didn't notice anything unusual about her face."

Sarah blinked, realising he had taken her comment seriously. She shook her head, stifling a laugh. "No, Inspector, it was a joke. I get the impression that Emily's just naturally guarded."

Stanley's face remained blank for a moment longer before the realisation dawned on him. "Oh, sorry, I see what you mean. I'm not great with jokes."

Sarah chuckled, patting his arm lightly. "It's all right. But seriously, I think I could get Emily to open up."

Stanley nodded, looking a bit more relaxed. "If you think you can get her to talk, it's worth a shot. Just be careful and don't push too hard. We need her cooperation, not her shutting down completely."

"Got it," Sarah said, her mind already planning. "I'll go see her tomorrow. And who knows, maybe I'll come back with fewer frown lines."

Stanley smiled faintly. "Just remember, it's about the information, not the Botox."

Sarah laughed, feeling a renewed sense of purpose. "Don't worry, Inspector. I won't lose sight of the mission. But I might still ask about those frown lines."

Stanley cleared his throat a bit awkwardly. "Anyway, if you think it could help, it might be worth a shot. Just be careful. If she's hiding something, she might not take too kindly to being probed, even if it seems casual."

Sarah nodded, determination setting in. "I'll be careful. I know Emily, and I can probably steer the conversation in the right direction without raising too many alarms. Maybe she'll let something slip."

Stanley finished his coffee and stood up. "I appreciate it, Sarah. Any lead, no matter how small, could make a difference. Let me know how it goes."

Sarah watched him leave, feeling a mixture of anticipation and anxiety. She had a plan, and now she just had to execute it. Taking a deep breath, she mentally prepared herself for the task ahead, hoping she could coax out the information that Stanley needed.

Sarah and Inspector Stanley stood outside the sleek, modern façade of *Parker Dermatology*, their expressions tense with anticipation. They exchanged a quick nod before stepping inside. The pristine white walls and calming decor did little to ease their nerves as they approached the reception desk.

"Ms. Parker is expecting us," Stanley informed the receptionist, who gave a curt nod and gestured toward Emily's office.

Emily Parker looked up from her desk as they entered, her professional demeanour giving way to a slight frown. "Inspector Stanley, Sarah, what can I do for you?"

Stanley took the lead, his tone firm but polite. "Ms. Parker, we need to discuss Terri's death. We understand you have an alibi for the time of Terri's death. However, we now know that the tanning bed was tampered with before she used it. Can you account for your whereabouts during that time?"

Emily's eyes widened briefly, but she quickly masked it with a calm expression. "I've already told you I was at a seminar. A room full of students can confirm it." Her voice was steady, but her fingers tapped lightly against the desk, betraying a hint of nervousness.

Sarah stepped forward, her voice softer, but no less determined. "Emily, they know you were at the seminar during Terri's death. But the tampering happened earlier. Can you prove where you were then?"

Emily hesitated, then sighed, motioning for them to sit. "I understand your concerns. The truth is, I've been worried about Rachel. She and Terri had unresolved issues from college, especially after Terri stole Rachel's boyfriend. I was worried Rachel might do something drastic out of jealousy."

Sarah's eyes narrowed. "Are you saying you think Rachel could be involved?"

Emily shook her head. "I don't know. But I can assure you, I had nothing to do with it. On the day the machine was tampered with, I was in a meeting with a supplier. We were discussing new dermatology equipment. I can provide you with the meeting logs and the contact information of the supplier."

Stanley leaned forward, his expression thoughtful. "We'll need to verify that. Can you get us the details?"

Emily nodded, turning to her computer. "Of course. Give me a moment."

As Emily pulled up her calendar and forwarded the necessary emails, Sarah studied her. She seemed genuine, but Sarah couldn't shake the feeling that something was off.

"Emily," Sarah said softly, "why didn't you come forward with this information sooner?"

Emily paused, her fingers hovering over the keyboard. "I didn't think it was relevant. And to be honest, I was scared. Scared that pointing fingers at Rachel or anyone else might drag me into something I had no part in."

Stanley took the printed emails from Emily, skimming through the details. "We'll verify this with your supplier."

He studied her face, as he said, "You've been very helpful."

"Of course." Her smile didn't quite reach her eyes. "It's strange," she said finally.

"What is?" Stanley asked.

"How quickly people assume it was murder." She glanced up. "Maybe it was just...bad luck."

Sarah frowned at Emily. "You don't think it was foul play?"

Emily hesitated, then gave a small shrug. "Even if it was, things like this don't happen in a vacuum. Actions have consequences."

There was something in her voice, an edge that hadn't been there before. Sarah's stomach twisted as she watched Emily's face.

"You're talking like she deserved it."

Emily blinked, then laughed lightly. "No, of course not. Just...people aren't always innocent, you know?".

Sarah and Stanley left *Parker Dermatology* in tense silence, the cool breeze outside doing little to ease the growing friction between them.

Finally, Sarah broke the quiet. "I think she's holding back. Emily knows more than she's letting on."

Stanley stopped walking and turned to her, his eyes narrowing. "Sarah, we can't afford to jump to conclusions. She gave us an alibi and forwarded the evidence. Let's verify that before throwing more accusations her way."

Sarah crossed her arms, frustration flickering in her expression. "Stanley, I'm not throwing accusations. But if we don't push a little harder—"

"You already pushed too hard in there," Stanley interrupted, his voice low but sharp. "Did you see her face when you started talking about Rachel? You nearly crossed the line with that comment about unresolved issues." His tone carried an edge of warning, and for a moment, the normally composed inspector looked genuinely angry. "I brought you along to help, not to risk tipping my hand."

Sarah froze, his words landing like a slap. She replayed the moment in her mind, realizing how her eagerness to press Emily might have come across. She'd got caught up in the momentum, too eager to crack the case, and hadn't considered how far she was treading into dangerous territory.

"I—I didn't mean to overstep," she said quietly, looking down for a moment before meeting his eyes again. "I just... I want to help. To get to the truth."

Stanley's gaze softened, but only slightly. He sighed, his shoulders relaxing just a fraction. "I know you do. And your instincts are good, Sarah, but you have to trust the process. If we push too hard, people will shut down, and we'll lose any chance of getting real answers."

She nodded, her frustration simmering into something quieter. "You're right. I'll be more careful."

Stanley studied her for a moment before nodding in return. "Good. Because the whole point of having you here is to get people to open up—not shut them down."

The words stung, but Sarah took them to heart. She knew he wasn't wrong. She'd let her emotions get the better of her, and it almost cost them a lead.

They walked in silence for a few minutes before Sarah spoke again, her voice steadier. "Do you think Emily's alibi will hold up?"

Stanley's expression grew thoughtful. "It might. Her story checks out on the surface, but we'll know more once we talk to the supplier. If she's telling the truth, we're back to square one. If she's lying..." He trailed off, leaving the thought unfinished.

"She didn't seem like she was lying," Sarah mused, more to herself than to him. "But she's definitely hiding something."

"Maybe," Stanley said. "Or maybe she's just scared, like she said. Fear can make people act guilty even when they're innocent."

Sarah glanced at him. "And what about Rachel? Do you think there's anything to what Emily said about her?"

Stanley hesitated before answering. "It's worth looking into. But we approach it carefully. Rachel might not take kindly to being dragged into this without solid evidence."

"Understood," Sarah said quietly. She hesitated, then added, "Stanley, I'll follow your lead from now on. I promise."

He gave her a sidelong glance, a hint of approval in his eyes. "Good. We're in this together, Sarah. But remember, sometimes less is more. The truth has a way of surfacing when you give it enough space."

Sarah nodded, her resolve renewed. They might have hit a rough patch, but she wasn't about to let it derail their investigation—or her partnership with Stanley. The truth was out there, and together, they'd find it.

Sarah sat at her kitchen table, the morning sun streaming through the window, casting a warm glow over the stack of papers spread before her. Missy snored softly at her feet, blissfully unaware of her owner's mounting frustration. Sarah absently sipped her coffee, her mind racing as she tried to piece together the puzzle of Marcus and his relationship with Terri.

"Why would Marcus think Terri owed him money?" she murmured to herself, her brow furrowed in concentration. She knew Terri had been successful, running a thriving business with the support of her husband. It didn't make sense that she would owe anything to Marcus, especially since her estate would likely go to her spouse.

Determined to understand it, Sarah decided to do some digging. She pulled out her laptop and began searching for any information about Marcus and his family history. After a few minutes of sifting through old articles and public records, she stumbled upon an old interview with Terri in a local business magazine.

In the interview, Terri spoke fondly of her parents, crediting them with helping her launch her first spa. They had invested their savings and even taken out a loan to help her get started. Sarah's heart ached at the thought of the sacrifices they must have made, all in the name of supporting their daughter's dreams.

But then she came across another article, this one a few years older, detailing Marcus's string of financial troubles. He had been in and out of debt for years, making one bad decision after another. Each time, it seemed, his parents had stepped in to bail him out, draining their resources to keep him afloat.

Sarah leaned back in her chair, a look of dawning realisation on her face. "Of course," she muttered. "He thinks it's unfair because they helped her get started, but they've also spent a fortune rescuing him from his own messes."

A soft knock on the door interrupted her thoughts. She looked up to see Robyn standing there, holding two cups of coffee in her hands. "Hey, I thought you could use a break," Robyn said with a warm smile, stepping into the kitchen.

Sarah managed a grateful smile. "Thanks, Robyn. I definitely could use one." Rubbing her eyes which were straining from staring at the screen, she gestured for her niece to sit, and they settled at the table, sharing the muffins and coffee.

After a few moments of silence, Sarah couldn't help but share her thoughts. "I've been trying to figure out why Marcus thinks Terri owed him money. It seems their parents invested heavily in her business, but they also spent a lot on him, bailing him out of his bad decisions."

Robyn nodded thoughtfully. "That makes sense. Marcus has always been a bit of a black sheep, hasn't he? Always in some kind of trouble."

"Exactly," Sarah said. "But he doesn't seem to recognise the help he's received. He just sees what they did for Terri and feels slighted."

Robyn sighed. "It's sad, really. That kind of resentment can eat away at a person."

Sarah's expression hardened with determination. "I need to talk to Marcus, understand his perspective better. Maybe there's more to this than we realise."

Reaching across the table, Robyn squeezed Sarah's hand. "Be careful, Auntie Sarah. Marcus isn't exactly the most stable person. But I know you'll handle it."

Sarah nodded, feeling a renewed sense of purpose. "Thanks, Robyn. I will." She glanced at the clock and stood up. "I think it's time I paid Marcus a visit."

As she gathered her things, Sarah couldn't shake the feeling that she was getting closer to the truth. And whatever she found out, she was determined to see it through, for Terri's sake and for her own peace of mind.

The sun filtered through the large front windows, casting a warm glow on the cosy interior of *Sarah's Secrets*. As she glanced out of the window, she spotted Dave, the local delivery man, pulling up with his usual stack of supplies. Wiping her hands on a towel, Sarah moved to the door with a welcoming smile. "Morning, Dave!" she called out.

"Morning, Sarah," Dave replied, hefting several boxes into the shop, and setting them on the counter. "Got the usual for you today."

"Thanks, Dave," Sarah said, signing off on the delivery slip. She locked the front door behind him as he left, then turned back to the counter, ready to sort and stack the boxes.

Humming under her breath, she carried the supplies through to the storage room at the back of the shop, checking off items on her inventory list as she went. But as she reached the last box, her hand froze. Several essential items were missing—particularly the coffee beans she'd ordered in bulk just last week. Her heart sank.

"Robyn," Sarah called out sharply. Her niece appeared moments later, wiping her hands on her apron.

"What's up?" Robyn asked, noting the concern on Sarah's face.

"We're missing supplies. The coffee beans, sugar sachets, and those biodegradable takeaway cups—I know they were delivered," Sarah said, her voice low and urgent. "They were all here yesterday. I checked."

Robyn frowned. "Are you sure someone didn't just move them?"

"I'm sure," Sarah said firmly. "Come and look."

Together, they combed through the back room. But it wasn't just the supplies that were missing. The faint chill of unease grew stronger when Sarah noticed something else— just beneath the shelves, a series of muddy footprints leading from the delivery access door to the storage area. The back door was unlocked, its latch broken.

"Someone was here," Sarah whispered, her voice tight. She crouched to examine the footprints. They were uneven, smudged, like someone had tried to wipe them away—but the streaks only made the evidence more damning.

Robyn gasped. "Are you saying someone broke in?"

Sarah nodded grimly. "And they didn't just take anything random. They went for what we need most. It's deliberate."

"Sabotage," Robyn said, her tone darkening. "Who'd want to sabotage us? This isn't just theft—they're trying to ruin opening day."

"I don't know," Sarah said, standing and brushing off her hands, though her fingers trembled slightly. "But whoever it is knows exactly what they're doing."

Robyn turned to her aunt. "You said there were threats before. Do you think this is connected?"

Sarah hesitated. The memory of the message in the scrawled note came rushing back, *Stay closed, or you'll regret it.* She'd brushed it off as a prank. Now, the weight of it felt heavier.

Before she could answer, the sounds of keys jangling in the lock broke the tense silence. Sarah and Robyn exchanged a look. It was Charlie, bursting in with his usual energy, but his face dropped the moment he saw them.

"What happened?" Charlie asked, taking in the broken lock and Sarah's pale face.

Sarah gave him a brief rundown. "We're missing stock—someone broke in last night. They went after the coffee beans and essentials. It's no coincidence."

Charlie's hands balled into fists. "This is crossing a line. We need to put cameras out back and make sure everything's locked tight."

"I'll call the police," Sarah said, trying to keep her voice steady, though the knot of fear in her stomach twisted tighter. She thought of the note again. She thought of the shadows she'd seen one night out of the corner of her eye, brushing it off as paranoia. This was no coincidence, no prank.

"We're not backing down," Sarah said, her voice stronger now as she met Charlie's and Robyn's determined gazes. "Whoever's behind this—they picked the wrong family to mess with."

As they walked down the cobbled street towards their car, Sarah couldn't shake the feeling that someone was watching them. She glanced around, her eyes scanning the shadows, but saw nothing out of the ordinary. Still, the sensation lingered, a prickling at the back of her neck.

Mike noticed her unease and squeezed her hand. "What's wrong?" he asked, concern evident in his voice.

Sarah forced a smile. "It's nothing," she said. "Just a feeling."

Mike nodded, not pressing the issue, but Sarah couldn't help but wonder if the threatening note and the missing supplies were just the beginning. As they drove home, Sarah's eyes lingered on the rearview mirror. The sensation of being watched clung to her, impossible to shake. Just before she turned onto her street, a dark figure appeared in the distance, silhouetted against the fading light. Someone was watching and they wanted her to know it.

Chapter 18

Charlie steered the trolley through the narrow aisles, clutching the list of supplies. The hum of fluorescent lights faded into the background as his attention snagged on a familiar figure, Rachel, deep in conversation near the refrigerated section.

He hadn't expected to see anyone he knew here, and he instinctively slowed his pace, not wanting to interrupt their conversation. He reached for a pack of creamers on the shelf, his attention divided between his task and the familiar voice. The other shopper, an older man with a gruff voice, leaned closer to Rachel. "I guess Terri's death has solved that planning problem you had, eh?"

Charlie froze, his hand hovering over the creamers. He strained to hear more, his heart pounding with curiosity and a hint of dread. Rachel's response was muffled, but the tone was unmistakable—defensive and terse.

"That's not what this is about," Rachel replied, her voice low and edged with irritation. "It's complicated, and I didn't wish for any of this."

The man shrugged, unconvinced. "Complicated or not, it sure came at a convenient time for you."

Charlie pretended to busy himself with the items on the shelf, his mind racing. Rachel had been dealing with a planning issue. And Terri's death had somehow resolved it? This was news to him, and it felt like a significant piece of the puzzle.

Rachel glanced around, clearly uncomfortable with the conversation. Her eyes briefly met Charlie's, and she gave him a tight, distracted smile before turning back to the man. "I have to go. I'm busy today." She started to walk away, her pace brisk.

Charlie watched her leave, his thoughts a jumble of suspicion and concern. He quickly finished his shopping and headed to the checkout, his mind replaying the overheard conversation. As he loaded his purchases into the car, he knew he had to share this with Sarah.

Driving back to the coffee shop, Charlie couldn't shake the feeling that something important had just clicked into place. The tension between Rachel and Terri, the planning problem, and now this unexpected resolution—it all seemed to point to deeper, hidden motives that needed to be uncovered. He parked the car and hurried inside, eager to share his findings with Sarah and hopefully make sense of this new piece to the puzzle.

Inside the coffee shop, Sarah was busy making herself familiar with the new till. She looked up as Charlie entered, noting the urgency in his expression. "What's up, Charlie? You look like you've seen a ghost."

Charlie set the bags down and took a deep breath. "You won't believe what I just overheard at the cash and carry. Rachel was there, and someone told her that Terri's death solved her planning problem."

Sarah's eyes widened in surprise. "Rachel? What planning problem?"

Charlie shook his head. "I don't know the details, but it sounded serious. And it seemed like Terri's death somehow fixed it for her. Rachel got defensive when the guy mentioned it."

Sarah frowned, her mind working quickly to piece together the implications. "This changes everything. We need to find out what that planning problem was and how Terri's death could have possibly solved it."

Charlie nodded, his determination mirroring Sarah's. "Agreed. It's certainly a lead that we shouldn't ignore. I'm happy to help you dig deeper and see what we can find."

As they stood there, the sense of urgency was palpable. The mystery of Terri's death was growing more complex by the minute, but Sarah and Charlie were more determined than ever to uncover the truth, no matter where it led them.

Sarah sat at her cluttered desk in the tiny office at the back of the coffee shop, her laptop open in front of her, surrounded by half-finished to-do lists and paperwork. She typed in the local planning office's website, hoping to find the information she needed without leaving the comfort of her shop.

She frowned slightly as she clicked through the online records, her eyes scanning the pages for anything that might give her the information she needed. She had hoped she could find everything online, but the more she looked, the more it seemed like there was no substitute for going to the planning office in person.

She sighed and leaned back in her chair, a sense of purpose settled over her. She wasn't just working on the coffee shop anymore. There was more to be uncovered, and she was ready to dive in, no matter where the next step led her.

She closed her laptop with a soft click, the decision made. She would head to the planning office this afternoon, hoping to dig up the information she needed. The sooner she could confirm the details, the sooner she could move forward with finding answers.

The planning office was a modest building, its brick facade blending seamlessly with the other municipal structures in the area. Sarah entered, immediately struck by the quiet, almost sterile atmosphere of the place. She approached the reception desk where a middle-aged woman with glasses and a warm smile greeted her.

"Good morning, how can I help you?" the receptionist asked.

"Hi, I'm looking for information on a planning application for the *Lotus Blossom Wellness Centre*," Sarah replied. "I saw some records online, but I need more details."

The receptionist nodded, typing quickly on her computer. "Sure, let me pull up the records for you. You'll need to sign in and take a seat while I get everything sorted."

Sarah signed in and waited, her mind racing with possibilities. A few minutes later, the receptionist returned with a folder in hand.

"Here you go. This file contains the details of the planning application and the correspondence related to it," she said, handing over the folder.

Sarah found a quiet corner and began to go through the documents. The application was straightforward enough—a proposed extension to Rachel's salon to include a new treatment room and additional storage space. However, as she flipped through the pages, she found a series of bitter complaints that stood out. Each one was typed meticulously and signed by the same person, Marcus Combes.

Sarah's eyes widened as she read through the complaints. They were filled with accusations of noise pollution, disruption to the neighbourhood, and claims that the extension would be an eyesore. It was clear that Marcus had been relentless in his attempts to block the planning permission.

Returning to the receptionist, Sarah asked, "These complaints from Marcus Coombes, have they been holding up the planning permission?"

The receptionist sighed, clearly familiar with the issue. "Yes, unfortunately. He's been very vocal about his opposition. It's been a real headache for us, to be honest. His complaints have caused significant delays in the approval process."

Sarah nodded thoughtfully, her mind piecing together the implications of this new information. "Thank you for your help. This has been very enlightening."

Leaving the planning office, Sarah's thoughts were a whirlwind. Marcus's constant complaints had been a major obstacle for Rachel, and Terri's death seemed to have removed that obstacle. It was a motive, albeit a complicated one, but it was enough to warrant further investigation.

As she made her way back to the coffee shop, Sarah couldn't shake the feeling that she was getting closer to the truth. Marcus's bitterness and sense of entitlement, combined with his financial struggles, painted a troubling picture.

She knew she had to share her findings with Inspector Stanley and continue to dig deeper into Marcus's past and his relationship with Terri. The puzzle pieces were slowly coming together, and Sarah was determined to see the whole picture, no matter where it led her.

Driving back from the planning office, Sarah gripped the steering wheel tighter than she needed to, her knuckles pale against the leather. Her mind wouldn't stop circling back to Edward Barnes' visit. His stern warnings about the changes she was making to Castle Road had unsettled her, sure, but there was something else. The note.

She could still picture it—folded in half and left on her counter as if someone had just slipped inside and vanished. *"Castle Road doesn't need you."* The words had been scribbled in jagged handwriting, the ink pressed so hard it had bled through the paper.

Vague. Cryptic. But hostile enough to leave her lying awake at night.

Thinking about Edward's resistance, the way he had watched her so closely during their last conversation, she couldn't shake the thought, did he know something? He'd been on Castle Road longer than anyone. If there were whispers going around, surely he'd have heard them. The thought left a sour taste in her mouth.

Sarah bit her lip, debating, before her resolve hardened. She'd talk to him. Not accuse him outright, of course—she wasn't ready for that. But she'd find a way to steer the conversation, to gauge his reaction. Even if she couldn't prove anything, she needed answers.

Ahead, the light turned red. She tapped her fingers against the wheel, a quiet rhythm to the storm inside her head.

The next day, she made her way to *Barnes Curiosities*. The scent of polished wood and aged paper greeted her, the shop filled with a myriad of antiques, each piece meticulously curated by Edward himself.

Edward was behind the counter, carefully inspecting a small brass telescope. He looked up as Sarah entered, his expression unreadable. "Mrs Meadows," he greeted her with a nod, setting the telescope aside. "What brings you here today?"

Sarah offered him a warm smile, trying to keep her tone light. "I just wanted to stop by and see how you're doing, Mr. Barnes. And maybe ask you something that's been on my mind."

Edward raised an eyebrow, his eyes narrowing slightly. "Ask away," he said, though there was a hint of wariness in his voice.

Sarah hesitated for a moment, then plunged ahead. "I've been receiving some… notes," she began, keeping her tone casual. "Anonymous ones. They've been left at my shop, warning me about changes and suggesting that my presence here might not be welcome."

Edward's reaction was subtle, but Sarah didn't miss it. His eyes flickered with something—unease, perhaps—and his posture stiffened just a fraction. He quickly regained his composure, though, brushing off her words with a wave of his hand.

"People can be superstitious, Mrs Meadows," he said, his voice gruff. "They don't always take kindly to change, especially not on a street like this. I wouldn't read too much into it."

Sarah nodded slowly, watching him carefully. "I understand that" she replied. "But the notes... they're more than just complaints. They feel personal, almost like someone's trying to intimidate me."

Edward shifted slightly, his discomfort more apparent now. "I wouldn't know anything about that," he said, his tone a bit too dismissive. "This street has its quirks, and people talk, but I doubt anyone around here would do something so... underhanded."

Sarah kept her gaze steady on him, her voice soft but probing. "Do you think there's anyone who might want to see me fail? Maybe someone who's worried about the changes my coffee shop might bring?"

Edward's eyes narrowed, and he leaned in just a little closer, his voice lowering. "Mrs Meadows, you're new here, and I'm sure you're eager to make friends. But sometimes, the people who seem the friendliest can have other motives. You might want to look a little closer to home. Sometimes it's those who are already inside the gates who cause the most trouble."

Sarah's heart skipped a beat as she tried to decipher his meaning. "Closer to home? What do you mean?"

Edward's gaze was steady, almost piercing. "You've been spending a lot of time with that ceramics shop owner, haven't you? Miss Carmichael. She's a bright one, full of energy and ideas. But don't let her cheerful demeanour fool you. People in this town have long memories, and not everyone is as they seem."

Sarah was taken aback. Amy had been nothing but supportive, a constant source of encouragement. The idea that she might be behind the notes was almost unthinkable. Yet, Edward's implication hung heavy in the air.

"I find that hard to believe," Sarah replied cautiously, her mind racing. "Amy's been a good friend. I can't imagine she'd have any reason to..."

Edward cut her off with a wave of his hand. "I'm not saying she's the culprit, Mrs Meadows. I'm just suggesting that you be careful. Sometimes the people closest to us have their own agendas, especially when they feel threatened by change. Just something to think about."

Sarah stared at him, her thoughts in turmoil. Was it possible that Amy, with all her warmth and enthusiasm, might be behind the notes? The idea felt absurd, yet the seed of doubt had been planted.

"Thank you for your... advice, Mr. Barnes," she said, her voice tight. "I'll keep that in mind."

Edward nodded curtly, his expression unreadable. "Just trying to help, Mrs Meadows. This street has its ways, and it's best to keep your eyes open."

With that, Edward turned back to the brass telescope on the counter, effectively ending the conversation. Sarah took the hint and made her way out of the shop, her mind now swirling with uncertainty.

As she stepped out onto Castle Road, the sun shining brightly, everything suddenly seemed a little less certain. She couldn't believe that Amy would do something so underhanded, but Edward's words echoed in her mind. Could there be truth in his warning, or was this just another attempt to unsettle her?

Sarah stood behind the counter of her coffee shop, her heart pounding in her chest. The warm surroundings did little to calm her nerves as she watched Amy enter, her usual cheerful demeanour replaced with visible tension. Amy wore her signature oversized shirt and colourful trainers, but today, they seemed out of place, a stark contrast to the weight of the conversation that Sarah knew she was going to have to have.

"Amy, can we talk?" Sarah's voice was firm, but wavered slightly, betraying her emotions.

Amy nodded, her eyes wide with concern. "Of course, Sarah. What's going on?"

Sarah took a deep breath, gathering her courage. "I need to ask you something, and I need you to be honest with me. You've been acting strangely, and we've been friends long enough for me to know that something is up. I know that you've done something. Did you send me that letter? The one with the threat?"

Amy's eyes widened in shock, and she took a step back, shaking her head vigorously. "No, Sarah, I swear I didn't. I would never do something like that to you. You're my friend!"

Sarah studied her friend's face, the tension in her chest tightening. "Then why have you been acting so off? I'm worried, Amy. You're hiding something, and I need to know what it is."

Amy's eyes widened in shock, and she took a step back, shaking her head. "Sarah, it's not like that. I swear, I haven't done anything to hurt you."

Sarah's voice rose, the frustration in her chest threatening to spill over. "If it's not about the letter, Amy, then what is it? I need to know—no more secrets." Her heart pounded as she searched Amy's face for an answer, torn between anger and a desperate hope that her friend wasn't lying.

A long silence filled the space between them, the tension palpable. Amy looked down at her feet, struggling to find the words. Finally, she pulled herself together and turned to face Sarah, her eyes brimming with tears.

"Sarah, the letter had nothing to do with me," Amy admitted, her voice barely above a whisper. "I need to confess that I found some fliers that had been left in the street and posted through shop doors. When I saw them, I knew how upset you would be and just wanted to hide them from you.

But the real confession is that I think I might know who sent it. Or at least, I have a suspicion."

Sarah's eyes widened with concern as she reached out to grip Amy's trembling hands. "Amy, who do you think it is? If someone is trying to scare me, I need to know who it might be."

Amy hesitated, her gaze darting to the window as if expecting shadows to appear. "I don't want to say anything until I'm sure," she admitted. "The thing is… whoever is behind this, they've helped me before. They did something for me when I really needed it, and I can't believe they'd do something like this. I need to talk to them first, give them a chance to explain."

Sarah frowned, the pieces not quite fitting together. "Amy, if someone is targeting me, we don't have time for you to dance around this. If you know something, you need to tell me."

Amy shook her head, her face pale, her lips quivering as if she were holding back a flood of emotions. "I just need to be sure. I don't want to believe it's them, and I don't want to accuse someone who may not be involved. But if they are… then I need to know why. I owe them that much."

Sarah's heart sank. Amy's shop, the cozy haven she'd always admired, suddenly seemed fragile, teetering on the edge of collapse. "Why didn't you tell me?" she asked softly. "I could have helped."

"I didn't want to scare you off," Amy admitted, her words tumbling out in a rush. "You're about to open your own place, and I couldn't stand the thought of you looking at me—at my failures—and thinking, 'What if that's me in a year?' You don't deserve that, Sarah. You deserve to believe you can make it."

A knot of doubt twisted in Sarah's stomach. Amy's words hit too close to home, stirring fears she'd kept buried under her excitement. "Amy… Do you really think I can do this? I mean, if it's this hard…"

Amy grabbed Sarah's hand, squeezing it fiercely. "Yes. Yes, I do. You're smart, and you've got the drive. Just don't make the same mistakes I did."

Sarah sighed, her heart aching for her friend. "Promise me you'll be careful. And if things get out of hand, you'll let me or Mike know immediately."

Amy nodded. "I promise. And thank you, Sarah, for understanding. I'll talk to them and see if I can find out anything that might help us."

Sarah stepped forward, pulling Amy into a tight embrace. "You don't have to go through this alone, Amy. We'll figure it out together. You're my friend, and I'm here for you, no matter what."

Amy clung to Sarah, her relief evident as she finally let go of the secret she had been carrying. "Thank you, Sarah. I don't know what I would do without you."

As they stood there, the weight of their worries momentarily lifted, Sarah realized that the letter was still a mystery to be solved. But at least she knew one thing for sure, Amy wasn't the enemy.

Amy pulled back slightly, her eyes searching Sarah's face. "Sarah, there's something else. I'm worried about you getting so deeply involved in this case. I mean, what if you end up suspecting the wrong person? Or... what if someone dangerous is behind all of this?"

Sarah took a deep breath, considering Amy's words. "I understand the risks, Amy. But I can't just ignore what's happening. Terri's death, the letter... it's all connected somehow. And if I can help find the truth, I have to try."

Amy nodded, her face lined with concern. "Just promise me you'll be careful. This is more than just a puzzle to solve, it's about people's lives. I wouldn't want you to get hurt, or to mistrust someone who might be innocent. Especially now, with everything we've been through... I'd hate to think you might suspect me again."

Sarah squeezed Amy's hand. "I promise I'll be careful. And I'm sorry for doubting you, even for a moment. This has been hard on all of us, but I won't let it come between our friendship again."

Amy gave a small, grateful smile. "Thank you, Sarah. I'll help in any way I can. Just, let's make sure we stay on the right side of things. We're in this together, and that's what matters."

Sarah nodded, but as Amy left, doubt lingered in her mind. The letter was still a mystery, and Amy's suspicions raised more questions than answers. For all her resolve, Sarah couldn't shake the feeling that the real threat was closer than she'd dared to imagine.

Chapter 19

Amy left Sarah's coffee shop with a heavy heart, her mind buzzing with anger and confusion. The conversation with Sarah had shaken her resolve, but it had also strengthened it. Edward Barnes needed to answer for his behaviour.

As she made her way down Castle Road, the wind picked up, brushing damp air against her cheeks. Clouds rolled overhead, a thick, grey blanket that mirrored the heaviness pressing against her chest. She clutched her coat tighter, her thoughts racing.

Why had Edward been so generous to her, only to turn so bitter toward Sarah? None of it made sense—unless there was something Edward was hiding.

When she reached *Barnes Curiosities*, she paused on the threshold, her hand hovering over the door handle. Taking a steadying breath, she stepped inside, and the bell above the door jingled faintly, its sound sharper in the stillness.

The shop smelled of aged wood and metal polish, but something felt different. The once-meticulous displays were slightly askew, a set of dusty books piled haphazardly in one corner, an ornate clock stuck at 11:17. In the dim light, Amy noticed a brass lamp on the counter, its finish dulled by neglect.

Behind the counter, Edward was polishing a candlestick, his movements slow and mechanical. When he looked up, his expression softened slightly.

"Amy," he said, setting the candlestick down with deliberate care. "What brings you here?"

Amy stepped forward, her voice steady despite the tightness in her throat. "I need to talk to you, Edward. About Sarah... and the notes she's been getting."

His face hardened, but he didn't respond immediately. Instead, he picked up a cloth and began polishing the candlestick again, his eyes fixed on the tarnished surface. "I don't know what you mean."

"Don't," Amy said, her voice sharper now. "Don't lie to me. I know it was you. Sarah showed me the letter that she received and I recognised your handwriting. I just don't understand why. You've always been kind to me, even helped me when I needed it. So why are you doing this to Sarah?"

Edward's hand froze mid-polish. For a moment, the only sound was the faint tick of an old wall clock behind him. Then he resumed, his movements tighter, more forceful. "You're mistaken."

"I don't think I am," Amy pressed, stepping closer to the counter. "I think you're scared of something—something to do with her. But whatever it is, it doesn't justify what you've done."

Edward let out a short, bitter laugh, setting the candlestick down with more force than necessary. "You think you know me, Amy? You think you understand what it's like to lose everything?"

Amy hesitated, taken aback by the anger in his voice. But she steadied herself. "I don't know what you've been through, Edward. But I know this isn't who you are. Whatever's going on, talk to me. Help me understand."

Edward turned away, gripping the edge of the counter as if it were the only thing keeping him upright. "It's not about Sarah," he said finally, his voice low and rough. "It's about... Margaret."

Amy frowned. "Margaret?"

"My wife," he said, his voice breaking on the word. "She had this dream—a coffee shop. We used to talk about it for hours, planning every little detail. But then she got sick. And suddenly... all those plans were just dreams. Dreams we'd never get to live."

The room seemed to close in on Amy as his words sank in. She could see the weight he carried in the slump of his shoulders, the tremble in his hands.

"When she died," Edward continued, "I threw myself into this shop because it was the only thing I had left. But when I saw Sarah, with her bright ideas and her coffee shop, it felt like... like she was stealing what was left of my wife's dream. And I couldn't bear it."

Amy's throat tightened, and she stepped closer. "Edward... I'm so sorry. I didn't know."

He let out a shuddering breath, his fingers gripping the counter until his knuckles turned white. "I didn't mean to hurt anyone," he whispered. "I just...seeing that shop, it was like losing her all over again."

Amy reached out, resting a hand on his arm. "Edward, your wife's dream isn't gone. It's not forgotten. And Sarah's shop—it doesn't take anything away from her. If anything, it's a way to honour her memory."

Edward shook his head, his eyes brimming with tears he refused to let fall. "I don't know how to let go, Amy. I've been holding on so tightly for so long... I don't know how to stop."

Amy gave his arm a gentle squeeze. "You don't have to let go all at once. But this anger, this hurt—it's not helping anyone. Least of all you."

For a long moment, Edward said nothing. Then, with a shaky sigh, he nodded. "You're right," he murmured. "I need to make this right. I just... don't know where to start."

"You start by apologizing to Sarah," Amy said softly. "Tell her the truth. She's a kind person, Edward. She'll understand."

Edward looked at her, his face etched with regret. "Thank you, Amy. For not giving up on me. I don't deserve it, but... thank you."

"We all make mistakes," Amy said, offering a small, reassuring smile. "What matters is what we do to fix them."

As she left the shop, Amy felt the tension in her chest ease just a little. There was still work to be done, but she believed Edward was ready to take the first step. And as for Sarah, Amy would stand by her side, ready to face whatever challenges came next.

Inspector Stanley stood in front of the modest suburban house where Rachel lived, his mind buzzing with questions. He knocked on the door, waiting patiently until it swung open to reveal Rachel, her expression wary.

"Inspector Stanley," Rachel greeted, her tone a mixture of surprise and apprehension. "What brings you here again?"

Stanley nodded politely. "Good afternoon, Rachel. I have a few more questions regarding Terri Treharne's death. May I come in?"

Rachel hesitated for a moment before stepping aside to allow him entry. "Of course. Come in."

Stanley entered the house, noting the tidy but modest decor. Rachel led him to the living room, where they both took a seat. He pulled out his notebook, ready to take down any new information.

"I wanted to clarify a few things," Stanley began, his tone professional. "First, can you account for your whereabouts at the time the tanning bed was tampered with? We're talking about the period before Terri's death, not just the seminar you attended."

Rachel's brow furrowed in thought. "I was at the clinic, working on paperwork and seeing patients. My schedule was pretty tight that day. I can provide you with my appointment book and the clinic's log."

Stanley nodded, jotting down her response. "We'll need to verify that. Now, I also need to ask you about something Emily mentioned. She said that you and Terri had unresolved issues from college, particularly over a boyfriend."

Rachel snorted, a bitter smile playing on her lips. "It's hardly something to murder someone over, is it? It was a long time ago. Yes, Terri stole my boyfriend back then, but she moved on and married someone else a long time ago. I've moved on too."

Stanley watched her carefully, noting the slight tension in her posture. "Did you hold any grudges about it?"

Rachel's eyes flickered, but she quickly masked any emotion. "No, Inspector. Like I said, it was a long time ago. People change, and life goes on."

Stanley nodded, though he couldn't shake the feeling that Rachel was holding something back. "Rachel, I understand that past grievances can sometimes linger, even if we think we've moved on. If there's anything else you can tell me, now would be the time."

Rachel shook her head, her expression resolute. "I've told you everything I know, Inspector. I had nothing to do with what happened to Terri."

Stanley stood up, closing his notebook. "Thank you for your cooperation, Rachel. We'll be in touch if we need any more information."

Rachel escorted him to the door, her face a mask of composure. "I hope you find out what really happened. Terri didn't deserve this."

As Stanley walked back to his car, he couldn't help but replay the conversation in his mind. Rachel's denial seemed genuine, but her reluctance to address the grudge issue left a nagging doubt. He knew he had to dig deeper to uncover the truth.

Driving away, Stanley resolved to verify Rachel's alibi and cross-reference it with the clinic's logs. He also made a mental note to revisit Emily and delve further into the dynamics of their college days. The pieces of the puzzle were starting to come together, but the full picture was still elusive.

With determination fuelling his every move, Stanley set off to continue his investigation, knowing that the truth was out there, waiting to be uncovered.

Inspector Stanley leaned back in his chair, staring at the mess of phone records spread across his desk. The muted hum of activity in the station filtered through his office door, but he hardly noticed it. His eyes flicked from one highlighted number to the next, tracing the sequence of calls leading up to Terri's death like a hunter following a faint trail.

Most of the numbers were routine—friends, family, colleagues—but one stood out. It wasn't just familiar, it was Emily's.

Stanley's brow furrowed, and he reached for her previous statement. Emily had been clear, she hadn't spoken to Terri in years. And yet, the log in front of him told a different story. A call between Emily and Terri, timed almost exactly to when Sarah and Robyn overheard that heated argument in the changing room.

He tapped his pen against the desk, tension building in his chest. It didn't make sense. Emily's alibi had checked out, and she'd seemed forthright during their earlier interview. Was this an oversight? A slip of memory? Or something more deliberate?

The pen stopped tapping as his gaze fell to his phone. He hesitated. Calling Emily would mean opening a can of worms—one that might lead to answers, or one that could blow the case wide open in unexpected ways. For a moment, he let his mind wander through the possibilities. Was Emily hiding something? If so, what? And why now, after years of silence?

His hand hovered over the phone, his thoughts running in circles. What if she shut down? Or worse, what if he alienated a potential key witness by pushing too hard?

But then Stanley thought about Terri, about the senselessness of her death. Whatever it took to get answers, he would do it.

He picked up the receiver and dialled Emily's number. The line rang twice before her familiar voice came through, calm and measured.

"Hello, Emily. It's Inspector Stanley," he said, keeping his tone steady despite the tension coiling in his stomach. "I need to speak with you about something important. Can you come down to the station?"

There was a pause, just long enough for doubt to creep in. "Is everything all right, Inspector?"

Stanley chose his words carefully. "It's regarding Terri. There's something in the phone records we need to discuss."

Another pause. Then, finally, "I'll be there."

When Emily arrived, Stanley led her to the interview room, his mind working through the questions he needed to ask. The sterile white walls and harsh fluorescent lighting seemed to sap the warmth from the room, and for the first time, Emily's typically unflappable demeanour showed a crack.

She took a seat opposite him, her hands folded neatly in her lap, though her fingers fidgeted ever so slightly.

"Emily," Stanley began, sliding the printout of the phone records across the table. "We've reviewed Terri's call history, and I noticed something... unexpected. There's a call from Terri to you on the day of her death. Can you explain why you didn't mention this before?"

Emily's face paled, and she blinked rapidly as if searching for the right words. "I... I didn't think it was relevant," she said finally, her voice quieter than usual. "We hadn't spoken in years, and then she called me out of the blue that day. It was... a shock."

Stanley raised an eyebrow. "Emily, this wasn't just a casual call. This lines up with the argument Sarah and Robyn overheard in the changing room. What were you arguing about?"

Emily's composure faltered. She looked down at her hands, twisting the edge of her sleeve between her fingers. "She was upset," she admitted. "She accused me of something—something untrue. It wasn't important, just... personal history between us."

Stanley leaned forward, his voice low but firm. "If it wasn't important, why didn't you mention it? You knew Terri was at the centre of this case. Why hide your connection to her?"

Emily hesitated, her lips pressing into a thin line. When she spoke, her voice trembled slightly. "Because I was scared, all right? I didn't want to be dragged into this. Terri and I— we had our differences. And I didn't think a stupid argument would mean anything."

Stanley studied her, the tension in the room thick enough to cut. "Emily, this isn't just a stupid argument. Withholding information like this jeopardizes the investigation. If there's something you're not telling me, now's the time to come clean."

Emily's eyes met his, glassy with unshed tears. "I didn't hurt her," she said softly. "I swear, I didn't. I was angry, yes, but I'd never... I just wanted to forget about it. About her."

Stanley leaned back, the weight of her words settling in his mind. He could see the guilt etched on her face, but was it the guilt of omission—or something darker?

"Emily," he said at last, "I need your full cooperation from here on out. No more secrets. No more omissions. We're trying to get to the truth, and that includes understanding what happened between you and Terri."

She nodded, her shoulders slumping. "I'll tell you everything I know," she murmured.

As Stanley closed his notebook, he felt the case shift, another piece of the puzzle snapping into place. But the picture it was forming was far from clear, and Stanley couldn't shake the feeling that Emily's role in all this was far more complicated than she was letting on.

Chapter 20

Sarah sat at her kitchen table, her thoughts swirling as she stared at the evidence spread out before her. The complaints, the planning application, and Marcus's undeniable link to Terri painted a far more complicated picture than she'd anticipated. The puzzle pieces were starting to fit together, but the image they revealed made her stomach churn.

A knock at the door startled her, pulling her from her thoughts. She glanced at the clock—it was late for visitors. Bracing herself, she crossed the room and opened the door to find Inspector Stanley standing on her doorstep, his sharp gaze fixed on her.

"Inspector Stanley," Sarah said, stepping aside to let him in. "I wasn't expecting you."

He nodded curtly, his expression unusually grave. "Sarah, we need to talk," he said, stepping into the hallway. His fingers drummed lightly against the edge of the doorframe, a telltale sign of his unease. She led him into the kitchen without a word, gesturing for him to sit. But before he could speak, she launched into her findings.

"I've been digging," she began, motioning to the papers scattered across the table. "And I think Terri was using Marcus to file those complaints against Rachel's salon. She promised him money—money he desperately needed—and he went along with it."

Stanley frowned, his fingers brushing against one of the documents. His analytical mind was already turning over the implications. "That would explain Marcus's sudden hostility toward Rachel," he said slowly. "And his persistence with those complaints. But why would Terri want to sabotage Rachel's planning application in the first place?"

Sarah leaned back in her chair, crossing her arms as she considered the question. "I don't know yet," she admitted. "Maybe she saw Rachel as competition. Or maybe... maybe it was personal."

Stanley's frown deepened. He tapped the edge of the table with his forefinger, his voice low and measured. "Terri didn't strike me as someone who acted without reason. If she went to these lengths, there's something we're missing—something bigger."

Sarah hesitated, debating whether to tell him what she planned to do next. She decided against it, knowing he wouldn't approve. "Terri definitely had more enemies than we realized," she said instead. "And Marcus was just a pawn. If we can figure out her motive, maybe the rest will fall into place."

Stanley stood, pacing slowly around the room as he mulled over her words. "Sarah, I know you're determined to help, but you need to tread carefully. If Rachel's involved in this, she's not just a suspect—she's dangerous. I don't want you putting yourself in harm's way."

Sarah gave him a faint smile, but it didn't quite reach her eyes. "I'll be careful," she promised, though the reassurance felt hollow.

Stanley paused by the kitchen counter, his gaze fixed on her. "Don't go digging on your own, Sarah. If you find anything else, you bring it to me first. Understood?"

"Understood," she replied quickly, though she had no intention of holding back if she uncovered something significant.

Stanley finally relented, nodding once. "We'll keep looking into Terri's connections. There's more to this than meets the eye, and we're going to get to the bottom of it. But I need you to trust me on this."

"I do," Sarah said quietly, watching as he left the room. The door clicked softly shut behind him, and she exhaled, the tension in her shoulders easing slightly. But she couldn't sit still. Stanley was cautious by nature—careful, methodical. She admired that, but sometimes it wasn't enough.

She glanced at the clock. If she left now, she'd have just enough time to make her appointment at *Lotus Blossom*. Something told her Rachel might have more to hide than Marcus or Terri ever did, and she wasn't going to wait around for someone else to figure it out.

Grabbing her coat, Sarah muttered under her breath, "This had better be less eventful than the last time."

And with that, she stepped out into the night, ready to see just how deep the rabbit hole went.

Sarah arrived at Rachel's salon, her heart pounding with a mix of nerves and determination. She approached the reception desk, where Rachel stood with a professional but welcoming smile.

"Good afternoon," Rachel greeted her warmly. "How can I help you today?"

"I have an appointment," Sarah replied, trying to keep her voice steady. "Under the name Meadows."

Rachel's eyes flicked over the appointment book. "Ah, yes, Mrs. Meadows. Welcome. We'll be starting with a brief consultation before your treatment."

As Rachel began the introduction, explaining the treatment process, she reached down absentmindedly and grabbed a tube of hand cream from the shelf under the desk. Flipping the lid open, she squeezed a small amount onto her palm and began rubbing it into her hands with practiced ease.

"Follow me, please," Rachel said, beckoning Sarah towards the treatment room. Her movements were smooth and confident, her demeanour completely at ease.

As Sarah followed Rachel down the hallway, a faintly sweet aroma tickled her senses. The smell intensified, heavy and unmistakable. Almonds. Her chest tightened as unease washed over her and her mind raced as she tried to connect the dots. The smell of almonds was often associated with cyanide, a fact she couldn't ignore. Hadn't Stanley mentioned that no cyanide had been found in the preliminary reports? But the scent was undeniable, and now it was here, in Rachel's salon.

Rachel led Sarah into a cosy treatment room, softly lit and filled with calming scents that were now overshadowed by the distinct smell of almonds. "You can make yourself comfortable on the table," Rachel instructed, her smile never wavering. "I'll step out for a moment while you get ready."

Sarah nodded, her mind buzzing with questions and suspicions. As she settled onto the table, she glanced around the room, trying to see if there was any other source for the smell. But everything seemed normal, innocuous even.

When Rachel returned, she continued to chat amiably, her hands now warm and fragrant from the hand cream. Sarah watched her every move, noting the casual confidence with which she handled everything. Was this the same woman who could have tampered with the red light therapy bed? The thought sent a shiver down her spine.

"How did you hear about our salon?" Rachel asked, her tone conversational as she prepared the treatment materials.

"Oh, a friend recommended it," Sarah replied, her mind quickly fabricating a plausible story. "She said you were the best in town."

Rachel's smile widened. "That's wonderful to hear. We always strive to provide the best service for our clients."

As Sarah lay back, feeling the warmth of the bed beneath her, Rachel continued, her tone casual yet inquisitive. "Sarah Meadows, your name sounds familiar. Have you recently been in the news, or is it just the local chatter? I feel like I've heard about you lately."

Sarah blinked in surprise. *Really*, she thought to herself, *I was just in here a couple of days ago, subtly poking around for information, and she doesn't even remember me?* She smothered a wry smile. *Clearly, I'm more forgettable than I thought. Maybe all middle-aged women blur together? Or maybe,* Sarah told herself, *she is a little bit distracted by the murder.* Forcing an easy-going chuckle, she replied, "Oh, really? Well, I've been busy lately with my new coffee shop. Maybe that's it?"

As the treatment began, Sarah lay still, her mind a whirlwind of thoughts and suspicions. The sweet smell of almonds lingered in the air, a constant reminder of the connection she was trying to make. She needed to find out more about Rachel, to see if there was anything that might link her to the incident at *Serenity Spa*.

Throughout the treatment, Sarah listened closely to Rachel, noting her mannerisms, her tone, and the way she interacted. It was a delicate balance, trying to appear relaxed and engaged while secretly scrutinising every detail.

Rachel's hands moved skilfully over Sarah's neck and shoulders, the gentle pressure and rhythmic motions designed to soothe. Normally, Sarah would close her eyes and let herself drift into a state of relaxation, allowing the therapist to work out the tension. But today was different. Today, she was on high alert.

Rachel's touch was firm yet gentle, her fingers finding and easing knots with practiced precision. Her voice, when she spoke, was calm and reassuring. But Sarah couldn't help but wonder if there was something more lurking beneath that serene exterior.

"Just relax and breathe deeply," Rachel said softly. "Let go of all your worries."

Sarah took a deep breath, but her mind refused to quiet. She needed to find a way to engage Rachel in conversation without arousing suspicion. Something casual, something that would allow her to gauge Rachel's reactions and perhaps reveal a hint of the truth she sought.

"You have such a calming presence, Rachel," Sarah said, her voice as casual as she could manage. "It must be rewarding, helping people find some peace and relaxation."

Rachel's hands didn't falter. "It is," she replied with a small smile. "There's something very satisfying about knowing you've made someone's day a little better."

Sarah nodded, her thoughts racing. "I imagine it must get quite busy, especially with everyone looking for a bit of escape these days."

Rachel's touch remained steady. "It does, but I enjoy it."

Sarah kept her tone light, as if making idle conversation. "Do you get to know your clients well? I mean, I'm sure some of them share quite a bit during their sessions."

Rachel chuckled softly. "Oh, you'd be surprised at the stories I hear. People do tend to open up when they're relaxed. It's almost like being a therapist in more ways than one."

Sarah seized the opportunity. "I bet you have some interesting stories. Have you ever had any, um, strange or unexpected experiences with clients?"

Rachel's hands paused briefly before resuming their rhythmic motion. "A few, here and there," she said, her tone still light. "But nothing too dramatic. Most people just want a bit of peace and quiet."

Sarah's heart skipped a beat at the pause. Had she touched a nerve? She decided to press a little further. "It must be a good community, though, all the wellness and spa professionals around here. Do you all know each other well?"

Rachel's hands moved to Sarah's temples, applying gentle pressure. "We do, to some extent. It's a small world, after all. We often refer clients to each other, depending on their needs."

Sarah closed her eyes briefly, considering her next move. She needed to ask about Terri without being too obvious. "I heard about the awful event at Serenity Spa. It's so tragic, what happened to Terri."

Rachel's hands stilled for a fraction of a second before continuing. "Yes, it's very sad. She was well-known in the community."

Sarah sensed an opening. "Did you know her well?"

Rachel's voice was calm, but there was a subtle tension beneath it. "Not particularly well. Our paths crossed occasionally, but we weren't close."

Sarah decided to take a risk. "Do you think there's any truth to the rumours? About her death, I mean. It just seems so... mysterious."

Rachel's hands moved to the back of Sarah's neck, kneading the muscles there. "Rumours are just that—rumours. It's best not to get caught up in them."

Sarah noted the deflection. Rachel was careful, measured. It was clear she wasn't going to reveal anything easily. "You're right," Sarah said, forcing a light laugh. "It's just hard not to speculate sometimes."

Rachel's tone softened, and she shifted the conversation. "How have you been managing with your coffee shop? It must be quite the adjustment."

Sarah allowed herself to relax a bit, letting Rachel steer the conversation away. "It's been a whirlwind," she admitted. "But I love it. There's something about making people happy with a good cup of coffee that's so fulfilling."

Rachel's hands continued their soothing work, and Sarah felt a moment of genuine relaxation wash over her. Despite her suspicions, Rachel was good at what she did. "It sounds wonderful," Rachel said. "I'll have to stop by sometime and try your coffee."

Sarah smiled. "I'd love that. You're always welcome."

As the session came to an end, Sarah found herself no closer to the truth, but she had planted a seed. Rachel was composed, skilled at maintaining her professional façade. But Sarah had noticed the subtle shifts, the brief pauses, and the underlying tension. It wasn't much, but it was something.

Rachel helped her sit up slowly, offering a warm towel to cover her shoulders. "How do you feel?"

Sarah stretched her neck and shoulders, feeling the lingering warmth of the massage. "Much better, thank you. You're amazing, Rachel."

Rachel smiled modestly. "I'm glad I could help. Take your time getting up."

As Sarah dressed and prepared to leave, she couldn't shake the feeling that there was more to Rachel than met the eye. The room's red glow had faded into the background, but the sense of foreboding remained. She would have to tread carefully, but she was determined to uncover the truth, no matter what it took.

Sarah exited the treatment room, the calming hum of the wellness centre enveloping her. She glanced back at Rachel, who was already preparing for her next client, her demeanour calm and professional. But Sarah knew better now. She would keep a close watch on Rachel, and she would find out what secrets lay hidden beneath that serene exterior.

"I hope you enjoyed your session," she said, her eyes meeting Sarah's with an earnest expression.

"It was lovely, thank you," Sarah replied, forcing a smile. As she left the salon, her mind was already racing with the next steps. She needed more information, more clues to piece together the puzzle.

Outside, the sun was sinking, casting shadows across the pavement. Sarah took a deep breath, feeling the weight of the investigation pressing down on her. She was getting closer, she could feel it. But there was still so much more to uncover.

As she walked away from the salon, she couldn't shake the image of Rachel's calm, smiling face. Was she truly as innocent as she seemed, or was there a darker side hidden beneath the surface? Sarah was determined to find out, no matter the cost.

Chapter 21

The next day, Sarah arrived at the coffee shop early, determined to tackle the final tasks before the grand opening. The quiet hum of the morning was usually comforting, a gentle prelude to a busy day ahead. But today, something felt off.

As she stepped behind the counter, her movements stilled. A package, small and meticulously wrapped, sat in the centre of the counter, its silvery ribbon catching the dim light filtering through the window. A flicker from the overhead bulb made the metallic sheen shimmer, as if the package were waiting for her.

Sarah's breath quickened. She hadn't been expecting anything.

The steady drone of the coffee machine seemed louder than usual, filling the silence with a mechanical whirr. A chill prickled at the back of her neck as she stepped closer, the hairs on her arms lifting beneath her sleeves. Her fingers hovered over the package before she finally picked it up. It was heavier than she expected, the weight solid in her hands.

Her brows furrowed as she turned it over, hesitating before peeling back the neatly folded note taped to the top. The paper felt smooth, expensive, and the handwriting inside was precise, almost too perfect.

Dear Sarah, just a little something to apologise for all the upset at your recent visit. Best wishes, Kerry.

She frowned. Kerry had never been one for elaborate gestures, and the elegant penmanship, combined with the meticulous wrapping, didn't match her usual style. For a moment, doubt pressed at the edges of her mind, a whisper of unease that she tried to shake away.

Maybe Kerry had felt guilty. Maybe this was her way of making amends.

Carefully, Sarah pulled at the ribbon. It came undone too easily, slipping away like silk. She lifted the lid, revealing an assortment of beauty products nestled inside—hand creams, lotions, perfumes—all encased in elegant packaging. The soft glow of the shop lights made them look luxurious, almost inviting.

Sarah inhaled slowly, her fingers hovering over the package for a beat longer than necessary. Curiosity tugged at her, tempting her to peel back the edges and take a look inside. But there were things to do. With a quiet exhale, she set it down and turned away—she couldn't afford to be distracted.

She was in the middle of preparing a last-minute shopping list when Robyn walked in, looking cheerful as ever.

"Morning, Auntie Scarah!" Robyn greeted, her eyes immediately drawn to the beautifully packaged beauty products on the counter. "Oooh, what's all this?"

"Oh, just a package from Kerry," Sarah replied. "I think it's a bit of a peace offering. I don't think it was necessary, but I'm not going to look a gift horse in the mouth."

Robyn barely hesitated before tugging at the package, her fingers already peeling it open before she even thought to ask. "These look amazing!" she said, rifling through the contents with unabashed enthusiasm. "Mind if I try some?"

Before Sarah could respond, Robyn had already opened a bottle of hand cream. smoothing it over her hands. The scent of marzipan filled the air, a sweet, almond-like smell that instantly made Sarah's heart race.

"Robyn, no!" Sarah's voice cracked. The sound of blood rushing in her ears as she instinctively knocked the hand cream from Robyn's hands. The bottle fell to the floor, its contents spilling out. Robyn frowned, wiping her hands on a napkin. "What's going on?"

Sarah lowered her voice, glancing around to make sure no one was listening. "I think that package might be dangerous. The smell of marzipan... it just brought back a bad memory for a moment. I don't know why, but I think you should wash your hands straight away and we should get Inspector Stanley to have a look at this package."

Before Robyn could protest, Sarah grabbed her wrist and pulled her towards the sink. Robyn stared at her aunt, her face pale, the carefree smile wiped from her face. "But... it's just hand cream," she stammered. "How could it—what could it do?"

"Just wash," Sarah urged, twisting the tap on and guiding Robyn's hands under the stream of water. She reached for the soap, lathering it between Robyn's fingers as if scrubbing away something far worse than hand cream.

A sense of panic flickered in Robyn's eyes. "Auntie Sarah, you're scaring me."

"Good," Sarah muttered. "Because I have a bad feeling about this."

Drying her hands on the nearby towel, Sarah grabbed her phone and quickly dialled Stanley's number, her fingers shaking slightly. When he answered, she explained the situation, her voice urgent and filled with concern.

"Inspector Stanley, it's Sarah. I received a package at the coffee shop, supposedly from Kerry, but I am a little worried that there might be something suspicious about it. The smell... it's like marzipan. Robyn used some of it."

Stanley's tone became immediately serious. "Sarah don't touch anything else. I'll send someone over right away to collect the package and analyse its contents. Stay where you are and make sure no one else comes into contact with it."

"Understood," Sarah replied, feeling a bit more at ease knowing help was on the way. She hung up the phone and turned to Robyn. "Stanley's sending a team. We just need to stay clear of the package until they get here."

Robyn nodded, her expression a mix of fear and gratitude. "Thank you, Auntie Sarah. I didn't realise..."

"Neither did I," Sarah said, giving her a tight smile. "But we'll get to the bottom of this."

As they waited for Inspector Stanley's team to arrive, Sarah couldn't shake the feeling that Rachel was behind this.

Sarah sat anxiously in the back room of the coffee shop, her mind replaying the events of the day. Robyn sat beside her, still pale and shaken, her fingers nervously twisting the corner of a napkin. The tension in the room was heavy, and when Sarah's phone finally buzzed, switching it to speaker so that Robyn could hear what the Inspector had to say.

"Inspector, any news?" she asked, her voice tight.

Stanley's tone was grim. "Yes, Sarah. You were right to be suspicious. The package contained several beauty products, and preliminary toxicology results confirm that the hand cream was laced with botulinum toxin."

Sarah's breath caught. "Botox? Isn't that... cosmetic? How could it be dangerous in this way?"

Stanley exhaled audibly, his voice taking on an explanatory tone. "Normally, Botox—the trade name for botulinum toxin—is used in extremely small, controlled doses for aesthetic treatments. But in this case, the toxin concentration in the cream was far higher than what's used medically. Absorbed through the skin, it could have caused severe harm—paralysis, respiratory failure, or worse."

Sarah's heart raced. "Absorbed through the skin? I thought it could only be dangerous when injected."

"That's true for typical cosmetic use," Stanley clarified. "But at high concentrations, the toxin can permeate the skin barrier. Once in the bloodstream, it can interfere with nerve signals just like an injection would—only with far more widespread and unpredictable effects. Whoever tampered with that cream knew exactly what they were doing."

Robyn gasped, her hand flying to her chest. "I put that on my skin," she whispered, her voice trembling. "I could have—" She didn't finish the sentence, and Sarah squeezed her hand tightly, her own fear threatening to bubble over. "You're ok, Robyn. We caught it in time."

Stanley's voice softened slightly, though his words remained measured. "Robyn was lucky. Absorption depends on a lot of factors—time, the amount applied, even the condition of the skin. But make no mistake, this wasn't an accident. Whoever sent that package intended for it to cause harm."

Sarah's mind raced. "Inspector, this isn't something just anyone could get their hands on, is it?"

"No," he agreed. "Botulinum toxin is tightly regulated. The average person couldn't source it legally, let alone at such a high concentration. Whoever did this has access through professional means—likely someone in the aesthetics or beauty industry."

Sarah frowned, her brow creasing. "But why use hand cream? Wouldn't it have been easier to tamper with something else?"

Stanley hesitated, his tone becoming contemplative. "It's possible they wanted it to seem harmless—something Sarah wouldn't think twice about using. But the choice of a beauty product, particularly one like hand cream, also suggests they knew enough to exploit its potential as a delivery mechanism."

Robyn shuddered, her eyes wide with horror. "Who would do something like this?" she whispered.

Sarah squeezed her niece's hand reassuringly. "We'll find out, Robyn."

Sarah's thoughts immediately turned to Kerry. "Could Kerry be behind this? She runs a clinic... she'd have access, wouldn't she?"

Stanley exhaled sharply. "That's exactly what I'm worried about." His voice was grim, the weight of yet another issue tied to Kerry pressing down on him. "First, the inconsistencies in her statements. Now, a package supposedly from her containing a toxin only a professional like her would have access to. This isn't looking good for her, Sarah."

"I need to speak with Kerry again," he said, his tone leaving no room for doubt. "But not at her clinic. Not in passing. It's time to bring her into the station. No more polite conversations—this time, she answers properly."

Sarah swallowed hard, a cold knot tightening in her stomach. The implications of the package—what it meant, what could have happened—were terrifying. But for the first time, she felt a small measure of reassurance. Stanley wasn't brushing this off as an unfortunate mistake. He understood the gravity of it. He believed her.

As she ended the call, Sarah exhaled shakily and turned to Robyn, who still looked pale, her eyes wide with the lingering shock of what had almost happened. Without a word, Sarah pulled her into a tight hug, holding on just a little longer than usual.

How had it come to this? A coffee shop, a fresh start—that was all she had wanted. And yet, here she was, caught up in something dark and twisted, something that could have cost her niece her life.

She closed her eyes for a moment, steadying herself. Surely, it couldn't get any worse. But deep down, a part of her knew…it always could.

The interview room at the local police station was a stark contrast to Kerry's clinic—cold, clinical, and stripped of anything remotely comforting. The fluorescent lighting buzzed softly, casting sharp shadows against the walls. A metal table separated Kerry from Inspector Stanley, who sat across from her, arms folded, his expression unreadable.

Kerry shifted in her chair, the plastic creaking beneath her. Her usual polished confidence was slipping, replaced by something closer to unease. This wasn't a casual conversation at her clinic. She wasn't in control here.

Stanley studied her for a long moment before finally speaking. His voice was calm but laced with something heavier this time.

"Kerry," he began, his tone measured but firm, "Sarah received a package this morning. It was signed with your name and contained beauty products—products laced with botulinum toxin."

The words hung in the air, their weight palpable. Kerry blinked, her expression shifting from confusion to alarm. "Laced with Botox?" she repeated, her voice rising slightly. "I don't understand. I didn't send Sarah anything."

Stanley studied her closely, his gaze unwavering. "Are you sure?" he pressed. "It wasn't a small oversight, a sample basket you might've sent as a gesture?"

"No," Kerry said emphatically, her hands coming to rest on the edge of the desk. He noticed the slight tremor in her fingers as she spoke, but her eyes remained locked on his. "I would never send Sarah anything, especially something like that. Someone must be using my name."

Stanley let the silence stretch, allowing her words to settle. He watched her reaction carefully, noting the flicker of panic in her eyes and the slight crack in her voice. Was it guilt? Fear? Or simply the shock of being implicated in something so dangerous? He couldn't be sure.

"This package wasn't random," he said, his voice quiet but heavy with intent. "It was deliberate. And whoever sent it wanted Sarah to believe it was from you."

Kerry's breath hitched. "Why would anyone do that? Who would—" She stopped, her brow furrowing as if the thought alone was too overwhelming to finish.

"Kerry," he said, his fingers tapping once against the table, "this is serious. I need you to understand that. The case against you isn't looking good."

Her posture stiffened. "The case against me?" she echoed, incredulous. "I told you—I had nothing to do with that package."

Stanley leaned forward slightly, his eyes sharp, unyielding. "And yet, someone went to great lengths to make it look like you did. A package delivered directly to Sarah, filled with beauty products laced with botulinum toxin—something that you, as a professional in the aesthetics industry, would have access to." He let the words sink in before continuing, his tone tightening. "This wasn't some amateur's idea of a prank. This was planned. And right now, you're the one whose name is on that package."

Kerry shook her head, her hands gripping the edge of the table. "I don't know how many times I have to say this—I didn't send it! Someone's setting me up."

Stanley exhaled sharply, his patience thinning. "Then help me understand why someone would go to this much trouble to implicate you." He sat back, arms crossing over his chest. "Because from where I'm sitting, the more we look into this, the worse it's getting for you."

Kerry's eyes darted between him and the tape recorder sitting on the table, the red light blinking steadily. The weight of the moment pressed down on her, a realisation creeping in—this wasn't just about defending herself anymore. This was about proving she wasn't behind something truly dangerous.

As Sarah prepared to close the shop for the night, her unease only grew. The events of the day replayed in her mind like a broken record. The package, Robyn's close call, Stanley's measured words—they all pointed to one undeniable fact, whoever was targeting her wasn't going to stop.

The shadows in the shop seemed darker than usual as she locked the front door. Every noise felt amplified, every creak of the old floorboards a reminder that she was alone. She couldn't help but glance over her shoulder as she walked to her car, her keys gripped tightly in her hand, her thumb resting over the panic button.

As she slid into the driver's seat, her phone buzzed. A text from Robyn.

"Be careful tonight, Auntie Sarah. Love you."

Sarah smiled faintly, warmth flickering in her chest. But as she stared at the words, her grip on the phone tightened. The world felt different now—less certain, less safe. And somewhere out there, someone was waiting for her next move.

Just as she went to tuck her phone away in her bag, it buzzed again. Another message.

Her stomach tightened as she glanced at the screen. *Unknown Number.* Not good. Hesitantly, she tapped the notification.

"I underestimated you, Sarah. I thought you were just another nosy customer, but now I see what you were really doing at *Lotus Blossom*. Checking up on me. Digging where you don't belong. Consider this your only warning—stay out of things that don't concern you, or I'll have to take drastic steps."

Sarah's breath caught in her throat. A cold, prickling sensation ran down the back of her neck as her mind scrambled for an explanation. *How the hell does Rachel have my number?*

Then, in an instant, the answer struck her. *Lotus Blossom.* She had given them her number when she booked her appointment—when she had been pretending to be just another potential client. That meant Rachel hadn't gone searching for her contact details—she had them handed to her.

The realisation sent a fresh wave of fear crashing over her.

Her hands felt slick with sweat as she read the message again, the words pressing into her like invisible fingers tightening around her throat. *Drastic steps.* What did that mean? Was this just intimidation, or was Rachel truly capable of something worse? And then—the smell.

It hit her like a punch. That faint, bitter almond scent that had lingered in her mind ever since she opened the package of beauty products. Marzipan. Her stomach turned violently.

She hadn't let herself dwell on the thought before, dismissing it as paranoia, but now? Now, the pieces clicked together with sickening certainty.

Oh god. Was it Rachel that tried to hurt me?

Her breathing shallowed, her chest tightening as she tried to fight the rising panic. The interior of the car suddenly felt smaller, the darkness pressing in through the windshield. She fumbled to lock the doors, her fingers shaky as she pressed the button on the key fob.

Was Rachel watching her now? Did she know where she was?

She darted a look in the rearview mirror, half-expecting to see a shadow moving in the distance. But there was nothing. Just the dimly lit car park and the empty street beyond. Yet that did nothing to ease the weight pressing on her ribs.

Her phone buzzed again, making her jump. Another message. "You wouldn't want to make an enemy of me,

Sarah. Some things are more dangerous than you realise. Keep your nose out of this."

Sarah's pulse pounded against her temples. She couldn't stay here. She needed to get home.

She started the car, her heart hammering as she backed out of the parking space, eyes flicking constantly between her mirrors and the road ahead. Every parked car looked like a hiding place. Every pedestrian a potential threat.

She pressed the accelerator, gripping the wheel so tightly her knuckles ached. One thing was clear—this wasn't just about digging into a business rivalry anymore. She had put herself in real danger. And Rachel knew it.

Chapter 22

Sarah sat at her kitchen table, her hands wrapped around a cup of tea, the warmth doing little to chase away the chill that had settled deep in her bones. The weight of Rachel's threats pressed heavily on her, each word from the text replaying in her mind like a sinister echo. She knew she needed to take immediate action.

Setting her mug down with a soft clink, she reached for her phone and quickly dialled Stanley's number.

"Stanley," his gruff voice answered after a few rings.

"Inspector, it's Sarah," she said, her voice barely above a whisper. "I think I might be in danger."

There was a brief pause before Stanley responded, his tone serious. "What's happened now?"

Sarah glanced towards the kitchen window, the darkness outside feeling heavier than usual. "Rachel sent me a message. She knows I was looking into her, and she's made it very clear she wants me to back off. She said she'd take drastic steps if I didn't."

A sharp exhale came through the line. "Damn it, Sarah," Stanley muttered. "I told you to be careful. Did she say anything specific?"

"She implied I shouldn't trust what I think I know... and she mentioned the beauty products." Sarah swallowed, her stomach tightening. "I keep thinking about that smell—marzipan. What if it really was her?"

Stanley was silent for a moment before his voice returned, calm but edged with concern. "Where are you now?"

"I'm at home," Sarah said, gripping her phone tighter. "I've locked the doors, but I don't know if she's watching me. I just... I don't know what she's capable of."

"Listen to me," Stanley said firmly. "Stay inside. Don't go anywhere alone. I'll send someone to keep an eye on the house, and I'll look into this. Whatever you do, Sarah, don't engage with her again."

Sarah nodded, even though he couldn't see her. "I won't. But Stanley... I don't think she's bluffing."

"I don't either," he admitted. "Which is why you need to let me handle it. Just sit tight—I'll be in touch soon."

As the call ended, Sarah set her phone down on the table, her pulse still racing. The house suddenly felt too quiet, the distant hum of the fridge the only sound in the room. She wrapped her arms around herself, staring at the phone as if expecting it to buzz again.

Somewhere out there, Rachel was waiting. Watching. And Sarah had no idea what she would do next.

Sarah sat there, her fingers curled around the cooling mug, staring blankly at the phone on the table. Stanley's words echoed in her head.

Stay inside. Don't go anywhere alone. Don't engage with her again.

She exhaled slowly, rubbing her temple. She knew he was right, but the thought of sitting back and doing nothing felt impossible. Rachel wasn't just trying to scare her—she was sending a message. A warning. And if she'd already gone as far as tampering with beauty products, what else was she capable of?

She should have been thinking about her next move, but exhaustion was creeping in, fogging her thoughts. The weight of everything—the threats, the fear, the paranoia—pressed down on her shoulders. She shut her eyes for a moment, trying to ground herself. Then—click. A sharp burst of light flooded the kitchen. Sarah jumped, her pulse spiking as she whipped around.

Mike stood in the doorway, his hand still on the light switch, his face tight with irritation. His usual easy-going expression was gone, replaced with something darker, something edged with frustration.

"You're still up?" His voice was flat, but there was an unmistakable sharpness underneath.

Sarah forced herself to exhale, pressing a hand to her chest. "Jesus, Mike. You scared the life out of me."

He didn't answer right away. Instead, he moved to the counter, yanking open the cupboard and pulling out a glass with more force than necessary. The silence between them thickened, stretching uncomfortably as he filled it with water.

Sarah watched him carefully. "Are you ok?"

Mike let out a dry, humourless laugh, shaking his head as he took a sip. "You tell me, Sarah."

Her stomach twisted. She knew that tone. Knew that look. He was mad—and not in the fleeting, grumble-about-it-for-ten-minutes kind of way. This was deeper.

"What's that supposed to mean?" she asked cautiously.

Mike set the glass down with a dull thud, finally turning to face her properly. His jaw was tight, his eyes tired but sharp. "It means I came downstairs to get a drink and find you sitting here, in the dark, looking like you've seen a ghost."

He folded his arms. "I heard you on the phone earlier. Something about Rachel threatening you? Sarah, what the hell are you doing?" Mike's voice was a mix of frustration and worry.

"Mike, I..." Sarah started, but Mike cut her off.

"I warned you about getting too involved in this," he said, his voice rising slightly. "I told you it was dangerous, and now look what's happening.

"You're putting yourself at risk, Sarah. Do you even realize how worried I've been?" Mike's voice was rougher now, his fists clenched at his sides.

Sarah felt a pang of guilt. She knew Mike was right. He had always been cautious, always tried to protect her. But her drive to uncover the truth had pushed her to take risks she hadn't fully considered.

"Mike, I had to do this." She reached for his hand, but he pulled back, exhaling sharply.

"No, you didn't," he said, voice edged with anger. "You're not a detective. You're not invincible. You're my wife, and I don't know what I'd do if something happened to you."

The words hit harder than she expected. She had seen the frustration in Mike before, but not the fear. Not like this. Sarah reached out and took Mike's hand, her eyes pleading for understanding. "I know, and I'm sorry. But I'm in this now, and I need to see it through. I promise I'll be more careful. Stanley's sending someone to watch over me."

Mike sighed, his anger softening into resignation. "I just... I can't lose you, Sarah. You're too important to me. Please, promise me you'll be careful."

"I promise," Sarah said, squeezing his hand. "I won't do anything reckless".

Stanley felt a sense of grim determination as he approached Rachel's salon. He needed answers, and he needed them now. As he entered the chic, modern space, Rachel greeted him with her usual professional and welcoming smile, though a hint of curiosity flickered in her eyes.

"Inspector Stanley, how can I help you today?" she asked, her tone polite but guarded.

"I have a few questions regarding some recent events," Stanley replied, his voice firm. "We need to discuss the incident involving threats to Sarah Meadows and a package she received."

Rachel's smile faltered just for a moment, before her professional mask slipped back into place. "Of course, please come to my office," she said, her voice smooth and composed.

Once they were seated in her office, Stanley wasted no time getting to the point. "We found botulinum toxin in a package of beauty products sent to Sarah, supposedly from Kerry. You name has come up in connection with it."

Rachel's lips parted, and then, just as quickly, she pressed them into a thin line. "Botulinum toxin? Botox?" She exhaled, a soft breath escaping her. "Inspector, I think there's been a misunderstanding."

Stanley's eyes sharpened at the slight delay before her response. "What do you mean?"

Rachel folded her hands on the desk, fingers interlocked, but her thumbs moved—circling one another in a slow, rhythmic motion. "I don't offer Botox treatments at my salon," she said firmly. "My entire philosophy is centred on natural products and unlocking one's inner beauty. I've always been against using any kind of synthetic substances, especially injections."

Stanley studied her carefully. She didn't fidget—exactly. But there was something overly controlled about her stillness, something too careful in the way she held herself. He pushed forward, his voice unwavering.

"If you don't use Botox, then can you explain why someone might think that you are involved?" he asked.

Rachel's nostrils flared slightly. "I can't say for sure." She tilted her head slightly, giving him a look of feigned confusion. "But I suspect someone's trying to frame me or use my name to mislead you. I've built my business on trust and natural beauty. Injecting poisons into people would completely contradict everything I stand for."

Stanley watched her carefully, his mind running through the possibilities. He didn't believe in coincidences, especially not when they were so specific. "And yet, Sarah Meadows received a package that I have been led to believe is linked to your business, containing a dangerous toxin. That's no small coincidence."

Rachel let out a light laugh, but there was no humour behind it. "It's a coincidence, yes. And if I were you, I'd be asking myself who would benefit from making me look guilty."

Stanley's expression remained neutral, but something in his gut tightened. "And who do you think that might be?"

Rachel exhaled, shaking her head again as if mulling over the thought. Then she leaned forward slightly, her voice lowering to a confidential murmur. "Kerry, perhaps?" she murmured. "After all, that package came from her spa, didn't it? And from what I hear, she's been struggling. Desperate people do desperate things."

There it was. The subtle redirection. A perfectly placed seed of doubt.

Stanley held her gaze, studying her expression carefully. Was this genuine confidence, or was she performing for him? He wasn't sure yet. But one thing was certain: he would be watching.

Chapter 23

Stanley sat in his office, flipping through a stack of case notes, his pen tapping against the desk in a slow, steady rhythm. Something just wasn't adding up. Emily Parker had insisted that her history with Terri was nothing but a teenage heartbreak, a painful memory she had long since buried. But if that were true, why had she twisted the details when she told Sarah her version of events?

He pulled up a public records search, typing quickly. Matthew Evans. Married to Terri Treharne. The marriage certificate confirmed it. Stanley frowned. Emily had deliberately left that part out. She had let people believe that Terri had stolen Rachel's boyfriend when in reality, Terri had kissed Emily's boyfriend.

His phone buzzed, dragging him from his thoughts. He grabbed it, barely glancing at the screen before answering. "Stanley."

A pause. Then, Marcus's voice—low, unsteady. "Inspector... I need to talk."

Stanley sat up straighter. "Marcus?"

"I've been thinking," Marcus slurred slightly. "About Emily. About Terri. About a lot of things."

Stanley's brow furrowed. "Are you all right?"

A dry, humourless laugh came down the line. "Define *all right.*" Glass clinked in the background. Ice cubes against a tumbler. Stanley exhaled sharply. Marcus was drinking.

"Marcus, where are you?"

"In my flat. My rubbish little flat," Marcus muttered. "I—I know I should have told you sooner. I just—I didn't want to believe it."

"Believe what?" Stanley pressed, his grip tightening on the phone.

Marcus inhaled shakily. "Emily never let it go, you know? Matthew. Terri. All of it. She acted like she'd buried the past, but she hadn't. Not really."

A pit formed in Stanley's stomach. "Did she ever say she wanted revenge?"

There was a long pause, followed by a soft, bitter chuckle. "She never had to say it. She used to tell me Terri had it *easy*—success, love, respect. And when Terri came back to Southsea, Emily acted like she was waiting for her to fall."

Stanley felt his pulse quicken. "Why didn't you tell me this before?"

Marcus sighed. "Because... I didn't want to believe it. But now? I think she was obsessed, Inspector. I think she wanted Terri gone."

Stanley leaned forward, adrenaline surging. "Marcus, listen carefully. I need you to stay put. If Emily contacts you, don't engage—just call me."

Marcus let out a long exhale. "Yeah. Sure. Whatever."

But Stanley wasn't convinced. Marcus was unreliable, and there was a good chance he'd already said more than he intended.

His stomach twisted. Sarah had been so focused on Rachel. She had no idea how wrong she was. And if she decided to visit Emily again…Stanley grabbed his coat. He needed to move. Now.

Sarah walked into *Parker Dermatology* her pulse quickening. She had booked the appointment under the pretence of a routine treatment, but her real goal was simple—find the missing link. Find the proof that Rachel was responsible for Terri's murder.

"Good afternoon, Sarah," Emily said warmly. "Ready for your treatment?"

"Yes, thank you," Sarah replied, trying to keep her voice steady.

Emily led Sarah to a cosy treatment room, softly lit and filled with calming scents. "Make yourself comfortable on the table," she instructed. "I'll just go get a few things ready."

Sarah settled onto the table, her mind buzzing with questions and suspicions. As Emily busied herself getting a tray of equipment together, she left the room to collect a missing item, leaving the door ajar.

She settled onto the table, her mind buzzing. If Rachel had wanted Terri out of the way, there had to be one last clue, one final piece of evidence to tie it all together.

Then—muffled voices from the reception area. Sarah wasn't paying attention until she caught a few familiar words.

"… I always felt bad for Emily."

Her breath hitched.

"… Terri kissed him, and everything fell apart."

Sarah froze, her mind racing. Could she really have just heard that? She was sure that Emily had let her believe that Terri had stolen Rachel's boyfriend, but it was actually her own boyfriend. If she had been manipulating the truth about a detail like that, what else had Emily been keeping from them?

As Emily returned to the room, Sarah struggled to maintain her composure. She needed to confront Emily, but she had to be careful.

"Ready to get started?" Emily asked, her smile unwavering, unaware of the panic that was coursing through Sarah's body at this moment.

"Yes, all ready", Sarah answered, forcing a smile. As Emily leant across her, only inches away from her face, Sarah suddenly felt anxious and unable to hold in the questions that were racing through her mind.

Sarah hesitated, then sat up slightly. "Actually, Emily, can I ask you something first?" Emily stilled. "Of course."

Sarah took a slow breath. "I overheard something just now... about Terri. And Matthew." Emily's expression didn't change, but her grip on the tray tightened.

"What about them?" she asked lightly.

Sarah chose her words carefully. "When I saw Terri in the changing rooms on the day of her murder, she was on the phone. I didn't hear much, just a few words, but she said something like, *I can't believe you still care about that night.*"

Emily's fingers twitched.

Sarah's breath shallowed. *Emily knows what was said that day.*

And the only way she could know that... Was if she was the one Terri had been talking to.

The tray clattered onto the counter. Emily exhaled sharply, her mask slipping for the first time. Her gaze locked onto Sarah's. Cold. Calculating.

You shouldn't have come here Sarah, she muttered silently to herself.

Emily's small, sad smile faded quickly as her mind raced with the implications of Sarah's questions. She couldn't afford to let anyone dig deeper into her past, especially with Inspector Stanley's recent inquiries. The pressure was mounting, and she felt cornered. As she considered her options, a dark thought crossed her mind.

Emily moved towards the counter where her tools were laid out. Her hands trembled slightly as she reached for a small vial and a syringe, her mind made up in a moment of desperate clarity. She needed to take Sarah out of the equation before everything unravelled.

Sarah opened her eyes and turned her head slightly, sensing a shift in Emily's demeanour. She couldn't quite put her finger on it, but something felt off. "Emily, are you ok? You seem... different."

Before Sarah could react, Emily approached her with a forced smile. "Just need to adjust a few things here," she said, trying to sound casual. She stood over Sarah, the syringe hidden behind her back.

Sarah's instincts screamed at her, and she pushed herself up on her elbows, looking directly at Emily. "What are you doing, Emily?"

Emily hesitated, the syringe poised but hidden. "Just getting ready for the treatment, Sarah. Lie back down."

Sarah's eyes narrowed, and in a horrible moment of realisation, she shook her head. "Actually, I think I'm done for today. I'll just get dressed and head out."

Emily's face hardened, the facade slipping. "Are you sure, Sarah?"

In a flash, Emily lunged towards Sarah, the syringe raised. Sarah's eyes widened in shock, and she instinctively grabbed Emily's wrist, struggling to fend her off. The two women grappled, the small room suddenly feeling claustrophobic.

"Emily, stop!" Sarah yelled, trying to wrestle the syringe from Emily's grip.

"You don't understand," Emily hissed, her eyes wild with panic. "I can't let you ruin everything!"

The door to the treatment room burst open, and Inspector Stanley stood there, his eyes taking in the chaotic scene. "Sarah, get back!" he commanded, his voice sharp.

Sarah, still on edge, managed to twist Emily's arm, sending the syringe clattering to the floor. She stumbled back, breathing heavily, as Stanley moved between her and Emily. Two constables stepped into the room behind Stanley, quickly taking control of the situation. They moved swiftly, grabbing Emily by the arms and securing her. Emily's eyes filled with a mix of disbelief and despair. "I didn't mean to... I just..." she stammered, her voice breaking.

Stanley stepped forward, his voice firm and steady. "Emily Parker, you are under arrest for the attempted murder of Sarah Meadows and the murder of Terri Treharne."

As the constables led Emily out of the room, Sarah pressed a hand to her chest, her pulse racing. She had come here looking for proof against Rachel, but instead, she had found herself face-to-face with the real killer.

Stanley turned to her, his expression softening. "Are you ok, Sarah?"

She nodded, though her body trembled from the adrenaline. "I think so, Inspector."

Stanley gave her a reassuring smile. "Let's get you out of here. You've had quite the ordeal."

Together, they walked out of the salon, standing outside as a police car pulled up. Emily, her head hanging low in defeat, was shoved into the back seat. The officers closed the door with a firm thud, and shortly afterwards the car pulled away.

Sarah and Stanley stood there in silence, watching the car drive off. Through the rear window, Sarah could still see Emily, shoulders slumped in resignation.

As the car disappeared down the street, Sarah felt a heavy weight lift off her shoulders. The truth had been revealed, and the tangled web of lies and jealousy had finally unravelled. But the image of Emily, broken and defeated, lingered in her mind. She felt a bittersweet sense of relief, knowing that justice was being served, but still unable to shake the sadness of it all.

"We'll get her into custody," Stanley said, breaking the silence. "But it's over now, Sarah. You're safe."

Sarah sat quietly in the back of Inspector Stanley's car as they drove back to her home. The events of the past hour swirled in her mind, leaving her both exhausted and relieved. She glanced out the window, watching the familiar streets of

Southsea pass by, feeling a mixture of surreal detachment and deep gratitude for her safety.

When they arrived, Stanley turned to her, his expression gentle. "If you need anything, don't hesitate to call. And please, stay safe."

"Thank you, Inspector," Sarah replied, her voice barely above a whisper. She stepped out of the car and made her way up the path to her front door, where Mike and Charlie were waiting.

The moment Mike saw her, he rushed forward, his face a mixture of anger, frustration, and overwhelming relief. "Sarah! What were you thinking?" he burst out, his voice trembling.

Charlie stood a step behind him, his eyes wide with concern. "Are you ok, Mum?" he asked softly.

Sarah tried to hold back her tears, but the weight of everything that had happened finally broke through. She crumpled into sobs, her body shaking. Mike's expression softened instantly, his anger melting away. He pulled her into a tight embrace, holding her as she cried.

"I'm sorry, Sarah," he murmured into her hair. "I didn't mean to be so harsh. It's just... I don't want anything to happen to you. I was so scared when I heard what happened."

Sarah clung to him, her sobs gradually subsiding. "I know, Mike. I know. It's just... I thought I could help."

Charlie stepped closer, placing a gentle hand on her shoulder. "You did help, Mum. You helped bring the truth to light. But Mike's right. You must be careful."

Mike pulled back slightly, cupping her face in his hands. "Promise me you won't put yourself in danger like that again."

Sarah nodded, her eyes red and puffy from crying. "I promise."

Mike kissed her forehead tenderly. "Good. Now let's get you inside and take care of you."

They led her into the house, where the familiar, comforting surroundings of her home helped to calm her nerves. Charlie went to make her a cup of tea while Mike sat with her on the couch, his arm around her shoulders.

"You're safe now," Mike whispered, holding her close. "And that's all that matters."

Sarah leaned into him, feeling a deep sense of gratitude for the support of the two men who meant so much to her.

As Sarah settled onto the couch, Mike's arm remained around her shoulders, providing a steady source of comfort. The familiar aroma of Charlie's special blend of tea wafted in from the kitchen, and Sarah took a deep breath, trying to centre herself. The events of the day were still fresh and raw, but the warmth of her home and the presence of her loved ones helped to ground her.

Charlie returned with a steaming mug of tea, placing it gently in Sarah's hands. "Here you go. Drink up. It'll help calm your nerves," he said, his voice soothing.

Sarah managed a small smile. "Thanks, Charlie. I appreciate it."

Mike glanced at Charlie, then back at Sarah. "Sarah, I know you were trying to help, and I understand why you felt the need to get involved. But you have to realize that these things can be dangerous. Promise me you'll let the professionals handle it from now on."

Sarah nodded, sipping the tea. "I promise, Mike. I never meant to worry you. I just... I felt like I had to do something."

Mike sighed, pulling her closer. "I know. You have a good heart. But your safety is the most important thing to me. To us."

Charlie sat down on the armchair opposite them, leaning forward with his elbows on his knees. "He's right, you know. We're all just relieved you're ok. But maybe from now on, we can find other ways to help without putting you directly in harm's way."

Sarah took another sip of her tea, feeling the warmth spread through her. "You're both right. I got caught up in the excitement of it all, thinking I could make a difference. But I need to be more careful. I understand that now."

Mike kissed the top of her head. "That's all I wanted to hear. Now, let's focus on something else. How about we watch a movie or something to take your mind off things?"

Sarah looked up at him, her eyes still glistening with the remnants of her earlier tears. "That sounds perfect. Something light and funny?"

Charlie grinned. "I think I have just the thing. I'll go grab some snacks."

As Charlie disappeared into the kitchen, Mike helped Sarah settle into a more comfortable position on the couch. He tucked a soft blanket around her and then took his place beside her, keeping his arm around her shoulders.

"I love you, Sarah," he said softly, his voice filled with emotion.

Sarah looked up at him, her heart swelling with love and gratitude. "I love you too, Mike. Thank you for being here for me."

Mike smiled, kissing her gently on the lips. "Always."

Charlie returned with a bowl of popcorn and some chocolates, setting them down on the coffee table. "All right, I found the perfect movie. It's a comedy classic. Should be just what we need."

As the movie began to play, Sarah felt a sense of peace settle over her. The laughter and light-hearted banter of the characters on screen helped to distract her from the day's events, and she allowed herself to relax in the embrace of her loved ones.

For now, the mystery and danger were behind her. She was safe, surrounded by those who cared for her, and that was all that mattered. The road ahead might still hold challenges, but she knew she wouldn't face them alone. And with that thought, she allowed herself to smile, truly and freely, for the first time that day.

Chapter 24

Sarah stood outside *Serenity Spa*, inhaling deeply as she gathered her thoughts. The sun was rising higher now, casting long shadows across the pavement. She should have been at *Sarah's Secrets*, soaking in the joy of its first full day in business. But there was one last thing she needed to do first.

Before she could truly move on, before she could fully embrace this new chapter in her life, she had to make sure Kerry was ok.

She pushed open the glass doors, the soft chime ringing in her ears as she stepped inside. A sanctuary, she thought. That was what *Serenity Spa* had always been. But now, after everything that had happened, she wondered if Kerry would ever see it that way again.

Behind the reception desk, Kerry was flipping through the schedule, her fingers moving with a mechanical precision that didn't match her usual energy. The tension in her shoulders, the tightness around her eyes—it was clear she was still carrying the weight of the past few weeks.

Sarah stepped forward. "Hi, Kerry."

Kerry looked up, momentarily startled, but when she saw Sarah, her face softened. "Oh. Hi, Sarah."

"I just wanted to stop by," Sarah said gently, "before I get completely swept up in the coffee shop. I needed to see how you're doing."

Kerry gave a small, weary smile. "That's sweet of you, but I'm fine."

Sarah wasn't convinced. "Are you?"

Kerry sighed, rubbing at her temple. "I don't know. It still doesn't feel real. To think that everything happened right here, in my spa, under my nose... it's hard to process."

Sarah nodded, understanding. "I can only imagine. But, Kerry, you've built something amazing here. And I think, in time, people will remember that more than the tragedy."

Kerry's gaze drifted toward the large windows, where the world outside bustled on as if nothing had changed. "I hope so. We've had... curiosity bookings, you know? People just showing up out of morbid interest. Like this place is some kind of crime scene attraction."

Sarah's stomach twisted. "That's awful."

"It is," Kerry admitted. "But I'm hoping once the novelty wears off, some of them will stick around for the right reasons."

"They will," Sarah reassured her. "The people who matter—the real customers—they know what this place is. They'll come back."

For the first time since Sarah had walked in, Kerry's shoulders dropped slightly, a bit of the tension easing from her posture. "Thanks, Sarah. It means a lot, really."

They shared a quiet moment, the spa's peaceful atmosphere offering a rare pocket of calm after the last week's upheaval.

Then, the soft chime of the door rang behind them. A group of women entered, chatting excitedly, their energy instantly filling the space. Kerry straightened, her professional mask sliding back into place as she turned toward them.

Sarah knew that was her cue to leave. With a small wave, she gave Kerry a final smile. "I'll let you get back to it. But… if you ever need to step away, even just for a coffee, you know where to find me."

Kerry's lips twitched, the closest thing to a real smile she'd managed so far. "I'll hold you to that."

As Sarah stepped outside, the crisp air hit her, carrying with it a sense of closure. She had done what she needed to do. Kerry wasn't ok yet—but she would be.

And now, Sarah could finally walk back to *Sarah's Secrets*, knowing that she had tied up the last of the loose ends. The thought of her little coffee-shaped sanctuary, filled with warmth and friendly faces, pulled her forward like a hug.

This was it. The real beginning.

Sarah, Robyn, and Charlie stood in the middle of the newly renovated coffee shop, a quiet moment before the official opening. Mike was with them, standing off to the side, his eyes full of pride as he watched the trio check in with each other. The excitement in the air was palpable, but so was the undercurrent of nerves as they prepared to open their doors for the first time.

"Okay, let's do this," Sarah said, taking a deep breath and giving Robyn and Charlie a quick look to make sure they were all set.

Just as Sarah was about to unlock the door, Mike stepped forward, a slight grin on his face. "Hold on a sec. I've got one last thing to do before we can make this official."

Sarah stared at him in confusion, irritation flickering across her face. "Now? We're doing this *now*?"

But before she could say more, she watched as Mike casually reached up and disengaged the bell hanging above the shop door. Her eyebrows shot up in surprise, and the irritation melted into a chuckle.

"You're kidding," she said, laughter escaping her. "That's the last-minute thing?"

Mike shrugged, his grin widening. "Well, you know it would have driven you mad by the end of the day."

With a quick hug, Mike stepped back, giving Sarah a wink. She couldn't help but smile as she unlocked the door, feeling a wave of warmth and appreciation for the simple gesture that had taken some of the pressure off.

Sarah stood in front of the shop door, her fingers hovering over the lock. She could hear the gentle murmur of voices outside, the rustle of people shifting in anticipation. Her stomach twisted—not with fear, but with something close to awe. This was it. The moment she had imagined for months.

She turned to Robyn and Charlie, searching their faces for reassurance. Charlie grinned. Robyn nodded. Mike gave her a look that said, *You've got this.*

Sarah swallowed, took a deep breath, and turned the key.

Sarah stared into the mirrored surface of the espresso machine as she prepared the next set of drinks, her mind wandering back to the memory of her cluttered desk, perpetually surrounded by a queue of colleagues needing help, advice, or simply someone to listen to their gripes, flashed vividly in her mind. Every day had felt like an endless cycle of managing tasks, fixing problems, and answering questions. There were times she barely had a moment to sip her coffee, let alone enjoy it.

Now, as she looked out over the cheerful crowd in her coffee shop, she marvelled at the difference. Here, the line of people waiting was not a burden but a joy. Each person was a potential smile, a friendly exchange, a shared moment of happiness over a cup of coffee. The root of their satisfaction was so much simpler and more gratifying. Instead of dealing with complaints and crises, she was serving warmth and comfort in a cup.

Sarah watched as Robyn handed a steaming latte to a young woman who had just walked in, her face lighting up with gratitude as she took her first sip. This was what it was all about. The joy of making someone's day a little brighter, a little warmer. It was a far cry from her old life, and she couldn't be more grateful for the change.

As she moved behind the counter to help Robyn with the growing line of customers, she couldn't help but feel a swell of pride. The faces in front of her weren't just customers, they were neighbours, friends, members of her community. She knew their names, but now she would get to know their favourite drinks, their stories. And that connection, that sense of belonging, was something she had never experienced in her old job. The morning rush continued, but instead of feeling overwhelmed, Sarah felt energised.

"Congratulations, Mum," a voice broke through her thoughts. It was Charlie, grinning broadly as he approached her. "You've done it. The place looks amazing."

"Thanks, Charlie, but don't you mean we've done it!" Sarah replied, her smile reflecting her gratitude. "I couldn't have done it without everyone's support. It means the world to me."

Charlie nodded. "We're all behind you. This coffee shop is going to be the heart of Southsea, I can feel it."

The coffee shop buzzed with activity, the hum of conversation blending with the clatter of cups and the hiss of the espresso machine. Inspector Stanley stood near the counter, his posture slightly stiff as he tried to make small talk with Robyn, who was behind the counter cutting cakes into slices to serve.

Sarah, busy helping Robyn and Charlie serve customers on this bustling opening day, noticed Stanley's presence. She took a moment to finish up with a customer before beckoning the Inspector over to a quieter corner of the shop.

"Inspector, thank you for coming," Sarah said, offering him a warm smile. "Please, have a seat. I know you're probably here on business, but it's good to see you."

Stanley returned her smile, albeit a bit strained. "Thank you, Sarah. Congratulations on the opening. The place looks wonderful."

Sarah sat down across from him, her expression turning serious. "I appreciate that. But I'm sure you didn't come here just to talk about coffee. Tell me—what did Emily have to say for herself? I know she's responsible and some of the reasons why, but did she tell you how she managed it?"

Stanley sighed, leaning back in his chair. "Yes, she did. It's a rather tragic story, really. Emily didn't even try to deny it once she realized we had her. She admitted to being consumed by jealousy and bitterness toward Terri for years. When Terri returned, all those old wounds reopened, and she decided that if the opportunity arose, she would take it."

Sarah frowned, feeling a cold unease settle in her stomach. "Take it how?"

"She disguised herself," Stanley explained. "Dressed as a young man—short hair, loose clothes. It was convincing enough. She got information about the security system from Megan by pretending to be interested in a job at the spa. She even called ahead, pretending to be Terri, to confirm her appointment. Once inside, she slipped into the treatment room and tampered with the wiring on the infrared bed."

Sarah exhaled sharply. "She knew exactly what she was doing."

Stanley nodded. "She admitted that she wanted to give Terri a painful shock, something to 'make her feel a fraction of the pain she'd caused.' But when Terri touched the bed with her wet hands, the shock was far worse than Emily anticipated. It killed her instantly." He hesitated before adding, "The thing is, when she told us all this, she wasn't particularly upset about it."

Sarah's eyes darkened. "So, she didn't mean to kill her, but she didn't care that she had?"

"Exactly," Stanley said grimly. "She called it 'an unfortunate consequence.' Like knocking over a glass of water. No real remorse."

Sarah shook her head, both horrified and saddened. "It's tragic."

Stanley gave a small nod. "And as for the smell of marzipan? That was a complete red herring. Rachel had been developing a new line of natural beauty products, including a hand cream with a strong almond scent. Megan used some while setting up the treatment room, which is why it lingered. It had nothing to do with the murder, but it certainly added to the confusion."

Sarah absorbed all of this, then let out a slow breath. "At least we have answers now."

Stanley offered a reassuring smile. "Yes. And now you can focus on your coffee shop without this hanging over you."

Sarah returned his smile, feeling the weight of the case finally lifting. "Thank you, Inspector. I appreciate everything you've done."

Stanley glanced at her, something unreadable flickering across his face before he said, "Funny thing is, once we got Emily into the interview room, her biggest concern wasn't her trial, or what people would think of her. The only thing she seemed worried about was what was going to happen to her cat."

At the mention of the cat, Robyn, who had been quietly listening, perked up, wiggling her eyebrows suggestively. "I know someone who'd love a cat if there was one going spare."

Stanley chuckled, shaking his head. "Sorry, you're too late. She's already spoken for."

Robyn looked disappointed. "Seriously? Who?"

Stanley leaned forward slightly. "Emily asked us to contact Marcus."

Sarah raised her eyebrows. "Marcus? After everything?"

Stanley nodded. "It seems not all of Emily's relationships were completely burned. She still trusted him enough to ask that he look after Cinnamon."

Robyn sighed, slumping back in her chair. "Damn. I was picturing a future full of cosy nights and a cat on my lap."

Sarah gave her a knowing smile. "Maybe Marcus needs someone to look after more than you do, Robyn. After all, he just lost a sister."

Robyn pursed her lips, then shrugged. "Fair point. Still, if he ever changes his mind, tell him to call me."

Stanley smirked, standing up. "I'll pass that along."

"Thanks for your help along the way, Sarah. And now that the case is closed, maybe you could call me Luke." he said, turning to face her. "If I'm in the area, I'll pop in for a coffee occasionally. And if there's anything I can do to help, just shout."

Sarah raised an eyebrow, a playful look on her face. "Luke, huh? All this time of not knowing your first name and it sounds like you've got two of them. Well then Luke, you're always welcome here.

Luke let out a short laugh, shaking his head. "Well, I do aim for an air of mystery."

"Mission accomplished" Sarah said, grinning. "Actually, if you'd like something to do that would really help, you could take Missy for a walk sometime."

She glanced at Robyn, who was watching the interaction with interest. Sarah subtly nudged her, giving her a meaningful look. Robyn's eyes widened slightly, catching on to Sarah's unspoken suggestion.

"Yes, that would be great!" Robyn said, her voice just a touch too enthusiastic. She cleared her throat and tried again, more casually. "I mean, if you're up for it, I could show you some of Missy's favourite spots."

Sarah glanced over at Robyn, a playful glint in her eye. "It's been a busy morning so far, don't you think? Maybe you should take a break," she suggested, her tone light but carrying an underlying hint of encouragement.

Robyn caught Sarah's eye, rolling her eyes slightly in response, but Sarah could tell she knew exactly what was going on. There was no fooling Robyn. Sarah could see her niece was about to protest, but then she paused. A slight smile tugged at the corner of Robyn's lips, as if she were reconsidering.

With a sigh and a slight shrug, Robyn gave in. "Well, it is lunchtime, I guess."

Sarah's grin widened, and Robyn reached for the strings of her apron, untangling them from around her waist. "You'd better not get too used to working me so hard," Robyn added, a good-natured grumble in her voice as she hung her apron on a nearby hook.

"Take it easy," Sarah teased, watching Robyn head toward the little office in the back to fetch Missy's lead. "Just think of it as a chance to get to know the man a little more."

Robyn gave her a wry look but didn't respond, the corners of her mouth twitching into an amused smile. She reappeared a moment later with the lead in hand. "All right, all right," she said, shaking her head. "Let's go then."

Lukes's stiff demeanour eased just a fraction. He bent down to give Missy a quick pat. "Ready for a walk, girl?"

Missy wagged her tail furiously, clearly excited by the prospect. As he and Robyn walked out of the shop with Missy trotting happily between them, Sarah and Charlie watched from the doorway.

Charlie chuckled softly. "Think they'll be good for each other?"

Sarah smiled, watching the pair disappear down the street. "I hope so. They both deserve a bit of happiness."

Edward stood in his shop for what felt like hours, staring out the window at the bustling activity of Castle Road. His encounter with Amy earlier in the week had left him raw, his emotions laid bare in a way they hadn't been in years. He knew what he needed to do, but the thought of facing Sarah after everything he had done made his stomach twist with anxiety.

Finally, gathering his courage, Edward put on his coat and hat, grabbed the small, framed photograph of his late wife from behind the counter, and stepped out of *Barnes Curiosities*. The walk down Castle Road felt longer than usual, each step heavy with the weight of his guilt. As he approached *Sarah's Secrets*, he paused, taking a deep breath before pushing open the door.

Sarah looked up from behind the counter, her expression shifting from surprise to concern as she noticed the serious look on his face.

"Mr. Barnes," Sarah greeted him cautiously, setting down the cup she had been cleaning. "What brings you here?"

Edward removed his hat, holding it awkwardly in his hands. "Mrs Meadows... Sarah," he began, his voice shaky. "I owe you an apology. A proper one."

Sarah tilted her head slightly, her brow furrowing in confusion. "An apology? For what?"

Edward sighed, his gaze dropping to the floor. "For everything. The notes, the harassment... it was me. I've been trying to drive you away, and I'm so sorry."

Sarah's eyes widened in surprise, but she didn't speak, allowing Edward to continue.

"The truth is," he said, his voice thick with emotion, "it wasn't about you at all. It was about my wife—my late wife, Margaret. She... she had a dream of opening a coffee shop, much like this one. We planned it together, but she fell ill before we could really consider making it a reality."

Edward paused, his hands trembling as he held the photograph of Margaret. "When I saw you here, succeeding where she couldn't, it was like a knife to my heart. I couldn't bear the thought of someone else living the dream that she never got to fulfil. So I lashed out. I tried to scare you away, to make the pain go away, but all I did was hurt an innocent person. And for that, I am truly, deeply sorry."

Sarah's expression softened as she listened, her heart aching for the grief and loss Edward had carried for so long. "Mr. Barnes," she said gently, stepping around the counter to stand in front of him, "I'm so sorry for your loss. I can't imagine the pain you must have felt, or still feel."

Edward nodded, unable to speak as he fought back tears. He offered the photograph to Sarah, his hands shaking. "This is Margaret," he whispered. "She was everything to me, and I've failed to honour her in the way I should have."

Sarah took the photograph with the utmost care, her eyes filling with tears as she looked at the image of a smiling woman with kind eyes, standing in front of what must have been the antique shop in its early days.

"She's beautiful," Sarah said softly. "And she deserved to see her dream come true. I'm sorry that she didn't get that chance."

Edward wiped his eyes, nodding. "She did. And I've let my anger and grief consume me, instead of finding a way to celebrate her memory."

Sarah looked up at Edward, a gentle smile on her face. "I think there's still a way to honour her, if you'd like. How about we hang this picture in the shop, here in *Sarah's Secrets*? That way, Margaret can finally spend her time in the coffee shop she dreamed of, even if it's in spirit."

Edward blinked, surprised by the offer. "You'd do that? After everything I've done?"

Sarah nodded, her voice full of compassion. "Absolutely. This shop is meant to be a place of comfort and connection. If having Margaret here with us helps to honour her memory, then I would be pleased to do it."

Edward's hardened exterior finally cracked, and he let out a shaky breath, tears spilling down his cheeks. "Thank you, Sarah," he whispered. "Thank you for your kindness. I don't deserve it, but I'm grateful."

Sarah smiled, placing a comforting hand on his arm. "We all make mistakes, Mr. Barnes".

Edward nodded, his voice breaking as he spoke. "I promise I'll stop the harassment. No more notes, no more trying to drive you away. I see now that Margaret would have wanted to see this place thrive, even if it wasn't hers."

Sarah squeezed his arm gently. "I appreciate that, Mr. Barnes. And I hope you'll visit often. This shop will always have a place for you and for Margaret."

Edward managed a small, grateful smile. "I will. And thank you, Sarah. You've given me a peace I didn't think I'd ever find."

With that, Sarah led Edward to a spot on the wall near the entrance, where the light filtered in just right. Together, they hung Margaret's photograph, placing it in a spot where she could greet every visitor to the shop. As they stepped back to admire it, Edward felt a sense of relief wash over him, the burden of his guilt lifting ever so slightly.

The warmth of the moment lingered as Sarah and Charlie stepped back inside the coffee shop. Sarah had been busy all morning, setting the place up and getting things ready for the day ahead, while Charlie had made himself at home, flipping through a coffee brewer's industry magazine that had been delivered earlier. As he skimmed the pages, an advertisement caught his eye—a notice for a Latte Art competition, showcasing intricate designs and inviting baristas from around the region to participate.

Curious, Charlie leaned in closer, studying the details of the competition. Sarah, noticing his interest, walked over and peered over his shoulder.

"What's that?" she asked, tilting her head to get a better look.

Charlie pointed to the ad. "It's a Latte Art competition. Looks like it's a pretty big deal. They're holding it at the Queen's Hotel."

Sarah's eyes lit up with excitement. "You should enter! It'd be fun for you... and you never know, if you do well, it would be good publicity for the coffee shop."

Charlie hesitated, glancing back at the magazine. "Do you really think I should? I mean, I've never entered a competition before."

Sarah smiled encouragingly. "Yes, of course! What harm could come of it? You've got a real talent, Charlie. People love your latte art here. Plus, it could attract new customers and get our name out there."

Charlie looked thoughtful, weighing her words. "You think so?"

"Absolutely," Sarah said, her confidence unwavering. "You've got nothing to lose and everything to gain. And who knows? You might just surprise yourself."

Charlie chuckled, the idea starting to take root in his mind. "All right, why not? I'll give it a shot. It could be fun. Thanks for the push, Mum."

"Anytime," Sarah replied, giving him a playful nudge.

As Charlie flipped back to the magazine, skimming through competition details, Sarah bent down and pulled out a small stack of leather-bound notebooks from the shelves beneath the counter. She cradled them carefully in her arms, the rich, worn covers giving them a timeless feel.

Charlie glanced up, raising an eyebrow as she began placing the notebooks into the small holders where the coffee shop's menus usually sat. "What's all this?"

Sarah smiled, running a hand over the smooth surface of one before tucking it neatly into place. "Oh, just something I've been thinking about," she said, a glimmer of excitement in her eyes.

She placed the final notebook into its holder, then turned to Charlie with a satisfied nod.

"I think it's about time we put the secret in *Sarah's Secrets.*"

Charlie gave her a puzzled look, clearly intrigued. "The secret?"

Sarah winked and walked toward the back of the shop, her excitement bubbling underneath. "You'll see."

As she disappeared into the back room, Charlie walked over to the nearest table and, unable to resist, opened one of the leather-bound notebooks. Inside the front cover, a small, handwritten note caught his eye,

Tell me your secrets.

Charlie smirked, a mixture of amusement and curiosity stirring inside him. What exactly had Sarah been planning for their little shop?

Thank You For Reading!!

I hope that you enjoyed my first book in the Sarah's Secrets series! Writing Brewing & Betrayal has been a fun journey, and I'm so grateful to have you as a reader.

If you'd like to show your support, one of the best ways is by leaving a review on Amazon. Reviews, whether short or long, help authors more than you might think. They not only let me know what you liked, but also signal to others that Sarah's Secrets is worth discovering.

I'd truly appreciate any feedback you have, and if you'd like to see more from Sarah, Charlie, Robyn and Sarah's Secrets, your reviews are the best way to let me know!!

Thank you for being part of this adventure – I hope to see you again soon in Latte Legacies!!

Sarah

Coming Soon!!

Latte Legacies

A Sarah's Secrets Mystery - Book 2

Southsea's favourite coffee shop, Sarah's Secrets, is once again brewing up trouble.

When Sarah Meadow's stumbles upon an anonymous note hidden among the pages of her café's "secret" journals, its chilling message stops her cold:

I know what you did.

At first, she dismisses it as a prank – until there's a death at the Latte Art Championships. As whispers of scandal and sabotage swirl through the city's coffee scene, Sarah can't ignore the coincidence.

With her son Charlie, vying for victory in the competition and her niece, Robyn drawn in to the mystery, Sarah finds herself playing detective once more. But in a world where reputations are everything, and coffee if more competitive than ever, someone is determined to keep their secrets buried – no matter the cost.

Printed in Great Britain
by Amazon